Last Will and Testament

The death of old Lord St Blaizey and the mystery of his last will and testament was, in a sense the sequel to another death some twenty-five years before. Dr Benjamin Tancred, consultant detective, and his friend, Paul Graham, narrator of this story, had been concerned in the earlier death and now inevitably found themselves involved in this second Cornish mystery, set near St Blazey (the fictional name has been deliberately misspelt) and in the beautiful Luxulyan valley.

But the mystery surrounding Lord St Blaizey's death is only one of the three that go to make up this tangled tale. Together with two no less intricate – Was the St Blaizey will a forgery? and who killed the impecunious Sidney Galloway, his lordship's former secretary? – it is resolved at last by Dr Tancred's unflagging persistence and insight. The result is a triumphant end to his greatest case in which the claims of justice are fully and finally satisfied.

This title was first published in the Crime Club in 1936.

G. D. H. and M. COLE

Last Will and Testament

Dr Benjamin Tancred investigates

The Disappearing Detectives
*Selected and Introduced
by H. R. F. Keating*

COLLINS, 8 GRAFTON STREET, LONDON W1

William Collins Sons & Co. Ltd
London · Glasgow · Sydney · Auckland
Toronto · Johannesburg

First published in the Crime Club 1936
Reprinted in this edition 1985
Copyright reserved G. D. H. and M. Cole
© in the Introduction, H. R. F. Keating, 1985

British Library Cataloguing in Publication Data

Cole, G. D. H.
   Last will and testament.—(The Disappearing
   Detectives)—(Crime Club)
   I. Title   II. Cole Margaret   III. Series
   823'.912[F]   PR6005.0226

ISBN 0 00 231997 7

Photoset in Linotron Baskerville by
Rowland Phototypesetting Ltd
Bury St Edmunds, Suffolk
Printed in Great Britain by
William Collins Sons & Co. Ltd, Glasgow

INTRODUCTION
H. R. F. Keating

Dr Benjamin Tancred, consultant detective in the great tradition, made only two appearances in fiction, or three if you count a short story read, as they said in his 1930s days, 'over the microphone'. He is a detective, indeed, who has, all but for the tiniest traces, disappeared. I have chosen to revive him, however, in preference to the sleuth G. D. H. and Margaret Cole more usually wrote about because he has some smack of distinction about him, whereas Superintendent Henry Wilson has justly been described in that bulky tome *Twentieth Century Crime and Mystery Writers* as 'one of the most colourless detectives ever created'.

Yet in the Twenties and Thirties when our authors were in fullest flood readers seemed not to be very worried by character, or by the lack of it, either in the detectives whose exploits they were addicted to as their successors are addicted to *Dallas* or *Coronation Street*, or in any of the other persona in the books.

It cannot be denied that some of those you will meet in the pages ahead well qualify for the colourlessness stakes. They are stereotypes of stereotypes. Take, for instance, the tycoon's secretary who appears briefly about half way through. 'Ben . . . saw before him a rabbity little man, with a weak but rather sensitive face, mouse-coloured hair, and large owlish spectacles.' For one blissful moment on first reading that I thought I had spotted who done it, simply on the grounds that it was once shown by someone with a terrible tendency to statistics that in this sort of book the private secretary did it more often than any other of the statutory figures. But I give away no vital secret if I say now 'Look elsewhere.'

To judge by the very last paragraph of the book, 'I shall never weary of singing my friend Ben Tancred's praises,' the authors liked him and contemplated keeping him in business. Alas, they relapsed into Wilsonism, letting 'The Professor' sit there in his room at Scotland Yard painstakingly solving by logical inference every crime that came before him. So we know less than we might about Dr Tancred.

From *Dr Tancred Begins* we learnt that he likes to drink, of all things, rum, that he and his Watson, Paul Graham, twenty-five years before the present narrative begins were already close friends and that while Paul was convalescing then in Cornwall he had become involved with both romance and crime and had summoned expert assistance over the latter, even eventually bringing in a certain Detective-Sergeant Henry Wilson. We saw then that Tancred was very much in the Sherlock Holmes pattern, a superman with a few moments of doubt and weakness. In this story he has occasion to call himself 'a fool and a goop and a juggins' in much the manner that the great Sherlock once asked Dr Watson to whisper the word 'Norwood' into his ear if ever he became too impressed with his own powers. And at one point here Tancred becomes 'fagged out' and falls asleep in a field, a palish imitation of Holmes who 'for days on end . . . would lie upon the sofa'.

Tancred also favours a pipe, but seems not to use it as a really Great Detective should, to induce that state of trance in which intuition combines with the rational to produce the absolutely unexpected solution. The Coles, though they could deceive their readers nicely enough, seem to have preferred to lead us to the solution of their puzzles by plain deduction.

As here. This book only starts – be warned – as a whodone-it and in its last third turns plainly into the how-done-it. But that approach has its strong fascination, and it is a nice mental exercise to try and keep ahead of Ben Tancred, the tweed-clad 'humble seeker after truth', as he works out what ingenious methods the murderer used. And Tancred does have endearing human qualities. He has to 'repress a scruple' before he reads private correspondence, but repress it he does, and so another clue falls into his hands. And ours.

It is a bright spark amid passages where, it must be admitted, a certain sturdy ploddingness creeps in. Margaret Cole in her life of her husband, the last thing she wrote, describes their 30-odd detective stories as 'competent but no more'. She is too modest. There are pages where mere competence reigns. There are solid chunks of repetitive periodic summings-up (one is included to speculate that they are where the stern pen of G. D. H. took back command, but, statistician though he was, one might be quite wrong). There are clichés ('My hat, Jellicoe,' Tancred exclaims once, and once someone retreats 'like a whipped cur'). But there are also lively pages of dialogue (Margaret at work?), even a quite charming incidental character in Smith the tramp and a nicely sharp caricature in Colonel Gates-Cocker, the Chief Constable. There is even a neat crack at the Coles' own fervent Socialism when, after Ben Tancred has admitted to being 'rather that way' himself, the crusty old cobbler he is questioning replies 'Socialists are no better than a pack of fools.'

The Coles were, in fact, much more concerned with Socialism than detection. Margaret, indeed, devotes only a couple of pages in her biography of Douglas to their crime stories. He was president of the Fabian Society; she succeeded him. He wrote biographies of Cobbett and Robert Owen; she wrote a biography of Beatrice Webb. He was Chichele Professor of Social and Political Theory at Oxford; she was for long a lecturer at university tutorial classes in London and at Cambridge.

They were married in 1918. He had been born in 1889 and died in 1959, having suffered in his latter years from diabetes which, Margaret said, only had the effect of making him 'write faster and faster, larger and more complicated books'. She was born in 1893, sister of Raymond Postgate, author of a remarkable crime novel *Verdict of Twelve*, and died in 1980, a Dame of the British Empire. But it is perhaps a glimpse we have of Douglas in his between-the-wars Oxford days that is, for our purposes here, the most interesting thing about him. He was then the leader of an informal gathering that came to be called 'the Cole group'. It included among its adherents W. H. Auden and John Betjeman. And at it Douglas Cole was described as 'a dark and dynamic presence'. Bear that in mind when you picture to yourself Dr Benjamin Tancred.

PREFATORY NOTE

All the characters in this story are imaginary, and none is modelled on any living person. Some of them have, indeed, lived before, in a story called *Dr Tancred Begins*, to which this is a successor. But, though some of the principal characters appear again, the present tale stands by itself, and can be read without any acquaintance with the earlier 'canto'. The places, unlike the persons, are largely real, though we have again taken certain liberties with the topography. There is no such place as St Blaizey Castle, old or new—and, we trust, no such ancient family as the Viscounts St Blaizey. In order to emphasize our departure from sheer reality, we have, in fact, presented the village of St Blaizey with an extra letter which its original, St Blazey, does not possess. We say this, in order to save Cornish readers from wasting postage stamps on telling us that we have misspelt the name. We claim also a certain licence to rearrange the times of trains to suit our own convenience, with the proviso that we do not allow them to reach their destination any sooner than real trains actually do.

If any reader, having read this tale, would like to know more of Rupert or Helen Pendexter, or of their Aunt Sarah, or of Dr Tancred himself, they can easily gratify their curiosity by referring to *Dr Tancred Begins*.

G. D. H. and Margaret Cole.
Freeland, Hendon, May, 1936.

MAP OF THE COUNTRY
ROUND ST. BLAIZEY

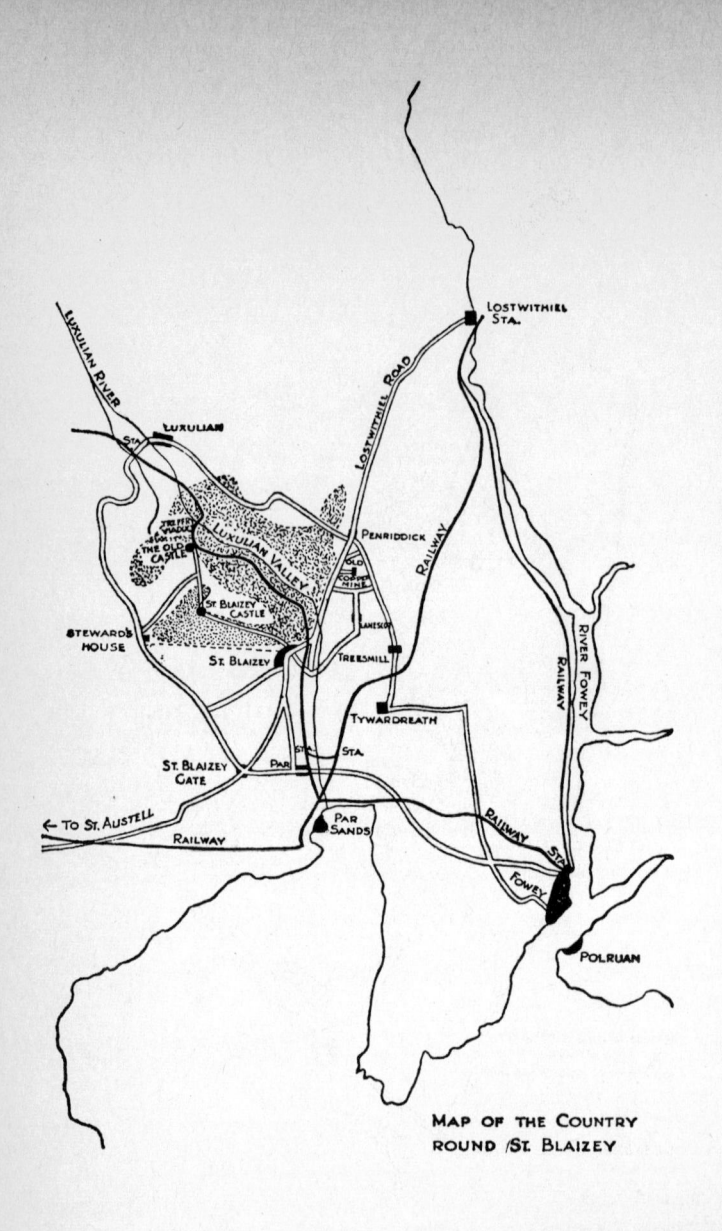

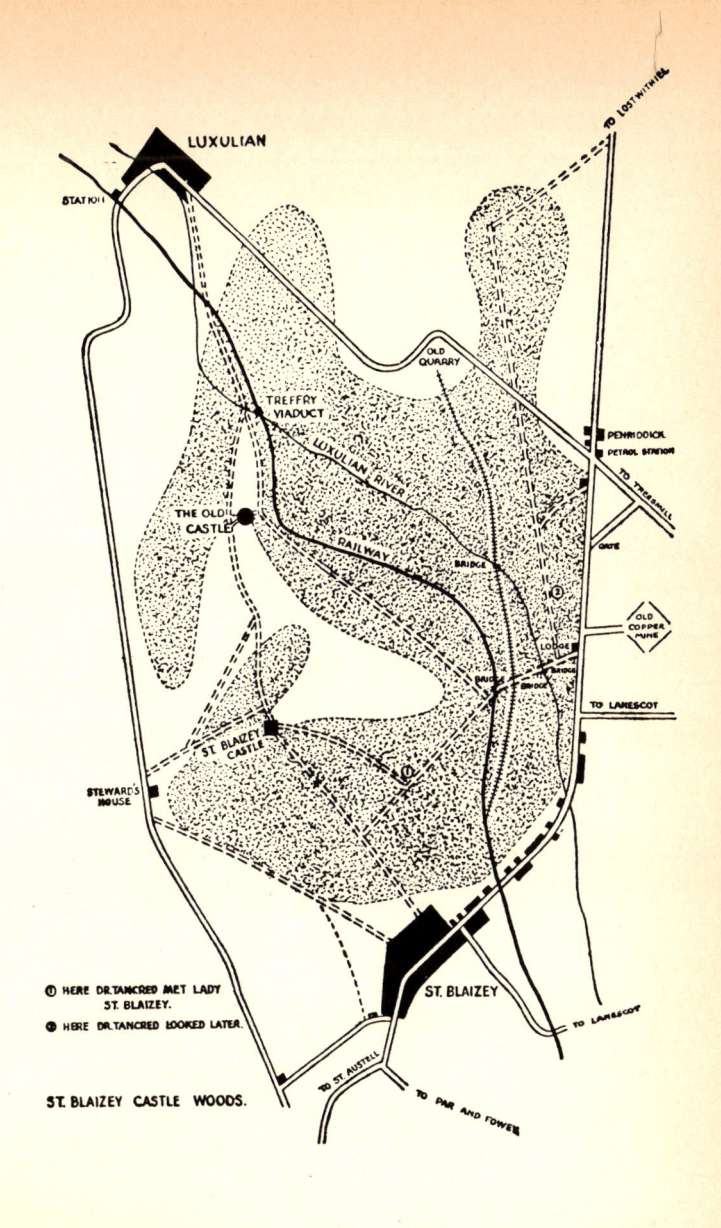

① HERE DR. TANCRED MET LADY ST. BLAIZEY.
② HERE DR. TANCRED LOOKED LATER.

ST. BLAIZEY CASTLE WOODS.

CHAPTER 1

THE PENDEXTERS AND THE DAMIANS

I fear it is indispensable for this story of old Lord St Blaizey's death and of the mystery of his last will and testament to open with a slice of history. For the death of Lord St Blaizey is in a sense a sequel to another death that happened five-and-twenty years before—when a certain Simon Pendexter, a retired master-builder from Truro, was murdered in the queer house he had built for himself by Blackbottle Rock, at Polruan, just across the river from Fowey.

The story of that murder, and of my friend, Dr Benjamin Tancred's, efforts to discover the murderer and bring him to justice, I have told in an earlier volume, entitled *Dr Tancred Begins*. Some of the readers of the present book may remember how suspicion in that case fell first on Helen Pendexter, Simon's stepdaughter, and then on her brother, Rupert Pendexter, but that, certain as Ben Tancred and I both felt about the murderer's identity, no proof could be found—though in the end there did come to light a fact, still far short of legal proof, that seemed amply to confirm our suspicions.

Simon Pendexter's murderer got off scot-free; and Dr Tancred had to wait for a quarter of a century before Simon's queer and half-mad sister, Sarah Pendexter, came to throw at his feet the chance of avenging that failure of his youth. That chance involved, alas, a second death—and even a third; and the story of these later tragedies stands, apart from the identity of certain of the actors, wholly distinct from the earlier events. It can be told as a tale by itself; and no one need fear, even if he has never set eyes on my earlier volume, that he will be less able to follow the story which is related in the present book. Two things only link the two books together—the same detective and the same criminal to be detected. For I think we can safely declare that the murderer of Simon Pendexter also murdered old Lord St Blaizey within a few miles of the scene of his original crime.

I have said already that twenty-five years separate the two cases, and I am under the necessity of bridging so wide a gulf with a slice of history. It is family history mostly; for the reader must know something of who the St Blaizeys were. They are all gone now, since the last Lord St Blaizey's death only a little while ago, and I can write about them freely, without the fear of hurting anyone's feelings or involving either myself or my publisher in an action for libel.

First then, you must know that the Damians were a very old family, and that the title of St Blaizey had been so long in their line that the old lord, whose death is the starting point of this story, was the sixteenth Viscount. Let me give him at once his full name—Augustus Gregory Concanen Damian, Viscount St Blaizey, of St Blaizey in the County of Cornwall. Let us call him Augustus, for short. To him and to his wife, Alicia, whose maiden name was Mangan, was born but one child, the Honourable Roderick Augustus Concanen Damian, who succeeded his father as the seventeenth viscount, and died childless, the last of his line. There were no relations left near enough to inherit the title. It died out, as so much else of old renown is dying out in these days of progress towards who knows what. Today St Blaizey Castle, the old family seat, stands empty, and so, a few miles away, does Blackbottle House, where Sarah Pendexter was dreaming her fantastic dreams in loneliness at the time when my story opens.

Between the Pendexters and the Damians there were two important connections, which serve to link old Simon Pendexter's end to Lord St Blaizey's. After the date of old Simon's murder, his stepdaughter, Helen Pendexter, married Roderick Damian; and her brother, Rupert Pendexter, became the close friend and associate of Roderick's father, the Lord St Blaizey of whose tragic death I am soon to write.

Roderick Damian and Helen Pendexter had been married

for the best part of twenty years at the moment when my story begins. But they had no child. Already the shadow of extinction was over the historic title to which Roderick was heir.

The second connection is even more important for the purpose of this story. At the time when my narrative opens, Augustus, Lord St Blaizey, in addition to being an aristocrat of ancient lineage, had a very different claim to count in the affairs of his country. He was generally reckoned one of the greatest figures in the financial world of London. Among many financial activities, he was best known as the very enterprising Chairman of Mangans', one of the greatest of London's private banking houses, and as the man at the back of the Metal Securities Investment Trust, its most important affiliate. In both these world-famous institutions Rupert Pendexter was one of the most active directors, having risen to that eminence from his start, about twenty years earlier, in a quite subordinate position in Mangans' office. That start he owed to his sister, shortly after her marriage to Lord St Blaizey's heir. But his rise was due wholly to his own very remarkable abilities. The city regarded him unquestioningly as Lord St Blaizey's right-hand man; and, now that Lord St Blaizey was getting old, the control of his vast affairs was passing more and more into Rupert Pendexter's hands.

It must be explained at this point how Lord St Blaizey, with his ancient title, came to be a leading figure in City finance; and incidentally the explanation will throw some needed light on the Damians and their ways.

The fifteenth Viscount, father of Augustus Damian, inherited a sadly embarrassed family estate and more than all the family pride. He was a stiff-necked fellow, of violent Tory opinions, possessed by the idea that the country was going to the dogs, and that it was all the fault of the Reform Act of 1832, which had put the financiers in the place of the old nobility. He had a passion for field sports, exacted the utmost deference from his tenants, and could seldom be persuaded to leave St Blaizey Castle for London, which he heartily disliked. His elder son, Thomas, took after him: the younger, Augustus, did not. Perhaps he got some of his qualities from his mother, who was a Carrick. At all events, in the quarrel I am just going to tell you of, she took his side.

Augustus, like his brother, who was two years his senior, went to Eton and Oxford. Thence Thomas duly returned to live with his father on the estate. Augustus, on the other hand, struck up a close friendship with Geoffrey Mangan, only son of the then head of Mangans' Bank. At Oxford he took first-class honours in 'Greats'—of which his father thought nothing. As soon as he was through his final exam, he announced his intention of accepting Geoffrey's offer to find him a position in Mangans' Bank.

There followed a terrific scene between father and son. Old Lord St Blaizey was far too impecunious to be able to offer his younger son any assured prospects in life. But despite his poverty, or perhaps all the more on account of it, he took the view that the family name would be for ever disgraced if any member of it lowered himself to have anything to do with so sordid a matter as finance. It was the country's duty to support the Damians; and if the country failed to do its duty adequately, the Damians should at least stay at home and cherish their pride.

Augustus remained quite unmoved by his father's tirades. He entered Mangans' Bank as little more than a clerk, with prospects; and six months later he married Geoffrey Mangan's only sister, Alicia, which made his prospects a great deal better. Then, within two years, both Thomas Damian and Geoffrey Mangan died—the first in a hunting accident, and the second of pneumonia. Augustus found himself unexpectedly heir both to the St Blaizey title and to the headship of one of London's foremost private banks.

Thomas Damian died a few weeks before Geoffrey Mangan; and Augustus, who had not seen his father since their quarrel, went down to St Blaizey Castle for the funeral. He found old Lord St Blaizey took it for granted that, now he had become the heir to the title, he would abandon banking and come back to live the life of a country aristocrat at St Blaizey Castle. On these terms the father was prepared to receive his erring son back into favour; and this time Augustus's mother joined her entreaties to her husband's commands. But Augustus had other views; he hated country life, loved his work in the City, and had great belief in his own financial abilities. The idea of giving up his business career, which promised great things, in order to take over at some indefinite time in the future the impoverished family estate did not appeal to him in the least. He refused flatly; and there was a second quarrel so ferocious that Augustus never saw his father again. His next visit to St Blaizey Castle was when he went down there to bury the old man, and take over control of what was left of the estate. His mother had died some years before; but Lord St Blaizey had absolutely refused even to have his apostate son to the funeral.

For generations, the Damians had been like that—headstrong, quarrelsome, never at peace one with another. It was part of the family tradition for father and son to be at loggerheads most of their lives. But it was also part of the tradition that death should wipe out old scores. No Lord St Blaizey had ever attempted to deprive his eldest son of the family fortune—unentailed as well as entailed. Augustus's father died intestate; and the son succeeded to the whole of the St Blaizey property, such as it was, as well as to the title.

By this time the family property, apart from sentiment, was to Augustus a matter of no account at all. Geoffrey Mangan's father had followed Geoffrey to the grave; and Augustus was chairman of Mangans' Bank and the possessor of a big enough fortune to make nothing of paying off the mortgages and putting the dilapidated Castle to rights. But he never lived there, save for a brief annual visit in the summer. Cornwall was much too far away for a man of his incessant business activity—especially as he was already at work on the first big transaction that went to the making of the Metal Securities Trust. He preferred living at Longridge Park, in Hertfordshire, the magnificent house and finely timbered estate that had come to him on old Mangan's death. On Longridge he lavished money; and there he put through many of his most spectacular business deals—for he loved to play host to the lesser fry whose fortunes he manipulated with so much skill.

Young Roderick Damian grew up at Longridge. Like his father, he was sent to Eton and to Oxford; and on leaving the University he too, celebrated the occasion with a family quarrel. But, whereas Augustus had outraged his father by entering business, Roderick outraged his by flatly refusing to have anything to do with it. He was a queer boy, with an ugly, flat face and a remarkable power of silent obstinacy that broke out occasionally into a cold and deadly fury; and these qualities did not desert him when he grew up. His mother had died when he was fourteen; and he was an only child. To her he had been devoted, but with his father he had little sympathy; nor did Lord St Blaizey, always immersed in business affairs, and making little of his ugly, obstinate, gawky, silent progeny, spare Roderick a great deal of human attention.

Augustus had always taken it for granted that the boy, when he became a man, would follow him into the City, and in due course succeed him in the control of his still rapidly expanding financial connections. Roderick, till the issue had to be faced practically on his leaving Oxford, did nothing to disabuse his father of this notion. He said nothing; and his father was too preoccupied to notice that he looked a lot. When Augustus talked of his future, Roderick let him talk; and Lord St Blaizey did not suspect that behind that rather sulky countenance, with its square-set jaw and its heavy unresponsiveness, there was a firm determination on Roderick's part to spend his life in very different ways from those which his father designed for him.

The quarrel came, as it was bound to come. When Lord St Blaizey announced his plans for putting Roderick through the mill in Mangans' Bank, his son simply announced to him that he did not propose to go into business, but would prefer, if his father agreed, to take up his residence at St Blaizey Castle and look after the estate. Augustus, taken thoroughly aback, tried to sweep his son's objections aside; but he soon found that neither reasonings nor commands were producing the smallest impression. He asked Roderick what, if he objected to business, he did propose to do with his life; and at that Roderick took him still more aback by announcing that he intended to go in seriously for anthropology, and to spend a good deal of his time exploring in Africa.

Now Augustus was in an even weaker position in relation to Roderick than his own father had been in relation to him. For though most of the Mangan fortune and his own very considerable additions to it were his to dispose of at his discretion, Roderick was financially in a position to go his own road. His mother had left a handsome sum in trust, to pass into his hands absolutely on his twenty-fifth birthday. For the next three years, indeed, Roderick would have only what he could persuade his father, or his mother's trustees, to disgorge—or, of course, what he could borrow on his expectations. But thereafter he would be quite independent financially, even to the extent of being able to gratify, in moderation, so expensive a whim as the promoting of an expedition to Africa.

Lord St Blaizey stormed—to no purpose. He refused to let his son live at St Blaizey Castle, and practically turned him out of doors. For the next three years Roderick, who had simple personal tastes, lived on next to nothing in a cottage just off the St Blaizey property in Cornwall, studying anthropology and preparing to do what he wanted as soon as he came into his mother's money.

These years were not uneventful in other ways. Roderick Damian lived the life of a retired scholar in his Cornish cottage: but at this time, before his accident, he was by no means the misanthrope he became later on. Having what his father regarded as 'low tastes' in human companionship, he mixed freely with the tenants on the St Blaizey estate, and got on with them very well. He learned to respect their somewhat narrow and gloomy religion and their staunchly independent Radical outlook in politics. He proclaimed himself a Radical and, to his father's deep disgust, went about with a fanatical cobbler, by name Reuben Amos, addressing political meetings and bringing discredit on the family name.

It was through some of his Radical acquaintances that Roderick Damian met Helen Pendexter, then working as paid nurse-companion to an old lady in Fowey. He fell promptly in love with her, proposed marriage, and was refused. Roderick was indeed anything but a ladies' man. He was shy and awkward in the company of women, and all too conscious of his own *gaucherie*. Perhaps he took Helen Pendexter's refusal more finally than she had intended. At all events, it seems to have precipitated his departure for Africa, on that ill-fated expedition on which his name as an anthropologist chiefly rests.

Roderick Damian had told his father nothing of his feelings for Helen Pendexter. But the affair, such as it was, was promptly reported to Lord St Blaizey by the steward of the estate. The young woman, he heard, was personally not ill-favoured or even unpresentable; and she had some good blood in her veins, and was even a distant relative of the Damians—for her mother had been a Carrick of Lostwithiel. But there was a great deal against her. Only a year or two ago she had actually been in prison on suspicion of murdering her stepfather—a retired builder of eccentric habits. She had been exonerated from this suspicion, and released; but the fact remained that the murderer had not been brought to justice. Lord St Blaizey's informant added that Helen had undoubtedly some most undesirable relations. Her brother, Rupert, was widely suspected of being the real murderer, though there was too little evidence to bring him to trial; and her aunt, one Sarah Pendexter, was a fanatical, trouble-making Methodist, whom many people regarded as more than half out of her mind.

Lord St Blaizey, unaware that Helen had refused his son, broke a long silence by dashing off an angry letter of protest against Roderick's entanglement with a person so plainly beneath him. Roderick replied shortly that he supposed he knew his own business best, and did not propose to enter into discussion with his father concerning his private affairs. Lord St Blaizey, hearing a little later that the affair was off, wrote again, attempting a reconciliation; but he got no answer. Immediately afterwards Roderick, having come into his mother's money, left for Africa.

Roderick Damian came back from Africa crippled for life, and poor as well. While he was in the middle of his expedition, word came to him that the lawyer with whom he had left a power of attorney had committed suicide after making away with most of his money, and that there was no hope of recovering more than a tiny fraction from the wreck. But that was not the worst. On his way home towards civilization he was so badly mauled by a tiger that it was a miracle he survived at all. He came home to his cottage on a stretcher, and lay there helpless for a year and more. And Helen Pendexter nursed him through his illness, and was married to him almost as soon as he was able to crawl about again with the aid of two sticks.

Suffering had done much by this time to change Roderick Damian's character; and if Helen's friends were surprised at her refusing him before, they were still more astonished at her marrying him now. For, during his illness, two things had happened to Roderick. His old headstrong sulkiness had turned into persistent ill-temper; and he had become a convert to an extreme and souring Calvinism, which henceforth absorbed more and more of his attention.

Lord St Blaizey had attempted reconciliation with his son when he came back from Africa, but had been ungraciously repulsed. Now, hearing of his marriage, he made yet another attempt to re-establish friendly relations, for, thanks perhaps to his business training, he knew how to face facts when he must. He made up his mind to swallow his anger, to recognize his son's wife, and to offer the young couple St Blaizey Castle as a home, and therewith to make another effort to induce Roderick to change his mind, and become, immediately his health allowed, an active director of Mangans' Bank.

Lord St Blaizey went down to St Blaizey Castle himself, though it was winter, and invited his son and daughter-in-law to come and stay with him. They came: for Helen knew how to manage Roderick—up to a point. Lord St Blaizey was introduced to his daughter-in-law, and, immensely to his surprise, liked her very much and found her a thoroughly sensible woman, whose influence he felt sure would be cast on his side when he put forward his proposals. With unusual tact, he said nothing for the first few days, and even let Roderick talk about the new expedition to Africa on which he had set his heart—though there was really no chance of his ever being fit again for such a venture. For the moment everything seemed to be going smoothly. Even Roderick was comparatively amiable, in his sour way; and when Rupert Pendexter came to see his sister at the Castle, and was presented to Lord St Blaizey, he too won his way at once into his lordship's good graces.

But Lord St Blaizey was fretting all the time to get back to Longridge and to London, where there was money waiting to be made. Before tackling his son, he spoke seriously to Helen about the future, telling her how vital it was for him to have some one to succeed him at the head of his various enterprises, and asking her to use all her influence to make Roderick show a little common sense. He found Helen very sympathetic, and, when at length he did tackle Roderick, his hopes ran high.

But Roderick would not budge. He would gladly occupy the Castle if his father wished; but he had no head or taste for business, and nothing would induce him to take any part in it. He would have enough for his needs, in any case; and he had no interest in making money for its own sake. He was sorry not to oblige his father—but there it was.

On this occasion Lord St Blaizey did not storm at his son. With considerable difficulty he governed his anger, offered Roderick the Castle for a home in spite of his refusal, and put as good a face on his disappointment as he could manage. His son thanked him, none too graciously, and Helen thanked him too—with a charm that did much to reconcile him to the marriage; and Lord St Blaizey went back to Longridge Park with his tail between his legs.

Thereafter, Roderick Damian slowly mended in health; but it became clear, even to him, that there was no chance of his ever visiting Africa again. He worked hard at his book, in which he set down the results of his observations; and the book, when published, brought him some *kudos* in the learned world. But, when he knew that his days of fieldwork were definitely over, Roderick Damian gave himself over more and more to religion; and Helen found living at peace with him a harder and harder task. A few months after their installation at the Castle, her first—and only—child was stillborn, and after that she and Roderick drifted further apart.

Meanwhile, Rupert Pendexter, whom Lord St Blaizey had met and liked while he was in Cornwall, had been invited to visit Longridge Park. After that first visit, he gave up his position as clerk to a Truro lawyer, and began work as a clerk in Mangans' Bank. Rupert took to the City like a duck to water. Before long, he was invited to Longridge again. On that occasion Lord St Blaizey, bitterly disappointed in his own son, began to feel that he had found some one to replace Roderick in his daughter-in-law's altogether charming and accomplished brother. Rupert, for his part, made the most of his opportunities. Young Pendexter soon began that meteoric rise in the City which made him within a few years Lord St Blaizey's most trusted lieutenant and raised him in due course to the position of managing director both of Mangans' Bank and of the already gigantic Metal Securities Investment Trust, which, although Lord St Blaizey had nominally nothing to do with it, was in fact now easily the most important of his numerous financial ventures. Lord St Blaizey had a supreme faith in Rupert Pendexter; and that helped, more than once, to prevent a renewal of his quarrel with Roderick. For Helen saw to it that Rupert was on Roderick Damian's side; and Lord St Blaizey, as he waxed in years, got more and more into the habit of taking Rupert Pendexter's advice.

CHAPTER 2

ACROSS THE YEARS

The facts related in the last chapter came to my knowledge piecemeal—mostly after Lord St Blaizey's death had re-opened the Pendexter case. But it seemed best to put the reader in possession of them at once, because they form in a sense the background against which my story has to be set.

In that far-off murder of Simon Pendexter, neither Ben Tancred nor I had felt any real doubt who the criminal was. But the villain had got cleanly away with it; and it was a long time after the events at Blackbottle House before either of us heard of Rupert or Sarah Pendexter again. Nor did I hear any more of Helen Pendexter, with whom, in those old days, I had fancied myself very much in love. I had quite recovered from my infatuation, and got married to the right person, some time before I had any further news about the Pendexters.

Then, one morning, I saw in my newspaper the announcement of Helen's marriage. She seemed to me then to have done very well for herself, in a worldly sense; for the Honourable Roderick Damian, only son and heir of the sixteenth Viscount St Blaizey, seemed a very good catch. I read the news without a tremor; but it set me wondering what had happened to the rest of Simon Pendexter's curious household at Polruan, and not least how Helen Pendexter had come to land quite so big a fish.

For Lord St Blaizey was, even in those days, a very well-known person. Even I, who know little enough of the great financial world, knew of him as a big figure in the City. I had, moreover, the curiosity to turn him and his son up in *Who's Who*; and I saw that Roderick Damian was heir to the title, and apparently a person of some importance on his own account. Under his name *Who's Who* recorded surprisingly several publications dealing with African tribal conditions.

I was then in the army as a temporary officer, and Ben Tancred was something unmentionable in the Secret Service. So I had not much leisure to inquire into Helen Pendexter's affairs, even if I had felt any strong inclination to do so. I was, in fact, due to set off again for France on the following day. I did wonder idly why the book made no reference to any war service of Roderick Damian's; but of course there might be several explanations of that. He might be unfit, or merely have omitted to revise the entry in *Who's Who*.

The war was over before I heard of any of the Pendexters again. Then, when I had settled down once more to my job as a University lecturer, and Ben Tancred was back at work making a name for himself as a private detective, I began to read about Rupert Pendexter in the newspapers. Those were the days of the great inflationary boom just after the war, when huge fortunes were being made by speculating in foreign currencies or buying up companies and refloating them on a credulous public at an exorbitant price. I confess that, unlike Ben Tancred, I like a flutter when I have a few pounds to invest; and that makes me a regular reader of the financial columns. It was there I found Rupert Pendexter's name cropping up quite a number of times, usually in connection with one of the more spectacular reflotations of those financially romantic days. There was something called the Metal Securities Investment Trust, of which he appeared to be managing director; and this concern was buying up businesses in the Midlands right and left, and then handing out shares to a public that seemed remarkably eager to buy. I kept off those shares myself, because of what I knew about Rupert Pendexter; and in the long run I was right, for many of them crashed pretty badly later on. But if I had sold, as well as bought, at the right time, I could have cleared a nice little sum, even with the small amounts that I could afford to venture.

On one or two occasions I saw Rupert Pendexter's name coupled with Lord St Blaizey's. Rupert, it appeared, was a director of Mangans' Bank, as well as managing director of the MSIT, with which Lord St Blaizey seemed to have nothing to do. Naturally, I spoke to Ben Tancred about this rise of Rupert Pendexter to a big position in the City; and, much to my surprise, he told me that Rupert was in high favour with Lord St Blaizey, and that he believed the old villain—for so he called the sixteenth viscount—was really behind the MSIT, working the market under Rupert Pendexter's name in order to avoid too deeply compromising Mangans' Bank.

Thereafter, I kept my eyes open for news of Rupert Pendexter's doings. I noticed that the MSIT, having traded off all its inflated shares on the public, came itself quite comfortably through the collapse of 1921, and settled down, to all appearances, to a blameless inactivity. Rupert's name appeared less in the papers after the boom was over; but I saw mention of him every now and then in connection with Mangans', and he seemed to be a director of quite a number of other companies of one sort and another. When his name was mentioned now, it was often in connection with Lord St Blaizey's; and Ben Tancred, who has to know quite a lot about these business people, though he never speculates himself, told me that Rupert was generally regarded in the City as Lord St Blaizey's *alter ego*.

Meanwhile, I had heard no more of Helen Pendexter, or rather Helen Damian, as she now was. I pictured her occasionally to myself as mixing with gay society, and being very much admired. Then I found out that I had been imagining everything quite wrong. I happened to come across a man who knew Roderick Damian; and he told me that Roderick was almost a cripple, who spent all his time working away by himself in a tiny cottage on the St Blaizey estate, and was as poor as a church mouse, because he had lost most of his own money and had quarrelled with his father, whose help he was too proud to accept. Roderick, of course, would be tremendously rich some day, when the old man died, unless Lord St Blaizey carried his anger to the point of leaving the unentailed property away from him. But my informant said he didn't think that would happen. The Damians were notorious for family quarrels; but the old man had no one else to succeed to his money, and possessed far too much family pride to wish the heir to the title to be unable to keep it up with proper state. The title, of course, was bound to go to Roderick, and with it the entailed estate; but most of Lord St Blaizey's fortune was his own, to deal with absolutely as he might choose.

These facts seemed to explain Roderick Damian's lack of war service. He had, it appeared, been badly mauled by a tiger in Africa, when he was out there in 1913 collecting data about tribal conditions. I asked my informant whether he knew Roderick Damian's wife. He had barely met her; but he believed Damian had got engaged to her during his illness. The woman had been his nurse, or something of the sort; and it had ended in his marrying her, greatly to his father's fury. But when the old man actually met Helen Damian, some time after the marriage, he had apparently taken a great fancy to her, and now it was Roderick's doing, and not Lord St Blaizey's, that they lived in poverty. Roderick Damian, it seemed, refused to touch a penny of his father's money; and of his own, which he had inherited from his mother, some had gone in financing the ill-fated African expedition which had ended in his disabling accident, and the rest been swept away by that defaulting solicitor, of whose doings the reader has already been informed.

That was all I learnt about Helen and her husband at that time. But I picked up a bit more afterwards when I went down for a few days to Fowey in Ben Tancred's company. His old aunt, who lived there, had just died; and he had to see her lawyer about the winding up of her estate. I met the lawyer, who came round to see Ben at our hotel; and he turned out to be the same Mr Polwhele who had represented Helen at the inquest on Simon Pendexter's body. Naturally, we asked him about the Pendexters; and he was able to tell us a good deal. Sarah Pendexter, he said —that is, Helen's aunt—had left Blackbottle House after her brother Simon's death; but she had afterwards gone back to live there alone, and was still there, with Simon Pendexter's old retainers, the Trevenas, still in her service.

Mr Polwhele told us that Sarah Pendexter had grown crankier than ever. She was still a pillar of the Methodist Church; but some of her views were said to be very wild. She believed implicitly in an early Second Coming, and was quite sure that the war had been sent to warn sinners of the speedy ending of the world. She was reputed too, to see visions; and there was no doubt of her believing that she was given some special sort of divine guidance.

I asked how she got on with Helen; and Mr Polwhele said he believed they were not on very good terms. He waxed enthusiastic at the mention of Helen's name, and said how wonderfully she had borne up in spite of all her troubles. She was, he said, as fresh and beautiful as ever, though her life with Roderick Damian must be enough to drive most people crazy. Roderick, I gathered, was 'difficult'—a morose semi-invalid, who had taken life hardly, and found in religion only a means of darkening the colours yet more. According to Mr Polwhele, he led his wife the life of a dog, but the lawyer said he heard she was always charming to Roderick, even in his worst moods. He opined that it was a shame for a fine woman like that to wear out her youth in unnecessary poverty, drudging for a perverse cripple who would not allow her so much as a servant in the house.

This was by no means the same view of Roderick Damian as I had got from my previous informant; and I was disposed to make some allowance for Mr Polwhele's evident partisanship where Helen was concerned. Still, it sounded as if she were having a pretty bad time. I asked whether her brother Rupert—who seemed to have managed very well for himself up in London—couldn't do something to help her. Helen had been very much attached to him in the old days; and surely he had been fond of her too, in his selfish way.

At Rupert Pendexter's name Mr Polwhele glowered. He shared my view that Providence ought to have managed better than to let the wicked flourish so profusely. But, as for Rupert helping Helen, his view was that Roderick Damian would absolutely refuse to let anybody help either himself or his wife. Perhaps Rupert did help surreptitiously, to some extent: he really didn't know. He believed he and Helen saw a good deal of each other when Rupert came down, as he sometimes did, to stay with Lord St Blaizey at the Castle. But that was not very often. The Castle was shut up most of the year; for Lord St Blaizey very much preferred living at Longridge Park, his other seat near London, where he could carry on his business affairs far more satisfactorily. Moreover, from all he had heard, Longridge Park, which had come to Lord St Blaizey through his wife, was a much more comfortable place to live in than the Castle, which was more of a medieval fortress than a dwelling-house.

Still, Lord St Blaizey did open the Castle once or twice a year; and, when he did, Mr Polwhele believed that Rupert Pendexter generally accompanied him. That young man seemed to be very much in his lordship's good graces in these days.

I asked the lawyer whether it was through Helen that Rupert Pendexter had got his position in Mangans' Bank. Mr Polwhele said he supposed it was, but he did not really know. He went on to abuse Rupert for having somehow succeeded in evading war service. He had apparently managed to get some sort of job in a government office, controlling something or other; and Mr Polwhele believed he had used his position pretty successfully for feathering his own nest.

All that, however, was hardly more than gossip; for the lawyer did not profess to know anything about it, except by hearsay. Sarah Pendexter, I gathered, was his principal informant; and from what I remembered of Rupert's aunt I felt it would be wise to take any evil she spoke of him with more than one grain of salt. I had not forgotten Sarah's vindictive hatred of Rupert; and, though I was sure he deserved it, I was not prepared to build much on facts about him that rested solely on Sarah Pendexter's evidence.

While Ben and I were at Fowey, we ferried over to Polruan, walked up the hill past Mrs Huggins's house, where I had lodged at the time of old Simon Pendexter's death, observed the Methodist chapel just opposite looking as ugly as ever, and went on to the headland from which we could get a view of Blackbottle House. It looked very forlorn, with the blinds down in most of the rooms, and the terrace rank with weeds. It had clearly not been painted for years, and the storms had buffeted it into a sadly dilapidated condition. No one appeared on the terrace while we were by; but smoke coming from one of the chimneys told us that the place was inhabited. Ben and I were rather silent on our way back to Fowey—which was unusual, for Ben is usually a great talker. I knew he was thinking of his failure to catch old Simon Pendexter's murderer; and as for me, I was thinking what a mercy it was that Helen Pendexter had refused to marry me when I flung my silly young heart at her feet.

CHAPTER 3

LORD ST BLAIZEY DIES

Ben Tancred and I paid our visit to Fowey nearly a dozen years ago. Thereafter, till last year, nothing at all happened to bring either of us into touch with the Pendexters or their affairs. Then began the rapid series of events which I am going to tell you about in this book, beginning with old Lord St Blaizey's death and ending with—but I mustn't tell you just how it all ended, or I shall spoil my story.

I read about Lord St Blaizey's death in the evening paper, and then more fully when the inquest was reported a few days later. The old gentleman—he was seventy-six—had died as the result of a fall from his horse. He had been out riding alone when it happened, though it came out at the inquest that he had no business to be riding alone. Old as he was, and feeble as he had been getting of late, Lord St Blaizey, it appeared, still insisted on going for a ride every morning, wet or fine. On these occasions he was regularly accompanied either by his private secretary, one Gregory Landor, or by a groom; and it had to be explained at the inquest how, on the day of his death, he had come to be riding alone.

The old lord was on one of his rare visits to St Blaizey Castle at the time of his death. I noticed with surprise, in the report of the inquest, that Roderick Damian, now the seventeenth Viscount St Blaizey, appeared to have been living at the Castle—or at all events staying there—when his father died. Apparently father and son had been reconciled; and Roderick and Helen were no longer living in the cottage in which they had passed their first years of married life. On the morning of Lord St Blaizey's death, Gregory Landor, who gave what sounded very nervous evidence, had gone out with his employer as usual for his morning ride; but he said that, when they had been out only a few minutes, Lord St Blaizey had sent him back to the Castle to put through an important business telephone call to London at once. Landor said that he had protested against Lord St Blaizey riding on alone, because he was too nearly blind to be safe on a horse by himself. But any allusion to his growing infirmity had always annoyed the old man; and it seemed from Landor's evidence that he had been sent back to the Castle with a flea in his ear.

At all events, according to his statement, he had ridden back, somewhat uneasy in mind, to put through his call to London. He had felt uneasy enough to look for Roderick Damian immediately upon his return, in order to tell him what had happened. But Roderick had been out; and he had therefore told Helen Damian, who had thereupon said that she herself would go off at once on horseback in the direction taken by Lord St Blaizey, in order to ensure that he should come to no harm. Having thus eased his conscience, Gregory Landor had put through his trunk call, which was a personal one; but it had taken him three-quarters of an hour to find the man he wanted and get his messages delivered. He had then gone to discover whether Lord St Blaizey had come back; but there had been no sign of him. He had ridden off down the drive, in the hope of meeting him coming back, but had met instead Helen Damian, looking very upset. She had told him that she had met with Lord St Blaizey's riderless horse at some distance from where Landor had left him; but there had been no sign of her father-in-law. She had ridden to a keeper's cottage to summon help, and the woods were now being searched. In the meantime she had come back to the Castle to tell Roderick and to fetch Gregory Landor to help in the search.

At this point Helen Damian—now Lady St Blaizey—took up the story, corroborating what Landor had already said. They had ridden back together towards the spot where Helen had seen Lord St Blaizey's horse; but on the way they had met a little group of men carrying a stretcher, on which was Lord St Blaizey's dead body, covered with a horse-blanket. The men had told her that they had found the body lying in one of the rides at the far end of the Castle woods. The old man had a broken neck, they thought, from the way his head was hanging; and there was a big weal across his forehead as well. Close by where he had fallen a branch forked out from one of the trees right across the ride. It looked as if his lordship must have ridden right into it without seeing that it was there. It was about at the height at which it would have caught him full in the face; and, of course, every one knew that his lordship's eyes had been very bad just lately. There had been no doubt of his being dead when he was found, so they had thought it best to bring the body straight back to the Castle, sending off one of the keeper's boys, on a bicycle, to tell Dr Andover to come to the Castle at once.

Next came some direct evidence from the men who had found the body. Unreasonably, as it seemed to me, they were taken somewhat to task by the coroner, who was sitting without a jury, for not having left Lord St Blaizey where he was, and summoned the doctor to the scene of the fatality instead of to the Castle. The head keeper's answer, repeated by his subordinates, was that, his lordship being clearly dead, and the nature of the accident plain, he had thought it more respectful to carry the body to the Castle at once, especially as the weather had looked threatening, as if a storm were coming up.

Dr Andover followed; and not till I read his evidence at the inquest did I realize that there was any suspicion of the accident not being just what it seemed. The headlines in the newspaper made no such suggestion, though the paper gave its very full report a prominent place. But, as soon as I read what the doctor had to say, I realized, from the way he said it, that he was far from satisfied. There is no need, here, to trouble the reader with technicalities. The gist of Dr Andover's evidence was that, when he examined the body at the Castle, the neck was broken, and there was also a large contused area on the forehead, clearly the result of a blow. The coroner asked him whether in his view the broken neck was such as could have been caused by Lord St Blaizey falling from his horse. Dr Andover replied that it could have been caused in that way. The coroner asked whether he could say positively that it was so caused.

To this the doctor gave a negative answer. He would only say that there was nothing in the nature of the fracture to exclude such a cause. Pressed farther, he agreed that it had probably been caused by the fall, but insisted that this could not be regarded as a strictly medical opinion.

The coroner then passed to the contusion on the forehead. Could this have been caused, as was suggested, by the deceased striking his head against the projecting tree-branch about which they had been told by previous witnesses? To this the doctor answered that there were some indications which seemed to point to that conclusion. He had found, on the surface of the wound, some traces of tree-moss, of the same sort as was actually growing on the branch to which reference had been made. 'Is not that fairly conclusive, doctor?' the coroner had said. 'I would not say that,' Dr Andover had replied.

Inevitably, this answer led to further questions. Were there any appearances inconsistent with the contusion having been caused by the projecting branch? 'Not positively,' said Dr Andover, 'but there were also upon the wound some traces of tree-bark which certainly did not come from that particular tree.' The coroner asked whether these fragments could have become attached to the wound after the blow—say, when the body fell to the ground. Dr Andover's very guarded answer was that, medically, such a possibility did exist. It was not his province to enter into the non-medical questions involved.

There was, of course, other evidence that I have not reported at this stage. Roderick Damian—or rather Lord St Blaizey, as he had now become—gave evidence, principally of identification; and one or two other people were also called as witnesses. But at the end of Dr Andover's evidence the coroner adjourned the court for a week—pending further inquiries. That, of course, was enough by itself to tell me that the supposition of accident was not being accepted without question. The coroner evidently thought that further investigation was called for. What the police thought I could only surmise; but I entertained a strong opinion that they must have inspired his attitude. Otherwise, there did not seem to be enough in the evidence to throw doubt on the idea that Lord St Blaizey had died a purely accidental death.

I had not seen Dr Tancred since I had read the first news of Lord St Blaizey's death, because he had been away from London on a case. But as soon as I had read the report of the inquest I rang up his flat in the Adelphi, where he had his offices as well as the comfortable, but always untidy, rooms which were his bachelor home. I found that he was out, but was expected back before long. I asked his secretary, Miss Jellicoe, whether she knew if he was busy, or would be likely to be free for a talk if I came round; and it ended in my fixing up to go and take my chance of finding him in at tea-time.

Tea-time, then, found me ensconced in a deep arm-chair in Ben's big sitting-room overlooking the river, eating buttered toast and drinking that very special China tea which was one of his extravagances. It is, I confess, wasted on me. I prefer Ceylon tea, made nice and strong, with plenty of milk and sugar. But Ben refused to have what he calls 'that poison' in his place: so when I go to see him I drink his brew and try to feel I might like it if only people wouldn't regard it as tea.

Ben grinned at me. 'I can guess what brings you round, Paul,' he said. 'I've been reading about it myself.'

'You mean the inquest on Lord St Blaizey?'

'Of course I do. If our old acquaintance, Rupert Pendexter, had been anywhere near the place when it happened, we might start imagining things, mightn't we?'

'How do we know he wasn't?' I exclaimed.

'We don't. But there's no mention of him in the proceedings so far.'

'Then you think it's murder?' I asked.

Ben made a gesture with his big hands. 'My dear chap, I don't think anything at all about it—except that the doctor thinks it's murder—or at any rate strongly suspects as much.'

'And the coroner, too,' I said. 'Or else he would hardly have adjourned the inquest, would he?'

'He had to, I should say,' Ben answered, 'after Dr Andover's evidence. I can't, of course, tell whether he knew beforehand what was coming. But one would have supposed the doctor must have warned the police of what he was meaning to say. At all events, they'll obviously be on to it now.'

'Of course, there may be nothing in it,' I said. 'I mean, the doctor may be making much ado about nothing.'

'Very likely,' Ben answered. 'Anyhow, it's no business of mine. Even if somebody did bump the old gentleman off, I'm not concerned.'

'Unless it was Rupert Pendexter who did it,' I said. 'In that case you'd want to be in at the death, wouldn't you—for old times' sake?'

Ben Tancred shrugged his shoulders. 'My dear Paul, your imagination's running away with you. Why should it be Pendexter—if it's anybody at all? From all I hear old St Blaizey's the very last person Pendexter would want to put out of business.'

'All the same,' I said. 'I've got a feeling . . .'

'Oh, rot!' Ben cut in. 'Bother your feelings.' And there,

for the time, we left the matter; for Ben had just finished off a most interesting case, and I spent the rest of my time with him hearing all about it. Not till I had got up to go was another word said about the St Blaizey case. Then Ben Tancred gave one of his big chuckles.

'There's one person, Paul,' he said, 'who'll agree with you about friend Rupert if the facts give her even half a chance. That's Sarah Pendexter, unless she's changed a lot since we knew her.'

'Oh, I shouldn't build much on Sarah Pendexter's opinion about it,' I said. 'She's prejudiced: besides, according to that Cornish lawyer she's more than half out of her mind. Heavens! She may be dead by now, for all I know.'

'So she may,' said Ben. 'Anyway, I don't suppose either you or I will ever run across Sarah Pendexter again. Well, so long, Paul.'

I heard Ben's telephone ringing as I left the flat.

CHAPTER 4

'I SAW HIM DO IT'

This next bit of my story I must tell you as I had it from Dr Tancred on the following day. The telephone bell I had heard shrilling as I left Ben's flat was actually the next important incident of the Pendexter Saga. It was Sarah Pendexter ringing up from Paddington Station, where she had just arrived from Cornwall with the demand that Dr Tancred should give her an immediate appointment. The old lady, Ben told me, sounded full of excitement over the telephone, and he at once agreed to see her, without asking her to explain what her business was. He could guess, without asking, that it had something to do with Lord St Blaizey's death. What, he would discover soon enough, without trying to get the information over the phone.

Naturally, Ben was surprised. It was nearly twenty-five years since he had seen Sarah Pendexter; and till Miss Jellicoe told him who was on the 'phone he had been without any expectation of the St Blaizey case coming his way. But Sarah's voice revived ancient memories. She must be an old woman now: she had seemed old to him at the time of her brother's murder a quarter of a century ago. Ben's failure to gratify Sarah's assurance by catching the criminal on that occasion could hardly have been expected to leave her with any great confidence in his prowess. Yet here she was, coming to him again, presumably on account of this other death which the doctor seemed to think was not really the accident it had been taken for at the first. Did Sarah Pendexter think more highly of him than he had supposed? Or was there some other and less complimentary reason for her coming in search of him now?

Ben told me that his curiosity was roused enough for him to await Sarah Pendexter's coming with not a little impatience. He had not long to wait. About twenty minutes after she had spoken to him on the telephone, a taxi drew up below, and he saw an old lady in a bonnet get out and pay the taxi-man. Ben could not see much of her from his window—only that she was dressed in black, and held herself as stiffly erect as in the old days.

Perhaps I had better describe Sarah Pendexter right away, not from what Ben told me, but from my own meeting with her later on in the case. In the old days, she had been tall and thin and angular; but now she seemed more like a scarecrow than ever. She had grown even thinner than of old, and, still holding herself very erect, she looked even taller than she really was. Her face had fallen away, and was heavily lined, and the scanty hairs on her head were quite white, and still combed straight back from her high forehead, showing spaces of bare scalp between. Her clothes were incredibly shabby and old-fashioned, but neat and prim, with no ornament except a big jet chain which she wore round her neck. It rattled when she was excited, for then her whole body seemed to heave and shake as she talked in the high, shrill voice that Ben and I both remembered so well. She wore steel spectacles, which looked as if they made the bridge of her nose sore; and she sometimes carried an ear-trumpet, having become very deaf as well as near-sighted with age. But for all her years, Sarah Pendexter still impressed one with a strong sense of vitality. Her speech was as sharp as ever, and she was as little able to keep still as she had been twenty-five years ago.

Such was the old lady whom Ben's clerk, Jellicoe, ushered into his sitting-room that evening. She wasted no time on ceremony. She began speaking before she was well inside the door.

'I have come to you, Dr Tancred, because I have been guided to come. As I lay in bed this morning, a voice said to me "Find Dr Tancred!": and I caught the first train to London and looked you up in the telephone book. The voices are always right. They told me to come to you; and here I am.'

Ben Tancred is one of the most matter-of-fact people I know; and he is the very last person who would be impressed by talk about 'guidance' and 'voices'. I think Sarah Pendexter's mode of address took him rather aback, even as coming from her. But he muttered something about being pleased to see her after so many years, and managed to induce her to sit down, though she was soon up again from her chair, and persisted in walking about the room in a disconcerting way as she talked.

'If I had not been guided, Dr Tancred, I should not have come to you,' Sarah went on. 'You were so unsuccessful in dealing with my wicked nephew when he murdered Simon that I should not have thought of asking for your services again. But the voice said I was to come; and, besides, I know of no one else who is in a position to give me any help at all.'

Ben thought privately that Sarah's last phrase gave a good deal more explanation of her presence than any 'voice' she supposed herself to have heard. But he did not say so. He merely reminded her that she had not told him yet about what she wished to consult him.

'You have seen the report of the inquest on Lord St Blaizey?' Sarah demanded.

'Yes.'

'He was murdered.'

'You know that?' Ben countered.

'Of course he was murdered,' said Sarah impatiently. 'Rupert murdered him.'

'The inquest,' said Ben, 'did not, if I remember rightly, bring up any mention of your nephew's name.'

Sarah brushed that aside. 'All the same I am certain Rupert killed him. Dr Tancred, this time I rely upon you to prove that he is guilty.'

Ben said, 'At present, madam, I know nothing about the case, beyond what appeared in the newspapers. You are asking me to take it up professionally?'

'Of course I am,' said Sarah impatiently. 'I do not mind how much money you spend, as long as you get Rupert hanged.' Her voice, Ben said, was so vindictive that she made him shiver.

'I take it you have some evidence, beyond what came out at the inquest.'

'I know that Rupert killed him.'

Ben felt an impulse to say, 'That's precisely what you said last time, without a tittle of evidence to back it up.' But after all he was pretty certain that on that occasion Sarah had been right despite her lack of evidence. Was she right again this time? By the same instinct? Or could she, on this occasion, tell him something that he could go upon if he decided to take up the case? For, though Ben disliked Sarah's manner, and thought her half-crazy, as she was, yet if there was the shadow of a case against Rupert Pendexter he would feel sorely tempted to take it up. Ben did not like being beaten; and that twenty-five-year-old defeat, now that he had been forcibly reminded of it, still rankled in his mind.

'But have you any *evidence*?' Ben persisted.

At that, Sarah Pendexter went off into a curious rigmarole. Some of it was obviously sheer fantasy: perhaps all of it. That was what, with a person of Sarah's mental composition, it was so difficult to tell.

'*I saw him do it,*' said Sarah. 'They were riding together —in the woods. They were talking. I saw Rupert look round, in order to make certain they were alone. Then he struck Lord St Blaizey across the face. I saw him fall off his horse on the ground. His neck was broken. Then Rupert rode away, as swift as the wind. He was gone in an instant and vanished out of my sight. Only Lord St Blaizey was left lying there, with no one to help him or to avenge his murder. But you must avenge him, Dr Tancred. He is watching and listening to us now; his murdered body is crying out to heaven for vengeance. I can hear him calling to me—and to you.'

'You say you saw all this?' said Ben Tancred, amazed. 'Of course you have told this story to the police?'

'I have told the police Rupert killed him.'

'And that you saw him do it?'

'No, no; not that! Only that I saw him riding away as swift as the wind.'

'But, my dear Miss Pendexter, surely when you told them that, they asked you . . .'

'They asked me nothing. They did not believe a word I said. They said I was only a hysterical old woman. They know I . . . hated Rupert. They think . . .'

Ben could supply the missing words, which Sarah could not pronounce. The police thought she was crazy. Was she? Or rather how crazy was she? Had she really seen . . .?

'*When* did you see all this?' Ben asked, fixing his eyes on Sarah's face.

'I saw it in a vision,' said Sarah Pendexter. 'I see many things in visions, when God allows.'

A vision! Then the woman *was* mad. She was as good as admitting that she had not really seen anything at all. She had simply reconstructed the scene, probably from what she had heard at the inquest, and then imagined she had seen it all really happen. Ben was deeply disappointed; for Sarah's assurance had roused hopes in him that she had some real evidence in her possession.

'*When* did you see this vision?' Ben persisted.

'I have seen it again and again,' said Sarah. 'It keeps on

coming back to me. I can see it now.' She stopped speaking, and stood staring straight before her into the distance, with a look of horror on her face, as if she were really watching the fatal scene.

'Did you first see this ... vision before or after you interviewed the police?'

'After ... No, it was before. I can't remember. It must have been before ...' Sarah floundered.

'Then why did you not tell them all about it?'

'I was not guided to tell them. I ...' Sarah's voice trailed away.

'What exactly did you tell the police?'

'That I saw Rupert riding away as swift as the wind.'

'Riding away from where?'

'From the murder.'

'Yes; but where exactly did you see him?'

'On the road to Lostwithiel.'

'Which road?'

'The road from St Austell. It runs along the boundary of the Castle grounds.'

Ben got up, and fished down, after a moment's hunting, sheet 143 of the inch Ordnance Map.* He spread it out on the table. 'I see the road,' he said. 'It runs through St Blaizey village, doesn't it?'

'Yes,' said Sarah. 'He was riding as swift as the wind.'

'Just where on the road?' Ben persisted. 'Can you point out the exact place on the map?'

'It was just to the south of the old copper mine,' said Sarah. 'Between the Porcupine and Penpillick.'

Ben bent over the map. 'I see,' he said. 'About a mile north of St Blaizey village?'

'Yes,' Sarah agreed. 'He came riding out of the Castle woods on to the road. He was gone in an instant.'

'This,' said Ben, 'is important. Can you fix the time—the day, I mean, and the exact hour when you saw this?'

'It was on the day of the murder. In the morning. It was between eleven and twelve o'clock.'

*See Map of the country round St Blaizey, p. 10.

'How did you come to be thereabouts, Miss Pendexter? Do you still live at Blackbottle House, by the way? It's a long way from there.'

Sarah said she did still live at Blackbottle House. That morning she had been over to visit a fellow-Methodist, who was bedridden, at a place called Lanescot, near the old copper mine, but off the main road. Her errand done, she had walked back to the main road, in order to pick up a bus that would take her into Lostwithiel, where she had a Methodist meeting to attend. She had walked along the road in the direction of Lostwithiel, waiting for the bus to overtake her, and had seen Rupert ride out of the eastern entrance to the grounds of St Blaizey Castle, beside the old lodge. She had caught no more than a glimpse of him; for he had been out of sight almost before she had been aware of his presence.

Now, this was all so circumstantial that it did not sound at all like a dream. Of course, even if Sarah had seen Rupert riding along the Lostwithiel road quite near the time of old Lord St Blaizey's death, that proved nothing in itself. But it was certainly worth verifying, if it could be verified, and following up—especially as nothing had been said hitherto, as far as Ben Tancred knew, to indicate that Rupert Pendexter had been anywhere in the neighbourhood of St Blaizey on that day.

Accordingly, Ben pressed Sarah hard, and succeeded, with the aid of the map, in fixing the exact place at which Sarah thought she had seen her nephew. He was disappointed to learn from her that there was no lodge-keeper at that entrance to the St Blaizey Castle estate. There had been once, but the lodge was now disused and ruinous. There was a gate; but there was no one to mark who went in or out by it.

Ben Tancred also pressed Sarah about the exact time at which she had seen Rupert. There he was able, by dint of careful questioning, to get a fairly precise answer. It had been about five minutes before the bus caught her up, and she knew the bus was due to leave St Blaizey at half-past eleven. It would have taken only a few minutes for it to reach the point at which it had overtaken her on the road.

That being ascertained, Ben had to tackle a harder task. He was now in no doubt that Sarah Pendexter did really believe she had seen Rupert on the Lostwithiel road on the morning of Lord St Blaizey's death. But was that all she had seen? Was all the rest of her 'vision' sheer imagination, or was there a substratum of reality beneath her vapourings? If she had come, as she said, from Lanescot straight to the main road, she would not have entered the Castle woods at all; for Lanescot lay to the east of the road, and the woods on the opposite side to the west.

'Did you go into the Castle woods that morning?' Ben asked. 'Or only along the main road?'

'It was in the woods I saw Rupert kill him,' said Sarah.

'Yes, but on that morning, when you saw Rupert on the road, had you been into the woods before you saw him riding away?'

That puzzled Sarah for a moment. Then she said, 'Of course, I must have been or I could not have seen him do it.'

'Yes, but do you remember when you went into the woods? You said you came straight from Lanescot to the main road. That wouldn't take you through the woods at all.'

'No, not then.'

'Then you say you turned up the main road towards Lostwithiel; and almost at once you saw Rupert Pendexter come out of the gate.'

'That's right,' said Sarah.

'Then there would have been no time for you to go into the woods, and actually see the murder,' Ben insisted.

'But I did see it,' Sarah answered. 'I see it now.'

Ben tried again, after that, but he got the thing no clearer. Two points did seem plain enough. One was that Sarah thought she had seen Rupert come out of the Castle woods on horseback, and that there was no question of this being merely a 'vision' in her mind. The other was that she had not seen the murder. Yet she was certain, if her testimony ever had to be used in court, utterly to destroy, with a jury, her credibility on the first point by her no less firm insistence on the second. Unless someone else besides Sarah Pendexter had seen Rupert Pendexter that morning, he might almost as well, from an evidential standpoint, not have been seen at all.

Ben Tancred tried, of course, to discover whether Sarah Pendexter had any further relevant facts to relate. He tackled, for example, the question of motive; but Sarah was unable to propound any motive, save innate wickedness, that could have prompted Rupert Pendexter to kill Lord St Blaizey. He did discover that she knew the Castle woods well, and was able to describe quite circumstantially the actual place where she said she had seen the murder done. He got the name of the bedridden friend whom Sarah had been visiting at Lanescot; and he also established the fact that, to the best of Sarah's belief, the bus had not overtaken Rupert anywhere on the road between Penpillick, where she had boarded it, and Lostwithiel. If, then, she had really seen him, he must have left the main road at some point not far north of where he had emerged from the woods.

The only other piece of definite information Ben got out of Sarah was that she had attended her Methodist meeting in Lostwithiel, and that one of the other people present at it had been Roderick Damian, the new Lord St Blaizey, who had been in the chair, but who had arrived a few minutes after the business of the meeting had begun.

The interview had already lasted a long time before all this information had been brought to light; for in the course of it Sarah had gone off into a number of excited digressions which I have suppressed in this report. But now came the critical question; for as soon as Ben had done with his circumstantial questions Sarah came back to her original demand.

'You will come down to Cornwall at once, and get Rupert hanged, Dr Tancred.'

Ben hesitated. The half-cracked Sarah was likely to prove a terribly troublesome client. Her entire story might be a mere mare's nest, and old Lord St Blaizey might have died a perfectly natural death. Even if he had been murdered, there was really nothing to show that Rupert Pendexter had murdered him. Yet assuredly, nothing short of a verdict of wilful murder against Rupert would satisfy this vindictive old lady, who had been cherishing her hatred of her step-nephew for nearly twenty-five years—ever since her brother had died unavenged.

There was all that to be taken into account against having anything to do with the case. On the other hand, Ben Tancred too had his feelings, and one of them was that he would dearly love a return battle of wits with Rupert Pendexter, if only there was half a chance of bringing him to book.

Ben made up his mind. 'I can promise nothing, Miss Pendexter. There is too little to go upon.'

Sarah interrupted fiercely. 'But I saw him . . .'

Ben Tancred had no desire to hear about Sarah's vision all over again. He went on swiftly, 'But I am willing to come down to Cornwall, and try to find out how matters stand. If I then think there is a case to investigate, I will do my best to discover the truth. Please understand, I make no promise at all to prove that your nephew murdered Lord St Blaizey. I have no notion yet whether he was murdered or not, and certainly none about your nephew's guilt. For all I know, Lord St Blaizey may have died an accidental death.'

'But I saw . . .' said Sarah.

'I have told you what I am prepared to do, Miss Pendexter. It is for you to decide whether you wish for my services on those terms.'

'I was guided to come here,' said Sarah. 'I will trust the Lord to guide you in your turn. You must come to Cornwall today.'

'Tomorrow,' said Ben. 'There are things I must clear up here before I leave.'

'Tomorrow, then, by the first train. You will stay with me while you are there.'

Ben had not the smallest intention of staying at Blackbottle House, not only because it seemed likely to be an exceedingly uncomfortable residence, but also because he could conceive of nothing more inhibiting to an investigator than Sarah's continual presence. He announced, firmly, that he would go to a hotel. Sarah tried to make him change his mind but at length she gave way. Ben also firmly resisted her desire to travel down with him by the same train.

'We had better not be seen together,' he said tactfully. 'I shall have a freer hand if I turn up as a mere visitor, with no known connection with the case.'

At long last Sarah Pendexter departed. She would return to Polruan at once, and would eagerly await Dr Tancred's first report on the affair. She was certain he would be guided to the dreadful truth. She had faith that the Lord would not allow Rupert Pendexter to escape justice a second time.

CHAPTER 5

SOMEONE IN THE CITY

As soon as Sarah Pendexter had gone, Dr Tancred rang up Scotland Yard. If the police had any serious thoughts of Lord St Blaizey's death being a case of murder, the Yard was practically certain to be called in; for the case would be of far too great national importance to be left to the local police. Wilson was the man to get hold of, if he could be found. Ben Tancred remembered how Superintendent Wilson, then a young sergeant, had shared his discomfiture in the Pendexter case of twenty-five years ago. Of course, Ben Tancred had come into contact with the Scotland Yard man many times since then. But now his thoughts went back naturally to that time in Cornwall when they had first met.

Ben was soon speaking to Superintendent Henry Wilson. Yes, the Yard had been called in: a man named Falcon—Chief Inspector Falcon—had been sent down yesterday at the request of the County Police. So Dr Tancred hadn't met him? Oh, he was quite sound: a bit of a queer fish, as Dr

Tancred would soon see for himself; but quite a sound man. Yes, Wilson would gladly give him a line of introduction to Falcon, and to the Chief Constable, whom he knew. But how did Dr Tancred come to be in on the St Blaizey case? One good turn deserved another. Who had called him in? Was it one of the family?

When Ben answered that he had been called in by Sarah Pendexter, whom Wilson might remember as old Simon Pendexter's sister, there was a sound of surprise at the other end of the wire. 'But what's it got to do with her?' Wilson asked. When Ben Tancred answered that Sarah had roundly accused Rupert Pendexter of the murder, Henry Wilson whistled.

'But he wasn't there, was he?' the Scotland Yard man inquired.

'He wasn't mentioned in the report of the inquest,' Ben answered, 'and so far, apart from Sarah, that's my only source of information. But she says she saw him, quite near the spot, round about the time when old St Blaizey perished.'

'I don't think the local police have got on to that,' Wilson commented. 'Their report says nothing at all about Rupert Pendexter—or Sarah. I've got it here, in front of me. Do you regard Sarah as what one would call a reliable witness?'

Ben Tancred laughed. 'About the most unreliable you can imagine,' he said, 'at any rate from the standpoint of a jury. She also had a vision vouchsafed to her of Rupert actually striking the old gentleman down; and she's got what she saw and what she fancied all mixed up. She's half-mad anyway. All the same, I'm sure she does believe she really saw Rupert Pendexter near the place where Lord St Blaizey died; and I'm inclined to think she did. The time fits too. I'm going down to St Blaizey to look into it.'

Wilson answered, after a pause, that if it really turned out that Rupert Pendexter had anything to do with the affair, he would be feeling sorry not to be in on it himself. Apart from that old affair down at Blackbottle House, he knew a thing or two about friend Rupert that would not bear repeating over the 'phone.

'City matters?' Ben Tancred asked; and Wilson said 'Yes.'

'If I come round, can you give me the dope?'

'I'll do better—drop in on you this evening after dinner, if I may. I've got to be round your way tonight.'

Ben said he would be delighted. He liked Superintendent Wilson, and the two men were often able to give each other help. In the meantime, if he was to get off to Cornwall on the following morning, he had a number of things to do first, in order to leave everything shipshape at the office. Jellicoe, who acted sometimes as chauffeur as well as assistant investigator, should, he decided, drive him down—or at any rate come with him and share the driving. It would be useful to have the car with him; and perhaps Jellicoe would come in handy too in doing some of the sleuthing, if there was any. So Miss Jellicoe would be left in charge of the office while he was away. Dr Tancred spent the rest of the time till Henry Wilson came in dictating and giving instructions to Jennie Jellicoe. He snatched a hasty meal of beer and sandwiches without interrupting his work.

'Well, Wilson, what's the lowdown on friend Rupert?'

'Nothing too definite, I'm afraid,' Wilson answered, taking a pull at the tankard beside him. He was drinking beer, whereas Dr Tancred preferred his inevitable rum. 'It's only that the Yard have had their eye on Rupert Pendexter for some time. Financially, I mean.'

'What, the Metal Securities Trust?' Ben Tancred asked.

'No, that's an old story; and it was never fraudulent—in a legal sense. Besides, that was really St Blaizey's concern, rather than Pendexter's, though Pendexter's name was chiefly used. I meant more recent doings. Ever heard of the Iridium Syndicate?'

Ben Tancred confessed his ignorance.

'Hardly any one has. But it's one of three or four City shows that have been up to some pretty queer doings just lately behind the scenes. They've been trying to corner the supplies of some fairly scarce materials—things there's little enough of on the market for a monopoly to be workable—and then force up the price sky-high—with the idea, of course, of unloading at the right moment.'

'You mean Pendexter's in on that?'

'The man behind it all, we're told, though he's keeping himself pretty well covered up.'

'Even if he is, that sort of swindling's quite lawful, isn't it? Regarded as thoroughly good business, if it comes off, and no worse than sharp practice even if it goes wrong. Why, your friend Lord Ealing's always doing that sort of thing; and he's in the Cabinet just now.'

Wilson gave a laugh. 'But sometimes people who start just the right side of the line step over it,' he said. 'Especially when things don't go off according to plan. We're waiting to see if Pendexter means to step over the line or not. I'm told some of his little speculations have got him into the deuce of a mess.'

'Iridium, for example?'

'Among others. You see, what is apt to happen in these cases is that, when the speculators think they have got the market safely cornered, a fresh supply turns up out of the blue, and they have got to buy it up, at whatever price they're asked for it, or sell off their own holdings at a loss, and chuck in their hand. That seems to be the choice in front of Pendexter in this case—unless he can find a way round it.'

'Who's the happy man with the extra iridium?'

'We don't know that yet; and it's possible there isn't any. It may be someone playing a game of bluff. But a firm of brokers called Wilkins and Leadem are selling large lots of iridium forward—for delivery in three months' time—and our news is that Pendexter and his friends are getting rattled. If that stuff exists, I think it must be Russian. That's what Venables suggests: he's our expert in that sort of thing.'

'The gist of it, from my point of view, being that Rupert Pendexter may be in a financial hole. At present, I don't see how it helps. He doesn't stand to gain by Lord St Blaizey's death, does he?'

'Not that I know of. Rather the reverse, one would think. I'm not suggesting anything—merely giving you the facts, as far as I know them.'

'Got any more of 'em?'

49

'Well, Pendexter's played a pretty daring game in the City for a long time past,' Wilson answered. 'Nothing positively unlawful; I mean, nothing you could charge him on. But he's a public danger, in my view. One of those men who love taking big risks—especially for other people.'

'But Mangans' name stands very high, surely. He's managing director of Mangans', isn't he?'

'Mangans' are sound as a bell, of course, in a City sense. Friend Rupert doesn't put any of these private deals of his through them. But he controls, behind the scenes, several smaller firms he can use for the sort of business Mangans' make a point of never touching.'

'Know their names?'

'Reed and Quencher, of Lothbury. That's one. And M.A.N.G.O.—known as Mango.'

'Sounds nasty. It's a foul vegetable. What's it stand for?'

'Mutual Alliance of National Gas Organizations, or something like that. It started with some idea of making a privately owned "gas grid", on the lines of the electricity grid, you know. That fell through; and now it's just a general predatory investment company. Pendexter controls it.'

'Up to anything special?'

'Only that he's been using it to finance these corners in commodities for him. Look here, I don't know the full facts. If you want them, now or later, you'd better see Venables. He knows everything about 'em.'

Ben said that he reckoned that would keep, until he discovered whether there was any case for him to investigate, or any likely connection between Rupert Pendexter's financial entanglements and Lord St Blaizey's death. He went on to give Superintendent Wilson a full account of his visit from Sarah Pendexter.

'I think it's pretty clear she didn't see the murder—if there was one,' Wilson commented. 'But it sounds as if you were right about her having really seen friend Rupert in the neighbourhood. Or thought she did,' he amended. 'She may merely have seen someone else, and mistaken him for Rupert. What about her sight?'

'She wears spectacles; but she doesn't seem at all blind.

Still, I know well enough it may be all moonshine. Only, I'm intrigued enough to go down there and try to find out whether it is moonshine or not.'

'Then I wish you luck,' said Wilson. 'I'd better write you those notes I promised now.'

Superintendent Wilson wrote a short note to Col. Gates-Crocker, the Chief Constable, asking him to give Dr Benjamin Tancred, who had a high standing as a private investigator, any help he could reasonably afford. Wilson paused.

'Shall I say whom you're representing?' he asked.

'Better not. I'll explain, if I have to.'

'Right.' Wilson finished his note, and wrote another, this time to Chief Inspector Falcon, in more familiar language. He handed them to Ben Tancred.

'You called Falcon queer,' said Ben. 'What's the matter with him?'

'Nothing except being queer,' Wilson answered. 'You'll soon see when you meet him.'

CHAPTER 6

MR POLWHELE DISCOURSES

Dr Benjamin Tancred got to Fowey in time for dinner on the following day. He had decided to stay in Fowey, rather than try to find quarters in St Blaizey itself, or at Par, partly because he knew a comfortable hotel in Fowey, where he would be welcome, and partly because he wanted to be able to make his first investigations without letting everyone at St Blaizey know of his interest in the case. He put up at The Three Cutters Hotel, where he had often stayed before, and soon he and Jellicoe were seated at a small table in an alcove of the big dining-room, which was nearly empty. It came back to Ben's mind, as he looked out across the river towards

Polruan, that he and Jellicoe had lunched at that very table, with Sarah Pendexter and the lawyer Polwhele, on the day of the inquest on Simon Pendexter's body. The hotel had been redecorated since then, in a more modern style, and there was a sound of wireless in the distance; but apart from that, nothing seemed to be greatly different. Ben looked down the wine-list. That too was much the same, except that the years of the vintages were later. He selected a Chambertin that looked promising, and not too revoltingly expensive.

On the way down in the car Ben had told Jellicoe most of what he knew about the case; and the telling had served to impress upon him how little it was. He went over it again now to his assistant, in order to get it in order, and see what lines it suggested for investigation on the spot. Lord St Blaizey had gone out riding with his secretary, by name Gregory Landor. A little later he had sent Landor back to the Castle, to put through a personal trunk-call to London, and ridden on alone. Landor had remonstrated with him, on the ground that because of the state of his eyes he ought not to be riding unattended, and had been told off for his pains. Helen Damian, informed by Landor, had ridden out from the Castle in search of her father-in-law, and had met with his riderless horse. She had summoned a gamekeeper, who had collected others; and after a search Lord St Blaizey's body had been found, with the neck broken and a nasty wound across the forehead. The body had been found lying in one of the rides in the Castle woods; and the presumption was that Lord St Blaizey had ridden, being nearly blind, into a branch which projected across the ride just by the place where he was found. So far, the thing looked like a mere accident.

'Well, Jellicoe, what does that suggest to you, up to that point? I mean, where can we make a start in checking up on it?'

'It doesn't suggest much, doctor, that I can see. We can have a look at the place where they found the body; but I don't suppose that will be much help.'

'No,' Ben Tancred answered, 'except that we can find out

whether it's the same place as the one Sarah Pendexter described in her "vision" of the murder, or whatever it was.'

'And I suppose we can have a look at the branch that they say may have hit him on the head?'

'Good, unless it's been sawn off. To see if it could have caused the accident, you mean? Anything else?'

'We can verify the secretary's story, doctor. Find out exactly when Mrs Damian—I mean Lady St Blaizey—saw the riderless horse. Work out the times of her movements, and Landor's, and see how they fit it.'

'Yes, of course. All the routine things. We shall have to consider how best to set about it. The obvious way is to go straight to the Castle and ask; but that gives away my interest at once. We'll leave that for the moment. Get on to the next point.

'As far as we know,' Ben Tancred continued, 'the first suspicion of foul play arose when the doctor expressed doubts whether the contusions on the forehead had been caused by the projecting branch. He found traces of some special sort of bark in the wound; and none apparently on the branch that was said to have made it. He may have had other reasons—probably had: we don't know that yet.'

'See the doctor,' Jellicoe commented.

'Yes, at some stage—unless the police can tell us all we want to know about it. Then comes Sarah Pendexter's story. Part I, she saw Rupert ride out of the Castle woods on to the Lostwithiel road at about eleven forty or eleven forty-five on the morning of the murder—or better say the death.'

'We must try to find out if anyone else saw him too,' said Jellicoe.

'Or a horseman who might have been mistaken for him,' said Ben. 'Also, if possible, where he went, as he doesn't seem to have ridden straight on to Lostwithiel along the road. That is, unless Sarah missed him when she passed him in the bus. I think all that's your job, Jellicoe. Make inquiries along the road; and, while you're about it, see the old woman Sarah visited near by, and verify her story.'

'Right you are, doctor. I'd better verify the bus times as well.'

53

'Do that. Then there is Part II of Sarah's story. I mean her "vision", as she called it. I think we'll leave that out for the time being, apart from seeing if the place she named in the story is the one where the thing really happened.'

'I might make a few inquiries about the lady, doctor. How cracked she is, and all that.'

'Leave that to me for the present,' said Ben. 'Well, I think that's all we have to go upon, and it's not much. The first thing for me to do is to see the police, and find out as much as I can of what they think. That's for tomorrow morning.'

At that moment someone came up to their table. 'Isn't it Dr Tancred? A long time since we met.'

Ben rose to his feet with alacrity, and greeted Mr Polwhele heartily. The old lawyer, who had been his aunt's man of business and concerned in the Simon Pendexter case all those years ago, was just the sort of person to give him some of the information he wanted. It was quite a few years since they had met, again by chance, on the occasion of one of Ben Tancred's brief holidays at Fowey.

'Delighted to see you, Mr Polwhele. Upon my word, you don't look a day older. May I introduce my friend, Mr Jellicoe? I'm just off a case—run down here for a few days' holiday and a breath of Cornish air.'

'None better,' said the old lawyer. He accepted an invitation to sit down and take a glass of wine. 'Then your presence has nothing to do with our local mystery?'

'Is there one?' Ben asked mendaciously.

'My dear doctor! I thought all England was discussing us. Though, if you ask me, there is nothing to discuss. Lord St Blaizey . . .'

'Oh, it was down here he fell off his horse, wasn't it? I remember now. I saw a report of the inquest. Adjourned, wasn't it?'

'It was. All Dr Andover's doing. A fine man in many ways; but too clever. Much too clever for a local GP.'

'It's not too common a fault,' said Ben. 'Let me see, what was the trouble?'

'Some nonsense about finding a spot of dirt in the wound that shouldn't have been there, and building up all sorts of fantastic theories on it. As if a spot of dirt mightn't turn up anywhere.'

'There are different kinds of dirt,' said Ben. 'Someone defined dirt as "matter in the wrong place". Wasn't that what Dr Andover thought?'

Mr Polwhele sipped his burgundy. 'Not bad this, for hotel stuff,' he said. 'But they've shaken it. They always do.' He took a deeper draught. 'Yes, I suppose that's what he thought. But why on earth anyone should want to murder Lord St Blaizey . . .'

'Come, come,' said Ben. 'When a man's as rich as Crœsus, and a banker as well, do you mean to say no one could have a reason for murdering him? I'm not saying anyone did, mind you. I know nothing about it. But plenty of people might want to. I've often thought I should like to make a holocaust of all the bankers myself. Who gets his money?'

'I suppose his son does, with the title. There's no one else, as far as I know. But I refuse to entertain the suggestion that Roderick Damian murdered his father, if that's what you're suggesting. To begin with, he couldn't. He's practically a cripple. And, apart from that, the suggestion is quite absurd. Roderick Damian has always been crotchety; but he's a man of the highest moral principles . . . A bit too high, sometimes, for my taste.'

'Is somebody accusing him, then?' Ben said, laughing. 'You're very hot about it.'

'I am. I know the new Lord St Blaizey quite well, and I respect him, in spite of his—er—peculiarities. He is the least mercenary man I know. He cares nothing for money. I expect you remember he married Helen Pendexter, whom we both had something to do with a good many years ago?'

Ben nodded. 'What's she like, in these days?' he asked.

Mr Polwhele hesitated. 'I confess I am not a fair judge,' he said at last. 'I cannot pretend to like Lady St Blaizey— as she now is. At one time, I felt very differently about her. But now—no. In my opinion, she is much more to blame than he is.'

'To blame for what?' Ben asked.

'Well,' said the lawyer, 'it's fairly common knowledge down here that they don't hit it off any too well. Lord St Blaizey—I mean the new viscount—is admittedly a difficult man to live with. He is—er—somewhat soured by suffering. But I cannot think she has made him a good wife. She is—er—I am afraid . . . flighty. And she refuses to take any interest in his religious work. But I had really better not discuss the matter. I am . . . not an unprejudiced witness.'

'Gentleman in the case?' Ben inquired. But Mr Polwhele refused to be drawn any further about Helen Damian's private affairs. 'What about her brother?' Ben tried another tack. 'Has our friend Rupert been down here lately?'

'I believe he was here a couple of weeks ago; but I am told he went back to London some days before Lord St Blaizey's accident. I have heard nothing of him since.'

Evidently, Ben thought, local rumour had not connected Rupert Pendexter with Lord St Blaizey's death. Apparently, it had fastened on Roderick Damian.

Jellicoe struck in at this point. 'The inquest report mentioned a secretary, sir. What's he like?'

'Oh, Landor! A decent enough young fellow, I believe. Very quiet and unassuming. I hardly know him personally. A great improvement on his predecessor, Galloway. Why do you ask?'

'Only that he seems to have been the last person who saw Lord St Blaizey alive.'

Mr Polwhele looked sharply at Jellicoe. 'My dear sir, ridiculous!' he exclaimed. 'Really, I have no patience with all this malicious talk about murder.' He drained his glass and got up to go. 'Well, Dr Tancred, pleased to have met you again.' The old lawyer hobbled off. Despite Ben Tancred's remark about his not looking a day older, he was getting very shaky on his pins.

'I'm rather afraid, Jellicoe, you gave Mr Polwhele a shrewd suspicion of our business,' said Ben Tancred, as soon as he was out of earshot.

'I, doctor? How?'

'By asking about the secretary. There was no earthly

reason for asking about him unless you were interested in the question of murder.'

'But you asked him about lots of people, too.'

'Only people it was natural for me to ask about, because of old times.'

'I'm sorry, doctor, if I put my foot in it.'

'Never mind, Jellicoe. What we know is that people down here suspect the new Lord St Blaizey of having murdered his father.'

'Which annoys Mr Polwhele a good deal.'

'Yes. And we know that Polwhele dislikes Helen—Lady St Blaizey—pretty strongly, and has some bit of scandal about her on his mind. That's new. He used to have rather a weakness for her.'

'Flighty was the word he used.'

'Quite. Finally, he believes the secretary, Gregory Landor, to be an inoffensive person, but strongly dislikes someone named Galloway, who preceded him as secretary. Galloway, if he is no longer there, presumably doesn't arise. Still, we may as well docket the name for reference.'

A page came into the dining-room, calling 'Doctor Tancred!' in a high piping voice. Ben answered, and the boy presented a letter. Ben tore it open, and read it through. 'No answer,' he said; and the boy withdrew.

Ben Tancred passed the note across the table to his assistant. It was written on very cheap notepaper, with the written heading 'Blackbottle House, Polruan.'

Dear Dr Tancred,
    The voices tell me you are to see Abel Galloway as soon as possible after your arrival. He is a bad man.
Yours sincerely,
Sarah Pendexter

'Galloway again,' said Ben. 'I suppose that's the previous private secretary. And Sarah doesn't like him either. We must find out a bit about Mr Galloway, even if it does mean obeying the "voices". But now, Jellicoe, let's go out and get a breath of air before we toddle off to bed.'

CHAPTER 7

LACONICS FROM SCOTLAND YARD

Dr Tancred called at Fowey Police Station early on the following morning, and asked where Chief Inspector Falcon was to be found. The chief inspector, he was told, was staying at St Blaizey itself, at an inn called The Damian Arms; but he was expected at Fowey later in the morning, and would be certain to call in at the police station. There was no one at the station whom Dr Tancred remembered in connection with the Simon Pendexter affair; and an inquiry for the chief constable produced only the information that he lived near Bodmin, and was not expected to come to Fowey unless there were further important developments. That was a nuisance. Ben supposed that it would be only tactful, at some stage, to present Wilson's letter of introduction to Col. Gates-Cocker; but he did not want to waste time journeying over to Bodmin instead of getting on with his job of finding out whether or not there was really a case for him to take up.

No one at the police station knew at what hour Chief Inspector Falcon was likely to arrive; and Ben Tancred had to make up his mind whether to wait for him at Fowey, or drive over to St Blaizey with a good chance of missing him on the way. His impatience to make a start on the case decided him to risk an immediate journey to St Blaizey; and he returned to the hotel and told Jellicoe to get out the car. He then drove straight out to St Blaizey, where he dropped Jellicoe, with orders to pursue his inquiries along the Lostwithiel road, while he went on to The Damian Arms and inquired whether Chief Inspector Falcon was in. The chief inspector, it appeared, was up at the Castle. The landlord, who gave Ben Tancred this information himself, looked at his visitor curiously. He was a rather surly-looking fellow, and Ben did not feel disposed to stop and attempt to pump him about the local gossip. Instead, leaving his car parked outside the inn, he sauntered off down the village street, on the lookout for someone who might prove more communicative.

Ben looked into the post office, which was also the general store; but the flashy young woman who was on duty there did not seem promising. By and by he spied a cobbler's shop, with a window full of boots in various stages of dilapidation, at which an old man in steel-rimmed spectacles sat hammering.

Ben went in; and the old man looked up from his work and asked him what he wanted.

'I'm a stranger here,' Ben answered. 'I wonder if you can tell me of any one named Galloway who lives in these parts.'

'Galloway!' said the old man. 'Would you mean Captain Galloway up at the Castle?'

'I understood he had left there.'

'Oh! You're wanting Mr Sidney Galloway, maybe—the Captain's brother—him who used to be secretary to his lordship who has passed away. Mr Sidney has left these parts, I believe. Here today and gone tomorrow, as the Book says. But the Captain's here still. Maybe if you were to ask him . . .'

'I didn't know there were two brothers,' said Ben. 'Captain Galloway has a job at the Castle, has he?'

'Aye! Steward they call him. And I'm telling you no secret when I say there's many hereabouts would have been a deal gladder to see him to go even than Mr Sidney.'

'Not popular, eh?'

The old man got up from his seat and gesticulated with his hammer as he spoke. 'I'm a man that holds with plain speaking,' he said. 'This shop's my own, and I say what I please. But I'm telling you no lies when I say Captain Galloway is no better than a bully and a tyrant. Ask any of the folk hereabouts—only they mostly won't dare tell you, because most of them rents their houses off the estate. Fair rack-rented they are too; and as for getting a bit of repairs done when it's needed, for all his lordship's rolling in money up in London, they can whistle for it.'

'Bit of a Socialist, aren't you?' said Ben. 'I'm rather that way myself.'

'I'm no Socialist,' said the old man disgustedly. 'The Socialists are no better than a pack of fools, leastways in these parts. Always talking about a heaven on earth, when they ought to be laying up treasure in heaven, and getting on with the jobs that want doing instead of blathering. I'm a Radical. That's what I am, the same as my father and my grandfather were before me. My granddad was a Chartist, if you know what that means.'

'Quite well,' Ben said. 'So you don't think much of Lord St Blaizey, or his steward?'

'I'm not saying a word against the new lord,' the old cobbler answered, 'or his father either, in a personal way. It's the system I'm against. What I say is, God didn't give the beautiful land to be made the private possession of a few dukes and such-like. He gave it to all of us, and bade us increase and multiply. Would He have done that, now, unless He had meant us to have the land to live by and feed our children? Have you read Henry George?'

Ben had. They discussed for a few minutes the economics of the Single Tax, in which the old cobbler had an undiluted faith. Ben edged him back to more immediate matters. 'But you seemed to be blaming Lord St Blaizey personally, as well as the system, in what you said just now.'

'For employing a bad steward, aye, I do blame him, and for not seeing the tenants got their rights, when he had more than his. But maybe that'll be different now, under the new lord.'

'You think better of Roderick Damian, then?'

'Aye, and so do we all. He's a righteous man, the young lord, and walks in the Lord's way—barring his infirmities having soured his temper. I'm in hopes he'll be sending that Captain Galloway to the right-about before long.'

'Couldn't he have done anything about it while his father was alive? He was living at the Castle, wasn't he?'

'Aye; but him and the old lord could never agree. It was

the Captain had the management, not Mr Roderick at all.'

The old man by this time had sat down again to his work. But he was none the less ready to go on talking. Dr Tancred learned quite a lot more about Captain Galloway's iniquities, and the cobbler's reasons for giving his approval to the new Lord St Blaizey, who had never been on good terms with the unpopular captain. He even introduced the name of Helen Damian, mentioning that he had met her a great many years before, when she was Helen Pendexter. The old man remembered Simon Pendexter's death quite well; for at that time he had been working in Fowey. It turned out that he had a deep respect for Sarah Pendexter, whose brand of Calvinism he apparently shared; and, rather to Ben's surprise, in view of what Mr Polwhele had said, he appeared to think highly of Helen. As for Sidney Galloway, the Captain's brother, he believed he might be living in Fowey now, but had not seen anything of him in St Blaizey lately.

Ben had been wondering whether to try to lead the old man on to the subject of Lord St Blaizey's death, but he let him run on, in the hope that he would in the end come round to it of his own accord. So he did at last, with the statement that now some fools were making a silly fuss about the old Lord's accident, as if everybody didn't know he was as blind as a bat, and it was natural he should come to grief if he would go riding about alone.

'Then the common opinion about here isn't that he was murdered?' Ben Tancred asked.

Some fools, the cobbler said, would say anything; and in St Blaizey, at any rate, they were most of them fools, ready enough to touch their hats to the gentry and then lick their lips over a scandal any time when they got a chance.

'These people are saying it was murder? Who do they think did it?'

'I can tell you one thing, mister,' the old man answered. 'There's not a soul hereabouts, barring one or two nobody takes no notice on, as thinks the new lord did it. Now, if it had been that Captain . . .'

'Do you know Rupert Pendexter?' Ben shot at him.

'Aye, I know him. I've seen him, that is.'
'Lately?'
'Were you wanting him?'
'I wondered if he was down here, or had been.'

There was no help there. The cobbler said he believed Rupert Pendexter had been at the Castle a matter of a fortnight ago, and been seen in the village; but he had not heard of him being seen in the neighbourhood since then. Suddenly the old man gave an exclamation.

'There's that air-balloon of a detective from London,' he said, jerking his head at a figure on the opposite side of the village street. Ben Tancred looked out, and saw an enormously fat man, dressed in very loud checks and walking with a rather ludicrous strut. He had long moustaches, with waxed ends, and was twirling a walking-stick.

'Poking his nose in where he isn't wanted, and asking a lot of fool questions,' the old man grumbled. 'I told him to take his fat face back where he came from; and he wasn't pleased.'

Ben, wanting to catch the detective before he left for Fowey, was now eager to be gone. He covered his retreat with a couple of sentences, and hurried out of the shop in pursuit. He noticed that the name over the door was 'Reuben Amos, bootmaker.'

He caught up Chief Inspector Falcon just outside The Damian Arms, and asked for a word. The Chief Inspector spun round and looked him up and down. 'Who may you be? he said brusquely.

'By name, Benjamin Tancred—bearer of a letter to you from Superintendent Wilson.'

Falcon's manner changed. 'Come right in,' he said. 'Super told me you'd be coming.' He led the way into a small room behind the bar, and motioned Ben Tancred into a chair, while he stood before the fireplace, twirling his moustaches and—sticking out. He had a really magnificent corporation, and he looked very hot. 'Well!' he said. 'What can I do for you, Dr Tancred?'

'Tell me as much about the whole thing as, in the light of this letter, you feel you can tell me.' Ben handed over

Wilson's note. 'I've come down here to discover whether there's any case for me to investigate or not.'

The Chief Inspector read the letter through, and then folded it up and put it carefully away. 'For whom are you acting?' he said.

'At the request of Miss Sarah Pendexter.'

'What business is it of hers?'

'Perhaps none; but she asked me to look into it.'

'What do you want to know?' Falcon dismissed the subject of Sarah, and flung this remark out as if he regarded Ben Tancred as a busybody who had to be ticked off as quickly as possible.

'First, whether there is a case at all. Do you think Lord St Blaizey was murdered?'

'Yes, I do.' Falcon, as he spoke, closed his eyes.

'By whom? If that's not premature?'

'It is. I don't know yet.'

'Any suspicions?'

'Plenty.'

'Very well. That means the doctor's view is confirmed, I suppose. About the blow, I mean. I take it, the blow was not caused by the overhanging branch.'

'It was not.'

'Have you found what it was caused by?'

'Yes. Got the weapon.'

'What was it?'

'Branch off another tree. Found it in the wood. Thrown away near. Blood on it.'

'Good enough,' said Ben. 'No finger-marks, I suppose?'

'None. Wouldn't be.'

'And the neck? Was that broken by the fall from the horse, or how?'

'Don't know. No evidence.'

'Is there any other evidence you feel like passing on? You see, now I know it is murder, I shall have to go into it.'

'What sort of evidence?'

'I was asking you. Opportunity, motive, positive evidence pointing to any particular person?'

'H'm!' said the Chief Inspector. 'Want a lot, don't you?'

'All I can get,' said Ben. 'It saves time. May I put my questions more specifically?'

'Fire away.'

Really, thought Ben Tancred, this fellow is about the most staccato talker I have ever met. 'Well, begin with motive,' he said. 'Who had a motive, that you know of?'

'Four,' said Falcon, ticking them off on his fingers. 'Heir, heir's wife, discharged secretary, discharged stableman. Possibly others.'

'In fact,' said Ben, 'Lord St Blaizey, Lady St Blaizey, Sidney Galloway. Who's the stableman? He's a new one on me.'

'Name of Amos,' said the Chief Inspector.

'That's the cobbler's name,' exclaimed Ben.

'Damned Socialist,' said Falcon. 'Half the village named Amos. Alfred Amos, this one is. Fred's Fred, they call him.'

Further questioning elicited the fact that Alfred Amos was under notice for an affair with a girl up at the Castle, whom he had 'got into trouble'. Captain Galloway had apparently tried to protect him, but old Lord St Blaizey had discharged the man himself. This, owing to the Chief Inspector's extremely laconic habit of speech, had to be elicited bit by bit. The only other evidence against Amos appeared to be the fact that he had behaved in a supicious manner when he was questioned, as if he had something to conceal. He had a bad reputation locally, and was a shifty-eyed little rat of a man.

'What about the others?' Ben asked. 'Sidney Galloway, for example?'

Captain Galloway's brother, it appeared, had been discharged by Lord St Blaizey for dishonesty some six months before, and Gregory Landor had been engaged in his place. Galloway had been hanging about in the neighbourhood since, sponging somewhat unsuccessfully on his brother and fishing up a little money in various rather disreputable ways. He had been heard to utter threats against Lord St Blaizey when they had met in the Castle grounds about a fortnight before, and Lord St Blaizey had brusquely ordered him off. But there was at present no evidence that he had been at St

Blaizey at all on the day of the old lord's death. 'Being looked into, that,' said Chief Inspector Falcon.

'Then Lord St Blaizey himself?' Ben asked. 'I mean the new lord.'

'Dead men's shoes,' was the answer, accompanied by a heave of the shoulders.

'You don't suspect him?' said Ben, going by Falcon's manner.

'Suspect everybody. Nothing against him, bar that. Except that he's like a bear with a sore head.'

'And his wife?'

'Same motive. She found the horse. Bit of a hussy, if you ask me. Between ourselves, of course.'

'Do you mean you suspect her?'

'Frankly, I don't like the woman. Don't like her manner. Stuck up—and hostile.' It was fairly clear that Falcon had his knife into Helen hard. Dr Tancred wondered whether he was destined, after twenty-five years, to see her charged a second time with murder, and perhaps to come again to her rescue.

'Hardly a woman's murder, is it?' he asked.

'Accomplice, perhaps,' said Falcon. 'No evidence yet.'

'Any other suspects?'

'The whole world. None specially.'

'H'm! Not got very far, have you? What about opportunity?' Ben inquired.

That, it appeared, was not easy to say; for the medical evidence had failed to reach any precision about the time of Lord St Blaizey's death. Roderick, the new lord, had gone on foot early in the morning—he was given to walking, despite his half-crippled condition, which allowed him to walk only very slowly. He had apparently walked up the Luxulian Valley through the woods to Luxulian village, whence a friend, whom he had been to see, had motored him into Lostwithiel for the Methodist meeting to which Sarah Pendexter had referred. Falcon had worked out the times, and got the friend's confirmation of Roderick's arrival at Luxulian. Unless the friend was lying, this appeared to leave him no time to have encountered his father in the St

Blaizey woods anywhere near where the old man's body had been found. Moreover, his physical infirmity made his guilt very improbable.

Helen, on the other hand, said she had been in the Castle till Gregory Landor came to tell her about her father-in-law riding on alone. If so, her only opportunity had been after that, when she rode out to look for him. About Sidney Galloway nothing could yet be said. As for Alfred Amos, he declared he had not left the Castle stables all the morning, or been anywhere near the part of the woods where the body was found.

'What about Landor?' Ben asked. 'He seems to have been the last person to see the man alive.'

'Could have done it,' Falcon answered. 'No motive. Rabbit. Not likely.'

'Anyone else at the Castle at the time?'

'Servants.'

'Where was Captain Galloway?'

'In Fowey, shopping. That's been verified. Pretty clear alibi.'

'Anything against him?'

'Not liked. Nothing else.'

'Were his relations with Lord St Blaizey good?'

'Dead one, yes. Live one, no.'

'Was Rupert Pendexter at the Castle when it happened, by the way?'

'Thought you'd be coming to that,' said the Chief Inspector, giving his moustache another twirl. 'Answer is, No.'

'Meaning that he wasn't in the neighbourhood, or that you don't know he was?'

'Wasn't. Left some days before.'

'He might have come back.'

'To kill his best friend? Why?'

'I'm not suggesting he did.'

'Cracked-brained lunatic,' said the Chief Inspector. 'Not you—Sarah Pendexter.'

'Have you discovered whether Rupert Pendexter has an alibi?'

'No reason to look into it, that I know of. He's not suspected.'

All this time, Ben Tancred was finding the extraction of information from Chief Inspector Falcon very hard and dry work. He was hoping the man, as he was staying in the house, would offer him a drink; but he could not order one himself, as it was not yet opening time. Ben had been watching the hands of the clock; they had just reached twelve. 'I could do with a drink,' he said. 'Have one on me?'

'Thanks,' said the Chief Inspector.

'What? Beer? Mine's a pint of bitter,' said Ben.

'Ginger ale,' said the Chief Inspector. 'Teetotaller. Drink's a curse.'

'Not to me,' said Ben. He rang the bell, and asked for a pint of bitter and a ginger ale. When they came, he drank deeply of the beer, and felt better. The Chief Inspector drained his ginger ale at a gulp, and ordered another. He did not offer to treat Ben Tancred; perhaps it was against his principles. Ben ordered another half-pint for himself.

'Is that about the lot?' Ben asked. 'I mean as far as you've got yet?'

'Pumped me dry,' said Falcon, thawing a little under the influence of the ginger ale, and giving half a smile that was more like a smirk.

'Dry's the word,' said Ben, attacking the half-pint with relish. 'Well, you've been very helpful. I'm very obliged.'

'My turn now,' said Chief Inspector Falcon. 'What's Sarah Pendexter's game?'

Ben explained that Sarah was convinced she had seen Rupert Pendexter leaving the Castle woods by the old lodge gates on the morning of the murder. He expressed frankly his uncertainty whether she had really seen him, or only mistaken someone else for him; but he said that he felt sure she had seen a horseman ride out of the gate at somewhere round about twenty minutes after noon.

'She told the locals that,' Falcon commented. 'They didn't believe her.'

'I do,' said Ben. 'Half off her head though she is.' He said nothing of Sarah's other 'vision' of the actual murder being committed.

'Suppose I'll have to look into it,' said the Chief Inspector. 'Got any more notions?'

'No,' said Ben. 'Not yet. I'll come to you with 'em when I have. Cards on the table—mine in any case, yours if you will.'

'Suit me,' said Chief Inspector Falcon, laconic to the last. On that, they parted.

CHAPTER 8

A WITNESS REMOVES HIMSELF

Emerging from The Damian Arms, Dr Tancred found Jellicoe standing beside the car. He had just got back, by bus, from his journey along the Lostwithiel road. He looked hot, and observed that he felt hot.

'Lunch-time,' said Dr Tancred. 'Get in. We'll go down to Par Sands.'

On the way, Jellicoe related his discoveries, which were not many. He had been to Lanescot, and established the fact and time of Sarah Pendexter's call there on her bedridden friend. She had definitely been there on the morning of Lord St Blaizey's death, and had left not very long after eleven o'clock. Next Jellicoe had come back to the main road, found the gate leading into the Castle woods, with the deserted lodge beside it, and walked slowly up the road towards Lostwithiel. A little way north of the gate into the woods he found a track leading off the road on the opposite side. This, he found, led to a disused copper mine and a few deserted buildings belonging to it. He retraced his steps, and again followed the main road to the north. So far, he had seen no houses north of the Lanescot turning; but about half a mile beyond the track to the copper mine he found a tiny group of cottages, one of which, apparently an old smithy, now displayed a couple of petrol pumps. At this point a byroad led off to the south-east, signposted to a place called Treesmill, and there was also a track going westward, which, he was told on inquiring of a woman at the petrol station, led to Luxulian. Further inquiry elicited the fact that the signed byroad was the shortest way to Fowey, *via* a place called Tywardreath, but was not a good road, so that most of the traffic went round by St Blaizey and Par.

Jellicoe had then started questioning the woman about the day when Sarah Pendexter said she had seen Rupert. He had seen no way of disguising the fact that his interest had to do with Lord St Blaizey's death; and it had seemed best to let the woman suppose that he was connected with the police. No, he had been careful not to say he was; but he was sure she had gathered that impression.

But he had gained nothing. No one at the petrol station or at any of the other cottages remembered anything of a horseman having passed that way on the day of Lord St Blaizey's death. Ordinarily, the failure to notice such things would not have meant much. But it happened that, on that particular morning, a railwayman from Par, who lived in one of the cottages and was convalescing after an accident, had been sitting continuously in a chair in front of his dwelling. The man was certain that no horseman had passed by at any time before one o'clock, when, being unable to move by himself, he had been helped in to his dinner by his wife. The man seemed straightforward; and, apart from the possibility of his having dropped off to sleep for some part of the time, his story seemed to mean that the horseman Sarah had seen had turned off the Lostwithiel road before reaching the cross-roads.

If he had done that, where had he gone? Jellicoe had seen no road between the track to the mine and the cross-roads. He said so; but the railwayman put him right. There was another way into the Castle woods by a rough, narrow track about half-way between the two points Jellicoe had mentioned; and just opposite it, another rough track led across to join the byroad to Treesmill and Fowey. Jellicoe had missed these because they were both gated, and looked like mere openings into fields. Neither was in use except for occasional farm traffic.

That, Jellicoe told Dr Tancred, left three possibilities. The horseman, if he existed at all and if the railway worker was right about his not having come to the cross-roads, could have taken either the track leading to the disused mine, or the track leading across country towards Fowey, or he could have doubled back into the Castle woods by the northernmost gate. Jellicoe had not explored the main road north of the cross-roads, on which he was told there were no houses for another mile or more, and then only a farm and a couple of cottages. Nor had he tried the Fowey byroad, which was also devoid of habitations for a mile or so till it reached Treesmill. He had thought it better to catch the bus, and come back to report progress.

Dr Tancred said that Jellicoe had done quite right in returning, and proceeded to tell his assistant what he had learned from the Chief Inspector. By this time they had reached Par, where they entered a small inn and called for lunch. Over bread and cheese and beer, Ben Tancred and his assistant studied carefully the ordnance map of the district, which Ben had brought with him. Except that the track to the old copper mine was not shown, everything that Jellicoe related could be easily followed from the map. There was the main road from St Blaizey to Lostwithiel, with the extensive Castle woods occupying a long stretch of the frontage on the west side. The Castle itself—that is, the inhabited building—lay almost due west of the old copper mine, about a mile and a half away, on the opposite side of the Luxulian Valley railway line, which ran beside the Luxulian River, right through the middle of the estate. River and railway could be crossed at several points inside the Castle grounds, the principal crossing seeming to be at a point less than half a mile from the main road and rather to the north of the road leading eastward to Lanescot. To the north-west the Castle woods extended up the valley almost to the Treffry Viaduct, where a disused mineral line running from a mine just at the edge of the woods crossed both railway and river. Here foot travellers from the Castle grounds could cross and so reach a track leading to Luxulian village a mile or so away.

The map made clear one thing that Jellicoe had not known. The horseman, if there had been one, could have doubled back into the Castle woods not only by the track of which Jellicoe had been told, but also by taking the left turn towards Luxulian at the cross-roads, and then re-entering the woods by a ride which actually crossed the side-road near their northern limit.

One other item of interest the map revealed. There were two St Blaizey castles—one the relatively modern house and the other a ruin. The old castle stood about three-quarters of a mile north of the newer building, at the edge of the woods quite near the railway and not far south off the Treffry Viaduct.

In the light of these topographical particulars, it looked most likely that the supposititious horseman, if he had not followed the main road as far as the cross-roads, had doubled back into the woods. But even if he had reached the cross-roads without being noticed, that possibility still remained; for he might have taken the leftward turn and still regained the woods farther north. That indicated that it was necessary, first, to try the main road past the cross-roads, in the hope of getting nearer certainty of his not having passed that way; secondly, to explore the sub-road towards Luxulian; and thirdly, to try the road to Treesmill and beyond towards Fowey. But Ben was not very hopeful of any of these methods yielding results. They had to be tried; but this search for traces of a horseman who might either be a mere figment of Sarah Pendexter's imagination or, even if he existed, having nothing to do with the case, seemed rather a forlorn quest.

Pending further exploration along the roads, Dr Tancred had at this point to make up his mind how to tackle the case as a whole. That there was a case to tackle he was no longer in doubt, after what the Chief Inspector had said, though it seemed very doubtful whether Rupert Pendexter had any part in it, outside Sarah Pendexter's dreams. Ben, however, meant to go on now, and do his best to discover definitely whether Rupert did come into the picture or not. The question was, how? For, though Chief Inspector Falcon, despite his curious manners, had really given him all the help he could, Ben Tancred had, in fact, no *locus standi*. He was there at Sarah Pendexter's behest; but from the standpoint of the people up at the Castle Sarah was a mere outsider—an interfering busybody if she or her emissary attempted to poke a nose in where she was not concerned. Ben, as her representative, would almost certainly be regarded in an unfriendly light. He had indeed the advantage of knowing Helen Pendexter—Lady St Blaizey as she now was; or, rather he had known her, and had done her a signal service, twenty-five years ago, when he had helped to demonstrate her innocence of her stepfather's murder. But she had been none too grateful to him then; and the very last thing he could do was to go to Helen and ask for her help on the ground that her aunt had called him in the hope of proving Helen's brother a murderer for the second time. In the Simon Pendexter case, Ben was sure Helen had strongly suspected, if not actually known, her brother's guilt, vehemently as she had denied it. In this new case, wherever she stood, she would certainly give him no help if he appeared as Sarah's emissary and as Rupert's pursuer.

Nor was there anyone else to whom Ben Tancred could easily appeal. The new Lord St Blaizey he knew only by repute; but he was not given out as being at all of an oncoming disposition. True, he had connections with Sarah Pendexter through their common religious activities; but these would hardly serve Ben as a useful introduction if he appeared as a pursuer of old Lord St Blaizey's murderer—especially if the new lord was aware of being under some suspicion himself. Of Gregory Landor and of Captain Galloway he knew nothing except what he had been told by others—certainly nothing that would serve to enlist their aid.

It was, in fact, a difficult situation, and Ben Tancred admitted to himself that he did not quite know where to begin. Finally, he came to the conclusion that he had better start lower down the social scale, and that the most hopeful person to tackle was the stableman, Alfred Amos, who had given Chief Inspector Falcon so strong an impression that he had something to hide. Amos was known to have been in dispute with old Lord St Blaizey shortly before his death. Such a man would need careful handling, and in some ways Ben would have preferred to defer tackling him till he knew better what he wanted. But there seemed to be no one else on whom a beginning could be made.

Accordingly after lunch Ben drove back with Jellicoe to St Blaizey, and sent his henchman to the post office to inquire where Alfred Amos lived. He would not be likely to find the man at home at that time of day, unless he had actually ceased to work at the Castle; but it would be worth while, perhaps, to spy out the land even if Amos was out, and to have a preliminary word with his wife, if he had one, or his landlady. Jellicoe came back with the news that Amos had a cottage just outside St Blaizey, on the side-road leading towards the Castle. It was, by estate numbering, No. 87, and could be easily found. Thereupon, Ben Tancred sent Jellicoe off with the car to pursue his further inquiries along the Lostwithiel road, with orders to meet him again in St Blaizey at half-past five. Meanwhile, after visiting Amos's cottage, he meant himself to do a bit of trespassing —if it was trespassing—in the Castle grounds, in order to get better acquainted with the lie of the land.

Ben Tancred found Amos's cottage without any trouble. As he came up, two women were standing at the door, deep in talk. Their high-pitched voices, with the sing-song intonation he remembered so well, floated over to him as he aproached.

'You didn't ought to put up with being put upon,' the rather slatternly middle-aged woman facing the door was saying. 'What I say is, it isn't right—not to let yourself be put upon.'

The tired-looking faded young woman standing framed in the doorway replied. 'I've told him a hundred times I won't put up with it no longer.' Her voice was tired, like her appearance.

'What's the use o' that, as long as you do put up with it?' said the other.

'Well, I won't—not no more,' said the tired woman. 'That's flat.'

At this point the two women became aware of a stranger's approach, and suspended conversation in order to have a good stare at him. Ben would have preferred to catch Mrs Amos, if the tired woman was Mrs Amos, alone; but he did not feel like parading past under their stare, as if he had no business with them, and then returning later. So he went up to them, and asked if they could direct him to Mr Alfred Amos's house.

The slatternly woman answered. 'This is Mr Amos's, and this is Mrs Amos.' She turned to her friend. 'Well, I'll be leaving you, dearie. But you mind what I say.' Basket on arm, she trudged away in the direction of the village.

'My husband's not at home,' said Mrs Amos. 'Was you wanting him about anything special?'

Ben answered that he did want a few words with Mr Amos, and asked if his wife knew where he was likely to be found.

At this, unexpectedly, the faded woman burst into tears, and ran into the house, slamming the door in his face.

Ben was rather nonplussed at this reception, and stood a full minute staring perplexedly at the closed door. Suddenly it was reopened, and Mrs Amos reappeared. 'I'm sorry, sir,' she said, still sniffling; 'but I'm not quite myself. What was you wanting my husband for, if I may ask? Was it about the insurance, because if so you'll have to give us time . . .'

Ben hastened to tell her that it was not about the insurance.

'You wouldn't be another of them policemen, would you?' Mrs Amos asked suspiciously. 'You don't look as if you was; but one never knows.'

'No. I'm not a policeman either. Do you know where your husband would be likely to be?'

Again the woman burst into tears. 'Oh, sir, I wish I did know,' she wailed. 'He's gone away without a word, and left me.'

'Gone away!' said Ben. 'When did he go?'

'Last night. And he's taken all the money I was keeping for the insurance with him. And his best clothes. And all the silver his lordship gave us when we married. Oh, sir, what can I do to get him back?'

Ben, as kindly as he could, advised her, if she had not already done so, to tell the police, who would do their best to trace her husband, if he really had gone away. But the mention of the police seemed greatly to alarm her.

'Oh, sir, I couldn't do that. I'm sure . . . I'm sure he wouldn't wish me to do that.' Clearly, Mrs Amos was in no doubt about her husband's dislike of the police.

This, however, might have more than one explanation. If Amos had been in trouble over one of the servants up at the Castle, his desire to escape from the police might be connected with his fear of an order for maintenance. It might have nothing to do with Lord St Blaizey's death.

'I'm afraid not much can be done to find him without the help of the police,' said Ben. 'That is, unless you have any idea where he has gone.'

Mrs Amos had none. Her husband was a local man, and had lived in St Blaizey all his life. He had, as far as she knew, no friends elsewhere with whom he would have been likely to seek refuge.

'Why do you think he has left you?' Ben ventured to ask.

At that question, Mrs Amos stared at Dr Tancred in a frightened way. She was not going to tell any stranger, however friendly he might appear, why she thought her husband had left his home. 'It's not like him at all,' she said at length.

After that, Ben Tancred could get no more out of her. He left his name, and his address in Fowey, with a request that he should be told if Amos came back to his house; and he repeated his advice to Mrs Amos that no one except the police would be likely to find her husband for her. With that he left her, and went back to the village. He called at once at The Damian Arms, and asked for Chief Inspector Falcon. But the Scotland Yard man was out; so Ben Tancred left a note, telling him that Alfred Amos appeared to have fled from his home, and that his wife did not know where he was. He added no comment; Falcon could be trusted to look into that for himself.

That done, Ben went out of the village along the main road towards Lostwithiel. He was going to have a look round that end of the Castle woods for himself.

CHAPTER 9

BEN TANCRED RENEWS AN
OLD ACQUAINTANCE

Ben Tancred went on up the main road. On his right was a row of cottages, mostly of recent erection—the post-war outcrop of the village. On his left was a stone wall, of great age, which marked the boundary of the St Blaizey Castle estate.* Presently, just past the last of the cottages, he passed the turn to Lanescot on the right; and then in a very little while he came to a gate leading into the Castle grounds. From this point a ride ran into the woods; but it curved out of sight at no great distance from the gate. Beside the entrance was a lodge, to all appearances empty and half-ruinous.

The gate bore a notice, with the word 'Private' on it. But there was no lock, and Ben swung it open and passed in. This, of course, must be the gate from which Sarah declared she had seen Rupert Pendexter emerge. Ben walked on up the ride to where it curved to the left, and saw a second ride from the north coming in to join it just past the bend. Leaving this, he followed the turn to the left, which went rapidly downhill, and soon led him to a narrow stone bridge across the river. Just beyond this was a railway, which was shut off by a fence and gates. Ben opened the gates and

*See Map of the St Blaizey Woods, p. 11.

crossed, noting the narrow gauge and the dilapidated appearance of the track. Almost at once, however, he came to a second railway, of the ordinary gauge and in much better order, and running on rather higher ground. The first must have been some sort of mineral line, probably now disused.

The ground between the river and the larger railway was clear of trees; but now, on rising ground, Ben was back in the woods. Here the track forked. Ben chose the right fork, which traversed the higher ground. As he strode on he caught an occasional glimpse of the railway below him, the ground falling away very sharply to his right among the trees. Ignoring several side-tracks to the left, he went on for about a mile and a quarter. Then he saw, through a gap in the trees, away in front of him to the left, a big building on an eminence. He could see that it was ruinous; evidently he had come upon the old Castle of St Blaizey. Presently the track led him right up to the front of the hillock on which it stood; but instead of mounting to explore it, Ben turned almost due south, along a better made road running through open fields. He had now left the woods behind him; but he could see ahead a second stretch of woodland, and in this he knew the more modern St Blaizey Castle must lie.

Ben Tancred soon covered the open space, and found himself back among high trees, advancing along a wide avenue. At the end of this there appeared in sight some sort of stone building; but not enough could be seen of it to form any judgment of its size or architectural quality. Not wanting to come right up to the house, Ben Tancred took a narrow turn to the left, which led him away from the Castle in an easterly direction. The track curved round the lower slopes of a considerable hill, and then, again turning due east, was met by several other rides coming up from the south-west. Ben continued to advance along it, until his attention was arrested by a tree on the left of the track, from which he noticed that a branch had been recently sawn about eight feet from the ground, which was at this point considerably trampled, with tracks worn through the undergrowth beside the road. Just ahead, Ben could see that the ride forked, the main ride continuing eastwards but bending slightly to the north, while a second ride went off due south, presumably towards St Blaizey village.

Ben Tancred went back a few paces, and for some time surveyed the scene. He felt convinced that this must be the place where Lord St Blaizey's body had been found. But what astonished him was that it was also precisely the place that Sarah Pendexter had described to him in her 'vision' of the murder. He had made her describe the scene as exactly as she could, precisely for the purpose of comparison with the actual spot; and she seemed to have got every detail right. There were the forking rides ahead, just as she had told him of them; and by the fork was a big tree broken off short, about six feet from the ground, with the logs into which it had been roughly sawn piled up beside it. Here too, was a stack of hurdles beside the road, again just as she had said. Sarah Pendexter had assuredly somehow or other visualized the scene with quite remarkable fidelity. Her 'vision', which he had not hitherto taken seriously, began to assume a new importance. Was it possible that, after all, Sarah had seen the murder, not merely in a vision, but in sober fact?

He was so absorbed in his contemplations that he failed to hear the approach of a horse's hoofs till the rider came actually round the bend from the track leading south towards the village. It was a woman, mounted astride a big roan. She rode towards him, and then stopped right beside him and said, 'Who are you? One of the police?'

Ben might not have recognized the rider after so many years; but he knew her voice in an instant. This was Lady St Blaizey—Helen Pendexter that had been. Ben raised his hat, looking sharply at her, and noting that she knew how to sit a horse. Helen had worn well. She had the same fair complexion as ever, without a wrinkle. She looked in perfect health—a fine woman, still fully capable of setting hearts aflame. No sign of trouble there, though by all accounts she had been through trouble in plenty with her morose and semi-invalid husband.

Ben made up his mind in a moment. 'You would hardly

remember me, Lady St Blaizey. My name is Benjamin Tancred.'

Helen stared at him, as if astonished. 'Dr Tancred! Whatever brings you here?' It was a question not by any means of welcome, but rather of displeasure—even resentment.

Ben did not answer it directly. He said, 'I recognized you; but I think you would hardly have known me, after all these years.'

'Oh, but I am sure I should, Dr Tancred—as soon as you spoke.'

'We have that in common then. We remember voices.'

'But what are you here for? You're not a policeman, are you?'

'I am sorry if I am trespassing.'

'Oh, that!'

'Your beautiful woods tempted me.'

'Especially this bit of them, I notice.'

'I am right, then? This is where Lord St Blaizey was found?'

'How clever of you to find out, Dr Tancred. I suppose you saw where they have cut off the branch up there. But, Dr Tancred, you have not answered my question. Why are you here? Don't tell me you have come out of mere curiosity, as a sightseer. I shall not believe you.'

'Then I will not waste breath in saying so,' Ben answered.

'It will not be waste of breath to answer my question.'

'Very well,' said Ben slowly. 'I want to know how Lord St Blaizey died.'

At that Lady St Blaizey leapt down from her horse, and stood beside him. 'Why do you want to know?' she said. 'What is it to do with you? He died by accident.'

'The police do not think so,' Ben answered.

'The police are fools. Dr Andover is a mischief-maker,' said Helen hotly.

'If so, you should welcome my presence. I only want the truth.'

'But why? What business is it of yours?'

'Murder is everybody's business, Lady St Blaizey.'

'But it was not murder.'

Ben stayed silent.

'I tell you it was not murder,' Helen repeated.

'Then help me to prove it was not.'

'But who brought you here? Why can't you leave us alone?'

Ben had been wondering whether to answer that question. 'Your aunt,' he said.

'Aunt Sarah!' At that Helen was really angry. 'I call it wicked of her. She's a wicked, vindictive, horrible old woman. Besides, she's mad. No one takes any notice of what she says.'

'Then you know what she is saying?'

'I know she went and told the police a lot of dreadful, insane lies. Oh, I suppose I ought not to be angry with her —only pity her for being off her head. But you—you are letting her pay you to do her horrible work.'

'I have made no arrangement with Miss Pendexter beyond promising her to come down here and have a look round. When I have done that, I shall either drop the case —or go on with it.'

'I tell you there isn't a case.'

'Oh, yes, there is, Lady St Blaizey, even if you are right. If the police wrongly suspect murder, there will be people under suspicion until they are proved to be wrong. If you are right, you ought to wish me to go on. I shall seek nothing but the truth—whatever it is.'

It was Helen's turn to fall silent. She stood, holding her horse's bridle, and stared straight into Dr Tancred's face, as if she were trying to read his thoughts.

'Your husband, for one,' Ben went on. 'He surely wants everything cleared up beyond a doubt.'

Helen gave a short laugh, with no mirth in it. 'You do not suspect him, then, of murdering his father? Some people do, I am told.'

'I have barely begun suspecting anyone yet,' said Ben.

Helen burst out, 'Of course Aunt Sarah would say it was Rupert. Whenever anything wicked is done, she always says he did it. Why, Dr Tancred, you must see how absurd it is. He wasn't even here. He was in London when it happened.'

'In that case no one can suspect him,' said Ben.

'It is ridiculous to suspect anybody.'

'No, Lady St Blaizey, pardon me, it is not. It may be wrong, but it is not ridiculous. There is a very strong *prima facie* case for believing Lord St Blaizey was murdered.'

'Oh, I have no patience with you,' said Helen.

'That's a pity; for I was about to ask for your help.'

'You can do your own dirty work, thank you, Dr Tancred.' Lady St Blaizey turned her horse's head, and with a graceful, athletic motion, vaulted back into the saddle. 'You can tell Aunt Sarah what I think of her,' she called back.

Ben Tancred stood, hat in hand, watching the receding figure. 'Forsooth,' said he, smiling to himself, 'my lady is wroth with me.' He shrugged his massive shoulders, as if dismissing the subject. He went on talking to himself. 'What I really wonder is, What did Aunt Sarah see that day?'

CHAPTER 10

THE FAIR YOUNG MAN

Dr Tancred returned to St Blaizey by the track along which Helen had come. This, he found, led directly into the village at the north end, by way of a narrow passage between two houses. He made his way to the centre of the place; but there was no sign yet of Jellicoe or the car. Ben looked in at The Damian Arms, and inquired whether Chief Inspector Falcon had come back. Falcon, he found, had returned, and had received his note; but he had gone out again at once.

So by this time the hue and cry would be out after Alfred Amos. Ben went back into the street, and paraded slowly along it past Reuben Amos's shop. The old cobbler was in his window, tapping away as before. Ben went in.

'Is Alfred Amos any relation of yours?' he asked. 'I suppose you don't know where he's gone?'

Reuben tapped away as he answered. 'The young man is no friend of mine, though we are cousins in a manner of speaking. Has he gone away?'

'So his wife says.'

'Poor lass. Not but what Alfred would be a good riddance to her. He is bad—like his father before him.'

'I heard something of some trouble with a girl up at the Castle,' said Ben.

The old man looked him up and down. 'You'll be wiser not to be believing all you hear,' he said.

'Do you mean that Alfred Amos didn't get discharged because of trouble of that sort?'

'I'm not saying that. But there's two sides to that story. Maybe you heard Captain Galloway's.'

'And Alfred Amos has another side? I'd be pleased to hear it from him.'

'See here, sir. This is the second time this day you've come in here asking me questions. Are you another of these detectives, the same as the fat man from London? I'm one as likes to know where I stand.'

'I'm no policeman,' said Ben. 'But I am looking into the St Blaizey affair on my own.'

'What be you? A lawyer?'

'No. I'm a doctor.'

'Whatever you are, don't you go for to believe his lordship was murdered. Mind, I'm not saying it would have been altogether surprising if he had been, from what one hears of the goings-on up in London these days; but as a matter of fact, he wasn't.'

'You're very confident. How do you know?'

'No matter for that,' said the old man. 'I do know.'

'I don't see how you can know, unless you actually saw the accident.'

The cobbler shook his head. 'No. I'm not saying I saw anything. But I know one who did, all the same.'

'Whatever you do know, it's your duty to tell the police.'

'I reckon I can tell my duty as well as you, sir.' Amos tapped away as he spoke.

'But if you know it was an accident, surely you want to come forward and clear the whole business up once and for all. People are being suspected . . .'

The old man shook his head. 'I reckon 'tis no business of mine,' he said obstinately. 'But I can tell you this, sir. I've advised the party that told me to tell the police about it.'

'Told you what?'

'Her that saw the accident happen, and ran away instead of going to help the old gentleman, being too scared-like, to do aught else.'

'But, if someone actually saw it, of course they must speak out. Who was it?'

'I'm not going to tell you that. 'Tis not my business to break a person's confidence, when I've been told it private. But I'll tell her again she ought to speak it out.'

Through the window, Ben saw his car going by, with Jellicoe at the wheel. He turned impatiently to the old man. 'Whoever she is, she's doing very wrong, to keep it back,' he said.

'Maybe. I'll be telling her.'

Ben went out of the shop, and found Jellicoe and the car outside The Damian Arms. 'You're late,' he said. 'Had any luck?'

'A bit, doctor. But I'm not sure it comes to much. I've found out which way the man on the horse went.'

'That's fine. It means there was a man on a horse, at any rate. We couldn't be sure of even that till now.'

'No doubt about that, doctor.'

'Then we're getting on. Which way do you say he went?'

'Down the lane that leads to the old copper mine. There's a tramp of sorts who saw him.'

'What on earth was he doing there? It's a *cul de sac,* isn't it?'

'Yes. He met a man there, who took his horse, and went off leading it. Then our man—the one who was on the horse —scrambled up into the Treesmill road. The tramp heard a car start up a few moments afterwards.'

'This is getting interesting, Jellicoe. Can the tramp describe these two men? Got his name, by the way?'

'He said it was Smith, doctor—Henry Smith. As for describing the men, he's not much of a hand at it; but he says he'd know them both again. Tall and dark, and well-shaved, like a gentleman—that's the man on the horse. The other was fair and slightly built, and walked in rather a tripping way. Gentleman, too, by the look of it. He was young, Smith said.'

'Did your man see where the second one went?'

'Only saw him lead the horse back towards the main road.'

'Well done, Jellicoe. What about finding your Mr Smith again? He'll be wanted.'

'Well, doctor, he's got no address, except "The Old Copper Mine"; but I reckon that'll find him. I suggested there might be money in it. I gave him five bob to be getting on with.'

So far, they had been standing beside the car, talking. But now Dr Tancred said, 'Hop in, Jellicoe, and we'll get back to Fowey. That's about all we can do for today. You drive.'

They got in, and Jellicoe started up the engine. 'We've really made the most astonishing progress, you know,' said Ben. 'But there's one thing worries me. If I put the police on to your tramp, he may give us the slip. His sort is apt not to like policemen. But I can't very well keep him up my sleeve. That's why I came away, for fear of Falcon showing up before I'd had time to think it out.'

Jellicoe said nothing; he was well aware that his employer was thinking aloud, and did not want an answer.

'You see, Jellicoe,' Ben Tancred went on, 'if I tell Falcon, he's bound to go after the fellow himself. Then, if he does give us the slip, we've no one at all but Sarah to say our mysterious horseman ever existed—much less to identify him. As for the fair young man who led the horse away, I haven't the ghost of an idea who he can be. We don't even know whether most of the other people we've heard of in the case are dark or fair, or slight or fat, or the first thing about 'em. Or whether any of 'em could have been there at the time. Let's see. The secretary, Gregory Landor? He seems out of it, according to Falcon's story. He rode back to the Castle and told Helen about the old lord riding out alone, and then was busy telephoning to London till he rode out again and met them bringing in the body. That seems to rule him out—as having been the other man at the mine, I mean. That is, if he's telling the truth. We shall have to get the times worked out more exactly, of course. One can't be sure of anything till that's been done.

'Then there are the two Galloways. I've no idea what age Captain Galloway is, or what he looks like. Sidney sounds as if he was young. There's no other young man in the case at all, as far as we know yet, barring servants.

'Still, we've got on a longish way. It looks as if our horseman—we won't call him Rupert Pendexter just yet—does really exist. Our idea is that he met the old lord in the woods riding alone, rode along beside him, and in due course bashed him over the head. Then he rode away, went to the old mine and handed the horse over to his fair friend, and made his getaway in a car that he'd got parked ready. Our next job, if we can do it, is to trace that car. Someone may have seen it standing, where he left it, though I expect he cached it pretty well.

'If that's right, and the murderer rode beside Lord St Blaizey before killing him, he must be someone the old gentleman knew pretty well. The next question is, did they meet by appointment? Did Lord St Blaizey send his secretary back to the house on purpose to meet someone he wanted to see alone? If so, how was the appointment made? There might be traces of that up at the Castle. A letter perhaps—only Falcon would have spotted that, if it had been on show. We must look into that.

'Or was it a chance meeting—from the old man's point of view, I mean? Did the murderer waylay him? In that case, the murderer must have known he would be riding there alone. But I don't see how he could have known. No, it looks more like an assignation—if my reconstruction is anywhere near right. We'll work on that hypothesis, at all events.

'And we've got to find that fair young man. I confess he surprises me. Murderers don't often have accomplices; at any rate, well-dressed gentlemanly murderers don't, except sometimes, of course, their wives. But the young man must be an accomplice, unless we're barking up the wrong tree.

'Suppose our murderer did have an accomplice. Why did he need one? Still, assuming we're broadly right, the answer's fairly clear. If the murderer had an assignation to meet Lord St Blaizey on horseback, he needed a horse. But he didn't want to be seen riding to his appointment or riding away on horseback afterwards, so he had to borrow a horse, and then get rid of it. That wouldn't be too easy for him, especially if he wanted to get right out of the neighbourhood as quickly as he could. That's where the car comes in, of course. But there had to be someone to supply the horse and then put it away for him where it belonged after the murder.

'Where did it belong? It came out of the Castle stables, maybe. But in that case would our murderer have taken the risk of riding it out of the grounds and by the public road over to the old mine before getting rid of it? Wouldn't he have handed it over to his accomplice without ever leaving the Castle grounds at all? It looks as if he would. If that's right, it looks as if the horse, and presumably the accomplice too, came from somewhere outside the Castle. But all that is conjecture. We're not nearly far enough on to be certain of any of it.

'Yes, Jellicoe, we must certainly try to get on the track of that fair young man. Let me see. Your railwayman at the cross-roads was quite sure nobody on horseback had passed that way all the morning, wasn't he?'

'Yes, doctor. He was very positive about it.'

'Unfortunately that still leaves our fair young man plenty of choice. He could have ridden back into the Castle woods, though, as I say, I'm inclined to think he didn't. Or he could have ridden back into St Blaizey village, along the road. If he'd done that, he'd have been certain to be seen, and probably Falcon would have picked up his traces before now. Or again he could have taken the gated track on to the Treesmill road.'

'Or got on to the same road by taking the Lanescot turn further south,' Jellicoe put in.

'Yes, and Treesmill, by either of those routes, looks the

most likely direction. You shall try for him first there, tomorrow, Jellicoe. If you draw blank there, we'll try St Blaizey itself. Meanwhile, I must find out if either of the Galloways fits your tramp's description. Or Landor. We mustn't quite rule him out yet. His alibi hasn't really been checked, as far as we know.'

'Mr Polwhele might know what most of them look like, doctor, if you don't want to ask the Chief Inspector.'

'That's what is still bothering me,' said Ben Tancred. 'I think I shall have to tell him all about the tramp. But not tonight. I'll sleep on it.'

By this time they were in the streets of Fowey. Jellicoe, at Ben's request, stopped the car at Mr Polwhele's office and, dropping his employer, drove on to the hotel to put it in the garage. The lawyer, who lived over his office, was at home, and Ben was soon with him in his shabby but comfortable sitting-room upstairs.

'You want to know what the two Galloways look like. Let me see. I believe they're both in this group. It was taken when Lord St Blaizey threw open the old Castle to the public last year. That's Captain Galloway.' Mr Polwhele pointed to a big, stout-built man with a broad face.

'Dark or fair?' Ben asked, though the Captain's bulk alone seemed to rule him out.

'Very dark. Sidney's the fair one. He's over in this corner.' Mr Polwhele pointed to a short, slightly built young man with a tiny moustache and a small, weakly pretty face.

That looked much more promising. But Ben went on with his inquisition. 'What's Landor like to look at?'

'He's not in the photograph. A recent importation, since young Galloway left. He's—well, small and insignificant.'

'Fat or thin? Fair or dark?' Ben asked.

'Neither to both,' said the lawyer. 'Mouse-coloured, and of very ordinary build. The sort of man you don't look at a second time. But he's not quite such a rabbit as he looks, I fancy.'

'Well, thanks very much,' said Ben, getting up to go. 'I won't keep you.'

'And I won't ask what makes you so inquisitive,' said Mr

Polwhele, smiling, 'because you probably wouldn't tell me if I did.'

'I probably shouldn't,' said Ben.

'Nevertheless, I will return good for evil,' said the lawyer. 'You may care to know that Mr Narroway, of Narroway, Narroway and Straight, is down here. He arrived last night.'

'Who's he?' said Ben.

'They're a very old firm indeed. Lord St Blaizey's family lawyers. Mr Narroway is to read the will tomorrow up at the Castle.'

'Oh! I suppose the new lord scoops the lot. Must be a pretty penny, even after the death duties have been paid.'

'I should imagine so. As to the nature of the will, I know nothing. But I understand Rupert Pendexter has been invited to be present; so I presume he gets some sort of legacy. He was a high favourite with his late lordship.'

'No accounting for tastes,' said Ben. 'I can assure you he's no friend of mine.'

'Nor of mine,' Mr Polwhele agreed.

'In fact . . .' Ben began, and then decided to leave it at that. After a few commonplaces, the lawyer saw him down to the door. Ben went back to his hotel to dinner, well pleased with what the day had brought forth, but wondering, all the same, whether all this promising material about the dark horseman and his fair accomplice might not yet be blown to nothing by the old cobbler's mysterious female informant who professed to have actually witnessed the accident.

CHAPTER 11

SARAH EXCELS HERSELF

Ben Tancred wrote to me, Paul Graham, that same evening, reporting progress, because he knew I should be eager to know how he was getting on. I must say his long letter convinced me that Rupert Pendexter was the murderer, and that Ben was well on the way to catching him and handing him over to justice. Chief Inspector Falcon did not sound to me impressive, though Ben said he seemed to him to be quite competent, despite his mannerisms. I was sure it would be Ben Tancred, and not the police, who would track the criminal down.

Of course, I saw that there was a great deal still to be done. At present only Sarah Pendexter had identified the dark horseman as Rupert; but it was a great advance to have had the presence of a dark horseman confirmed by the tramp, who had promised to be able to identify him when the time came. I was very much intrigued about the fair young man, especially as I entirely agreed with Ben Tancred that one would not have expected Rupert, in planning a murder, to take to himself an accomplice. But I was in no position even to begin to guess who the fair young man could be.

I saw that, even if the horseman could be proved to be Rupert Pendexter, that still left Ben a long way off proving murder against him. But all that might turn out to be plain sailing when the fair young man and Alfred Amos, the stableman, had been found. Was it possible they were the same person? Ben did not seem to have considered that notion. I thought I must write to him about it, though of course he might have information about Alfred Amos's personal appearance that put it out of the question.

Then there was the mysterious woman mentioned by the old cobbler, Reuben Amos, and her statement that she had actually seen the accident. I was disposed to dismiss that as mere romancing, probably by some other female, besides Sarah, who was addicted to hallucinations. Weren't Cornish people supposed to be rather given that way? My mind moved on naturally from that conjecture to Sarah Pendexter's 'vision', which had turned out so strangely accurate in its topographical detail. Surely one couldn't take that 'vision' seriously; or had Sarah really seen the murder committed after all?

My mind passed from that point to the loose ends—the things that at present seemed to have no place in the puzzle. The Galloways, whom Sarah had bidden Ben Tancred watch out for—they seemed to be always cropping up, and yet to have nothing to do with the case—unless, of course, Sidney Galloway could be identified with the fair young man. The secretary, Landor—where, if at all, did he come in? Lord St Blaizey himself—that is, the young lord—and Helen, with her sharply hostile attitude to Ben Tancred's investigations? One couldn't tell in the least where or how they all fitted in. Perhaps that was simply because they didn't fit in at all. After all, why should they—if they were innocent?

Well, of course, I had to admit that Helen's attitude fitted in well enough with my assumption that Rupert Pendexter was the murderer. It was just like her attitude all those years ago, when she had been ready enough to screen her brother from the charge of killing old Simon Pendexter, even at the cost of being suspected and arrested herself. If Rupert Pendexter had committed his second murder, I felt no doubt of his sister's preparedness to shield him again, though it did not enter my head to suspect that she could be in any degree a participator in his guilt.

All the time I was thinking about Ben's letter I was itching to be with him. Well, why shouldn't I? Term at the university was over, and I had finished lecturing and was to that extent master of my time. True, I had been promising myself to put in a fortnight's hard work at the British Museum over a book I was writing. But that would keep. Why should I slave away writing erudite volumes which, when they were published, almost nobody wanted to read? How much better to clear my mind altogether of things academic, and join Ben Tancred down in Cornwall, where I should get some sun and fresh air in addition to his delightful company and the pleasure of helping him and watching him at work. My wife would not object; for I knew I was always apt to be grumpy after a day's hard reading in the British Museum. Moreover, I could get back in plenty of time to go away with the children on the family holiday that had been already arranged.

Ben Tancred, indeed, had made no suggestion that I should join him; but I felt sure he would be glad of a second helper—especially of one who had known the Pendexters in the old days. I put the case to my wife, and she at once agreed to my going. I wired to Ben at Fowey, saying that I proposed to join him there on the evening of the following day, and asking him to book me a room at his hotel.

Ben Tancred, meanwhile, after writing his letter to me, had dined at The Three Cutters in Fowey, and had then made up his mind to go over to Polruan and see Sarah Pendexter, of whom he had heard nothing since her letter on the evening of his arrival on the scene. Accordingly, he walked down to the ferry, crossed the river, and climbed up the steep village street of Polruan past the house where I had lodged with that rare gossip, Mrs Huggins, a quarter of a century before. Soon he came to the gate from which the track over the fields led to Blackbottle House, perched on the very edge of the cliff. There had been some new building in Polruan, so that the houses now stretched right past the approach to Blackbottle House, giving the whole place an unfamiliar appearance. But the track was unchanged, except that the gate, no longer white, was badly out of repair and hung askew on a loose gatepost that looked as if it would tumble right over before long.

The evening was beautifully light and cool, and there was no difficulty in following the track. A few minutes brought Ben to the main door of Blackbottle House, which was at the side of the building. Everything seemed to be in darkness. Ben knocked sharply; for the old-fashioned pull-bell was out of order. He waited some time before he saw a moving light through the glass of the door, which was opened, a minute later, by Sarah Pendexter herself.

'What do you want?' she said, peering out at him.

'I am Dr Tancred,' said Ben. 'I thought you would like to know how I am getting on.'

Sarah bade him enter, and he followed her into the big room whose long windows looked straight out over the sea.

Everything in it seemed to be covered with the dust of years. Not a scrap of the furniture or decorations had been touched in all those years; the place looked as if it had been simply left to moulder away. All the windows were tightly shut; but Sarah now threw one of them open, and a fresh breeze came in from off the sea. She motioned to Ben Tancred to sit down in a window-seat and for herself drew up a hard chair facing him, on which she sat bolt upright.

'Well, Dr Tancred,' said Sarah Pendexter. 'Wasn't I right?'

'That it looks like murder, yes,' said Ben. 'At any rate, that is the opinion of the police.'

'And yours too?'

'Yes, and mine.'

'And that Rupert did it?'

'That certainly is not the police view.'

'But it is yours. It must be yours.'

'I think there is a case to investigate. I am prepared to investigate it, provided that it is clearly understood I have a free hand and my sole purpose is to find out the truth, whatever it may be.'

'I have told you I agree to that,' said Sarah. 'As Rupert murdered him, the point is of no importance.'

'Certainly I am not in a position to say that your nephew is the murderer.'

'But you will be. You have found out something already, have you not?'

'Perhaps something. Certainly not enough. I have found someone who saw a dark man riding on a horse just after you did and quite near the same spot.'

'If he saw Rupert, surely that proves that Rupert committed the murder.'

'The man does not know your nephew by sight. He saw a dark man on horseback, who met a small fair man, who took the horse from him and led it away. We want to know who the small fair man was. Can you help me there?'

But on that point Sarah offered no help at all, beyond saying that she believed Gregory Landor to be small and fair. Ben asked whether Landor was a friend of Rupert's;

but Sarah had no knowledge on that point. They were acquainted, of course. Ben then asked if she knew anything of Sidney Galloway's relations with Rupert. It appeared that they had been friendly; but Sarah knew no more than that. She had supposed that Sidney Galloway had left the neighbourhood, or she would have mentioned him as another possibility for the small fair man.

'You specially asked me to keep an eye on Captain Galloway. Why?'

'Have you seen him?'

'Not yet. I shall do so. I wanted to find out more about him first. At present, I do not see how he comes in.'

'I dreamt of him,' said Sarah. 'I dreamt of you chasing Rupert with a great sword; and Abel Galloway came between and knocked the sword out of your hand.'

So Sarah had no better reason than a dream for setting him in pursuit of Abel Galloway. Or had she? 'Is he a friend of your nephew's?' Ben asked.

'Yes. They have been friends from boyhood. Rupert was responsible for getting Abel Galloway his position as Lord St Blaizey's agent. If Rupert needed an accomplice in his wicked work, Abel Galloway is the man to whom he would go. Abel was a bad boy. His morals are notorious. He is not to be trusted with women. And he is an unbeliever.'

Knowing Sarah's standards, Ben Tancred discounted most of this. Still, if Rupert Pendexter and Abel Galloway were as thick as thieves, that certainly made the man worth studying pretty carefully.

'I'm afraid Captain Galloway doesn't fit the part of our small, fair man,' he said. 'But his brother does. Are the two Galloways on good terms?'

Sarah had heard they were not; but she did not appear to know much about the matter.

So far, Ben Tancred had been on easy ground; but he had a far more difficult matter to take up with Sarah. Now that he had found her description of the scene of the murder tally so exactly with the real spot, it was impossible to dismiss her 'vision' as wholly without importance. He had, if he possibly could, to make certain whether it was a mere dream-vision, or something more—in fact, whether Sarah had really seen the crime committed. But it was not at all easy to know how to set about such a matter. A direct question would be obviously useless; for to Sarah her visions were evidently just as true as what she saw through her material eyes.

'I want you, Miss Pendexter,' Ben said, 'to describe to me again, as exactly as you can, what you called your "vision" of the murder. First of all, where were you when you saw it?'

'In the woods,' said Sarah. 'There were trees all round me.'

'Were you on a path?'

'No, I don't think so. I was among the trees, I tell you.'

'Then you were not where you yourself could be seen?'

'No. God would not let me be seen. It was not His will.'

'But you could see plainly? Tell me what you saw.'

'I saw Rupert and Lord St Blaizey riding along together. They were coming towards me. Then, just as they came quite near, I saw Rupert strike him; and he . . .'

'One moment. Where did your nephew strike him?'

'Across the face. I saw the blood spurt out from the wound.'

'With what did he strike him?'

'With . . . with something dark and long. I don't know what it was with. Why should I know what it was? You are trying to confuse me. I tell you I saw Rupert strike him on the face.'

'Yes, and then?'

'He fell off his horse, and . . .'

'Did he fall forwards or backwards?'

'He fell. I do not remember which way he fell. How can I remember everything? His neck was broken.'

Ben pressed her; but he could get no account of which way Lord St Blaizey had fallen.

'What did your nephew do then?'

'He rode away, as swift as the wind.'

'What? At once? Didn't he get off his horse to make sure Lord St Blaizey was dead?'

'I didn't see him. No, he rode away. He was out of sight like a flash.'

Really, Ben thought, that all sounded most improbable. Surely the murderer would have got down to make sure his victim was dead. Unless, of course, he had seen Sarah and fled in alarm.

'And now, Miss Pendexter,' Ben resumed, 'I want to ask you again just *when* this happened. You see, the question of time may be very important. Was it before or after you had been to see your friend at Lanescot?'

'After,' said Sarah.

'How long after seeing the murder did you see your nephew riding along the road?'

'That wasn't afterwards,' said Sarah. 'It was before.'

'You mean you saw your nephew riding away from the murder first, and then saw him committing it afterwards?'

'Yes,' said Sarah Pendexter.

'But how could you?' Ben exclaimed.

'I have told you it was a vision. Times and seasons are nothing to the Lord.'

Ben Tancred cursed under his breath. He had been almost persuaded that Sarah had seen the real thing after all. And now this—idiotic anti-climax. But all the same there was Sarah's extraordinary fidelity in describing the actual scene to be taken into account. Ben took Sarah all over it again, getting fresh details which confirmed the accuracy of her vision. A suspicion formed itself in his mind.

'I suppose you have been to see the actual scene of the crime since the murder was committed?'

'Only in my vision,' said Sarah. 'Except in my vision, I have not been there at all. But the vision keeps on coming back.'

Really, what was one to do with the woman, Ben wondered? You couldn't possibly produce her in a court of law, even to say what she had actually seen, without having all this stuff flung at the judge and jury, so as utterly to destroy her credibility as a witness about anything. He had half a mind, after this further experience of Sarah Pendexter, to fling up the entire case. But, all the time, he knew he simply couldn't bear not to do his best to solve it now.

A good deal more passed between them before Ben Tancred made his escape. But all that need concern the reader is that he left pledged to see the thing through. Sarah's last words, as she let him out of the door, were, 'God tells me to trust you, Dr Tancred. He lets me see you pursuing Rupert with a shining sword. But He bids me tell you to beware of Abel Galloway, who is lying in wait beside the path to trip you up.'

Really, Ben said to himself as he went back towards Polruan, if this wasn't the twentieth century that woman would get herself burned as a witch.

CHAPTER 12

INTRODUCING ABEL GALLOWAY

On the next morning, Ben Tancred found a note from Chief Inspector Falcon waiting for him. Falcon's epistolary style was not quite so laconic as his speech; but he wasted no words. Alfred Amos, it appeared, had walked to Lostwithiel, and thence taken train to London. Scotland Yard were looking for him there. The Chief Inspector added neither thanks nor comment to this bare statement of the position. Still, it was satisfactory, as far as it went, though Ben would have been better pleased to hear that the absconding stableman had already been laid by the heels. His departure might have nothing to do with the murder: it might have arisen wholly out of that discreditable affair with a servant at the Castle to which Reuben Amos had said there was another side. But Ben had a strong feeling that somewhere Alfred Amos fitted into the puzzle he was trying to solve. He badly wanted him found; but he also realized that the police were far more likely to find him than any private sleuth. He would have to leave all that to Falcon and the Yard.

Over breakfast, Ben planned out the morning's work. Jellicoe, with the car, or if Ben needed it, with a borrowed motor-cycle, must scour the country for traces of the fair young man, or the dark horseman and the car in which he had driven away. Meanwhile he, Ben Tancred, must pursue that idea of his that if old Lord St Blaizey had met his murderer in the woods, it must almost certainly have been by appointment. That seemed to involve getting admission to the Castle, in spite of Lady St Blaizey's hospitality, and contriving to get a look round. But before that he must discover what sort of search Falcon had already made.

But how was he to get into the Castle at all? Ben had no more *locus standi* than before for a visit in that quarter. Moreover, he remembered that Mr Polwhele had told him how that morning Mr Narroway, Lord St Blaizey's family solicitor, would be at the Castle to read the old lord's will. It hardly seemed an opportune time for him to go butting in.

Ben decided to begin the morning with a visit to Captain Galloway. So far, there was nothing beyond Sarah's dream to indicate that the St Blaizey agent had anything to do with the case. But he was an old friend of Rupert's, and it would be as well to have a look at him; and Ben could see his way to a plausible pretext for seeking an interview. He decided to let Jellicoe have the car, after he had driven into St Blaizey, where he would be able to find out where Captain Galloway lived, and perhaps get a word with Chief Inspector Falcon, unless he had already gone out. Falcon had been very informative up to a point; but Ben realized that he had not gleaned from their previous interview any real idea of the line the Yard were taking. It would be useful to find that out if he could. He arranged with Jellicoe to return to St Blaizey for lunch, unless he found some trail which it was imperative to follow up at once. In that case, he was to telephone a message to The Damian Arms before half-past one.

They drove out to St Blaizey. The post office told Ben Tancred that Captain Galloway lived in a house on the estate at the extreme west end of the woods, beyond the

Castle, on the road running north to Luxulian, which made a big detour round the edge of the park. It was about two miles by road, or a little less by a path along the south edge of the woods. Ben got out his map, and established the position of the house and the ways to it. He elected to walk by the path beside the woods, and sent Jellicoe away at once on his search for traces of the fair young man or of the dark man and his car.

It was a pleasant way along the edge of the woods, and Ben, who was always a lover of walking, enjoyed his tramp. Once he heard a distant sound of woodmen felling a tree, and occasionally the hum of a car reached him from the road, which ran parallel to the path not very far away. But he met no one, until the path brought him out on the road, a little way past the end of the woods, and not far beyond where the road turned north in the direction of Luxulian village. Its last lap ran beside a stone wall; and inside this Ben could see a square-built stone house, with a good many outbuildings. This he guessed to be the house of which he was in search.

He reached the road, and turned off it almost at once up a short drive which brought him to the somewhat forbidding front of Captain Galloway's residence. Its appearance did not suggest that Galloway was gifted with much æsthetic appreciation. The striped purple window-curtains struck Ben as among the ugliest he had ever seen; and all the woodwork was painted a peculiarly loathsome yellow-brown. He knocked, and the door was opened by a forbidding manservant who looked, Ben thought, like a prizefighter addicted to hitting below the belt.

Ben asked for Captain Galloway, and was told that he was round at the back, in the yard. With this information, the man shut the door in his face. Ben, prepared already to dislike the Captain heartily went round the side of the house to look for him. He found himself in a big stone-paved yard, at the far end of which was a range of low stables before which he could see two men and a horse. One was a little, weasely fellow, who looked like a groom. The big man, who was prodding the horse, and talking in a loud scolding voice, was readily recognizable as Captain Galloway.

Ben advanced towards him; but before he was half across the yard Galloway saw him, and bellowed at him to know what he wanted. Ben made no answer, but continued to draw nearer.

'I asked you what the hell you wanted,' said the Captain, as Ben came up. 'Can't you see I'm busy?'

'I can wait till you're free,' said Ben Tancred easily. 'I wanted a word with you.'

'What about?' Captain Galloway slapped his leg impatiently with his riding crop.

'Well, let's say about a man called Alfred Amos, to begin with.'

'Another damned cop!' said the Captain. 'Haven't I had enough of you badgering me already?'

Ben observed that he was not a policeman, and gave his name.

'Then what in heaven's name are you?' Captain Galloway observed.

'Shall we say, a student of human nature? I'm at present studying yours.'

The Captain looked Ben up and down, and then guffawed. 'You've got a cheek,' he said. 'Come in and have a drink, if there's something you really want.' He turned to the groom. 'Here, you, mind. If I catch you at any more of these games . . .' The sentence ended in a growl, as Captain Galloway struck off in the direction of the house. Apparently the best way of dealing with the brute was to answer him back. Ben followed with his long strides, and overtook him just as he kicked the backdoor open with his foot.

Captain Galloway led the way into an unmistakably masculine room full of guns and fishing rods and loose cartridges and pipes and tobacco and papers strewn untidily on the big table, which also held a decanter, two syphons, and some glasses.

'Have a whiskey,' said the Captain. 'Irish, of course. The stuff they call Scotch is undrinkable nowadays. Here's a cleanish glass.'

Ben refused the drink. 'No whiskey for me,' he said. 'Mine's rum.'

'Haven't got any. Well, take a pew.' Captain Galloway mixed himself a stiff tot of whiskey and flung himself into a desk-chair. 'What d'you want?'

'A description of Alfred Amos, and anything about him you care to tell me.'

Galloway grunted. 'He's a lazy, undersized, sneakish sort of vermin,' he said.

'But I was told you were against his being discharged.'

'What's that got to do with you?'

'Perhaps nothing. But I was told you were.'

'So I was. He's a sight better than some of the others. Too many canting psalm-singers about these parts for my taste. Amos isn't a psalm-singer. Besides, he's good at his job—when he likes. He does understand horses.'

'What does he look like?'

'More like a weasel than most things. Dark complexion, black hair, cast in one eye, always dirty. What d'you want to know for?'

'To make sure he isn't someone I'm looking for. He isn't, so that's that.'

'What's it all about? Who are you, anyway?'

'If you want to know, I'm a private detective.'

'Then you can go to the devil. The regular police are more than I want without your sort butting in. Who shoved you on the job?'

'At any rate, somebody did. I also received a communication telling me to beware of you.'

Captain Galloway guffawed again. 'That's frank, anyhow. Who's got his knife into me this time?'

'I'm not proposing to tell you that,' said Ben. 'But it caused me to come round to have a look at you.'

'Well, what do you make of me now you've seen me?' Galloway asked truculently.

'Do you really want to know?'

Galloway laughed. 'Bad as that, is it? Come, what's the matter with me?'

'I don't like your manners.'

'Then you can lump them.'

'I *am* lumping them,' said Ben. 'The whole lump. Because I should rather like your help, if you'll give it to me.'

'What for?'

'To find out who murdered Lord St Blaizey.'

'Why do you think any one did?'

'I don't know the reason. If you mean the fact, I'm pretty sure of it.'

'Then think again.'

'I have.'

'Look here, Dr Tancred, or whatever your name is, let me give you a word of advice. Go back and tell your infernal employer, whoever he is, that everyone in these parts knows Dr Andover for a born fool. Tell him there isn't a scrap of evidence, apart from Andover's silly notions, to show Lord St Blaizey was murdered, and that every sensible person round here knows he wasn't. And you can also tell him to mind his own damn business.'

Clearly Captain Galloway had no suspicion who Dr Tancred's employer really was. Whom, then, did he suppose the unnamed employer to be?

Ben said, 'But if I do think there is other evidence pointing to murder, what then?'

'What is it?' Galloway asked. 'I shan't believe there is till I know it.'

Ben got to his feet. 'I won't waste any more of your time,' he said. 'Unless, that is, you can tell me anything more about Amos. He was sacked for getting a girl into trouble, wasn't he? Was he really guilty, do you think?'

Galloway rose angrily from his chair. 'So that's what you're really getting at, is it? And you have the cheek to come and ask me. Of course he was guilty. And now you can get out.'

Ben said, 'You have the manners of a pig, Captain Galloway. But I am glad to have met you. Good day.'

A curse followed him into the hall. He opened the front door, and went out and down the drive. So Captain Galloway was himself suspected of having got the girl into trouble. For that was surely the obvious inference from his behaviour.

If it was correct, it lent added interest to the search for Alfred Amos, though clearly he was not the man to whom Rupert Pendexter, if the dark man had been Rupert, had handed over his horse.

'Alas!' said Ben to himself, as he regained the road, 'in the engrossment of our talk I forgot to ask our friend for brother Sidney's address. Never mind. He probably wouldn't have given it me.'

CHAPTER 13

A SQUIRE OF DAMES

As Ben Tancred came out on to the road, a car drew up beside him, and a high, affected voice hailed him. 'I say, d'you know if my brother's at home?'

Ben saw, leaning out of the car, a hatless, fair young man, slightly built, and with what he described to himself as a nancy sort of look.

'If you mean Captain Galloway,' he answered, 'he's there. I've just left him.'

'What sort of a temper is he in?' asked the young man.

'Foul!' said Ben, succinctly.

'Bother!' said the young man. 'He always is, when I want him particularly. Not much use my going in.'

'Perhaps you might be more welcome than I seemed to be.'

'You been dunning him too? He's as skinny with his money as if he was a millionaire. I say, I suppose you couldn't lend me a fiver, and shove it on to whatever you get out of him.'

'I could not,' said Ben, for whom this ingenuous proposal had no appeal. 'But if, as I suppose, you're Sidney Galloway, I could do with a word with you.'

'I say,' said Sidney, almost in the same words as his

brother, but in a very different tone, 'you aren't another of these cops, are you?'

'No, I'm not,' said Ben. 'Have they been after you?'

'Oh, no, not after me. But Helen told me there were lots of them messing around.'

'You're a friend of Lady St Blaizey, are you?'

'Rather! She's a good egg. D'you know her?'

'We're old acquaintances. I knew her when you were wearing a bib.'

'It's too bad, people bothering her. What I say is, the old man was a jolly good riddance. It's ever so much jollier, now that she'll have lots of money.'

'Jollier for you?'

'Jollier for everyone. You're not a friend of Roderick's, are you?'

'If you mean Lord St Blaizey, I've never met him. Or his father, either.'

'I was the old chap's secretary for a bit, till he buzzed me out. Rotten job it was. He was a fiend for making a fellow work.'

'Look here,' said Ben. 'If you aren't going in to see your brother, what do you say to running me somewhere where I can stand you a drink?'

'Oke!' said Sidney. 'Hop right in.' Ben got into the tiny sports car—the very latest model—and Sidney Galloway turned her in a splutter of noise and fume. 'Where d'you want to go?'

'Anywhere. What about Par?' said Ben.

'Right-o!'

'This your car?' Ben asked.

'Wish it was. I borrowed it off a friend where I'm staying.'

'Where's that?'

'Fowey. I've got rooms—till something turns up. Better tell me who you are, hadn't you?'

'My name's Tancred. I'm in Fowey too. But I'm due for lunch in St Blaizey.'

'What did you want to see me about?'

'Perhaps I just felt lonely, and took a fancy to your face.'

'Oh, if you don't want to tell me, I don't mind. A drink's a drink, anyway.'

103

'You're a friend of Rupert Pendexter, as well as Helen, aren't you?' Ben asked, drawing a bow rather at a venture. Sidney Galloway did not appear to be at all discomposed by the question.

'Oh, yes. Rupert's a good sort, in his way. Of course he's a bit close-fisted, or he'd never have made all that money. But he's not at all a bad chap, really. What about him?'

'Only that I used to know him. Seen him lately?'

'Oh, yes. T'other day. Tried to touch him, as a matter of fact. No go! It's damned difficult to get hold of money when you want it.'

'And it doesn't last long when you get it, eh?'

'Too terribly true, in my case. Poverty doesn't suit me one little bit, you know.'

'That's true of quite a lot of people,' said Ben; 'but most of them seem to put up with it.'

The car drew up, with a screeching of brakes, outside the hotel at Par. They went in. 'What's yours?' Ben asked. 'Mine's a bitter.'

'Ask the chappie for a Cowboy's Dream,' said Sidney. 'They know me here.'

Ben ordered a Cowboy's Dream, and a pint of bitter. He watched Sidney Galloway taste the nauseous compound, as I feel sure it was.

'When did you see Rupert Pendexter last?' he asked. 'Has he been down here at all lately?'

'I saw him about a week ago.'

'Where was that?' Ben concealed the eagerness in his voice.

'Oh!' Was there, or was there not a hesitation about the answer. Had Sidney merely interrupted his speech in order to take another gulp of the Cowboy's Dream, or had he needed a moment to think out his reply? 'It was up in London. I was up there, after a job. I didn't get it.'

'Then Pendexter hasn't been down here lately?'

'I met him some weeks ago, up at the Castle. I say! What's all the inquisition about?'

'I just wondered if he was in these parts,' said Ben.

'He wasn't here when the old chap pegged out, if that's

what you mean,' said Sidney. 'He told me so. I say, d'you believe in all this stuff about Lord St Blaizey being murdered?'

'I don't know enough about it to have any opinion,' Ben answered. 'Do you?'

'I shouldn't be surprised. It all looks a bit fishy. But what I say is, if he was, who the deuce did it? Of course, Roderick's the obvious bloke; but Helen says she's sure he didn't. I don't know who else it could have been. I mean, one can see Roderick's motive for doing him in; but why should anyone else put him on the spot?'

'What about Alfred Amos, the stableman who got sacked? I'm told he had a grievance.'

'Ugly Alf? Yes, I suppose it might have been him. If he had the guts. But I should hardly have thought it of him. You see, he hadn't really anything much against the old man.'

'Lord St Blaizey sacked him, didn't he?'

'Yes; but it was really Roderick put him up to it; and Amos knew that all right. The old chap wouldn't have bothered, if Roderick hadn't nagged at him about the bad influence it would have on the other servants, if he didn't make an example.'

'I see. And Amos knew that, did he?'

'Everyone knew it.'

'What's happened to the girl, by the way?'

'Oh, Roderick's looking after her, body and soul. Especially soul, if I know him. He's strong on souls.'

'Your brother tried to stop Amos being sacked, didn't he? Why, do you know?'

'Just fellow-feeling, I expect. He's a bit that way himself.'

'No doubt that Amos did it, I suppose?'

'I should say not. Why?'

'I just wondered. What you say seems rather to wash him out as a suspect.'

'I never suspected him. You dragged him in. I say, you seem marvellously interested in all this. What's the game?'

'Ordinary human curiosity,' said Ben, grinning. 'Murders are fascinating, somehow. Why, I can't think.'

'Anything with a kick to it is,' said Sidney Galloway, trying his glass to see if he could squeeze another drop out of it. 'Life's so hellish dull: most chaps'll give anything if only something'll happen.'

Ben suggested a second round; and his guest accepted with alacrity. Just as the fresh drinks arrived, someone else came into the lounge, and greeted Sidney as an old friend. 'Saw Mildred's car outside,' said the newcomer, a dark young man otherwise much of Sidney Galloway's type. 'Thought it was probably you. Had any lunch?'

'Not a bean,' said Sidney. 'Dr Tancred, this is Clive Venner.'

Ben greeted the newcomer without enthusiasm. 'About time I was off,' he said. 'I suppose I can get a bus to St Blaizey?'

'Oh, I'd better take you up,' said Sidney. 'Coming, Clive? We might be able to cadge lunch off Helen.'

Mr Venner had his car, but said he would follow in a jiffy. Ben led the way out of the hotel, and Sidney Galloway and he got back into the borrowed car, which hurtled noisily to St Blaizey. There Ben got out, and watched Sidney drive away in the direction of the Castle. It was still too early for Jellicoe to be back, so he went into The Damian Arms, and asked if Chief Inspector Falcon was in. It appeared that he was; and a moment later he was greeting Dr Tancred in his normal laconic fashion. 'Hallo,' he said. 'Heard the news?'

'What news?' said Ben.

'About the will.'

'I've heard nothing.'

'Lord St Blaizey gets the title, and the entailed estate. All the rest goes to Rupert Pendexter, barring minor legacies.'

'What? Rupert Pendexter gets the old man's money?' asked Ben, really astonished for once. The idea that Rupert would be heir to Lord St Blaizey's great fortune had never so much as entered his head.

'Pretty nearly scoops the lot,' said the Chief Inspector. 'Wants thinking about, eh?'

'It does,' said Ben. 'It provides the one thing lacking—a motive!'

'Think Pendexter killed him? That the idea?'

'I thought that before,' said Ben. 'Now I'm sure of it.'

'Wasn't here, as far as we know,' said Falcon. 'Supposed to have been up in London.'

'Is there any proof he was in London?' Ben asked.

'None been looked for, so far. Have to look into it now, of course. Come to that, no evidence he was here, that I know of.'

'There's Sarah Pendexter's.'

'Not worth that,' said Falcon, snapping his fingers. 'Wash it out, doctor.'

Ben considered that the time had come to tell Falcon what the tramp had said. The news about the will put a new light on everything. He told the Chief Inspector of Jellicoe's discoveries, including what he had learnt from Mr Smith in the old copper mine.

'Ought to have told me at once,' said Falcon disapprovingly. 'Man may clear out, and be deuce of a job to find again.'

'That's just what I'm afraid of his doing,' said Ben, 'if the police start badgering him.'

'Oh, we'll keep tabs on him,' said Falcon confidently. 'See him myself, this afternoon.'

'For heaven's sake don't scare him off,' said Ben. 'He's practically our only witness.'

'Now about this fair young man,' Falcon inquired. 'Got any notion who he was?'

'No. My man's out now trying to pick up his tracks. The only person who seems to fit the description is Sidney Galloway, Captain Galloway's brother. He's a friend of Rupert's. As a matter of fact, I've just been talking to him; but he gave nothing away. Mind, I'm not saying he is our man. But no one else I know of fits the description. I suppose Landor might fit—I've not seen him yet. But I don't quite see how he could have been there at the time—unless his story about 'phoning to London is all lies.' But Falcon said that Landor had undoubtedly 'phoned. That had been checked up at once. Ben repeated the reasons for his view which he had given in his monologue to Jellicoe at an earlier stage.

'We'll lay hands on the chap, whoever he was,' said Falcon, no less confidently than before. 'Well, doctor, any more news for me? Anything else you're keeping up your sleeve?'

'No,' said Ben, 'but I'll offer you an idea.' He went on to tell Falcon his notion that Lord St Blaizey's murderer must have met him by appointment, as otherwise he could not have expected to find the old man riding alone, and that there might be a note, or something else referring to the appointment, somewhere at the Castle. 'I'd been trying to work out a way of getting up there and hunting for such a thing myself,' Ben went on; 'but, frankly, I didn't see how to manage it. I suppose you've been through old Lord St Blaizey's papers.'

'Yes, and found nothing of the sort,' said Falcon. 'Admit I wasn't looking for it. I'll have another shot. Something in what you say.'

'May I come with you?' Ben asked.

'H'm. Irregular. But I owe you a good turn. Provided you play fair.'

'It's one of my habits,' said Ben.

'Right. Lunch first; then we'll go up together,' said Falcon.

'That suits me. I'll just go outside, and see if my man's turned up yet with the car.'

Jellicoe was outside, in the car. 'What luck?' Ben asked him.

'Not a thing, doctor. I've drawn an absolute blank. Not a sign of the fair young man anywhere. But I've got this. The chap in the car drove off towards Lostwithiel.'

'Got got his number, have you?'

'No such luck, doctor. The chap that saw the car didn't notice it—the number. But he did see it was a low sports car of some sort. He couldn't say what make it was, more's the pity. He was just a labourer, and not much of a hand at descriptions.'

'I suppose you've got his name,' said Ben.

'Yes, and where to find him again.'

'Well, it's better than nothing,' said Ben. 'Come on in. You and I are lunching with Chief Inspector Falcon. Then you're driving up to the Castle.'

'What orders after that, doctor?'

'Heaven knows!' said Ben Tancred.

CHAPTER 14

THE WILL IS READ

The news that Rupert Pendexter, and not Roderick Damian, was to inherit old Lord St Blaizey's vast fortune put everything in a new light. Over lunch, Chief Inspector Falcon explained how he had heard the news. He had been up at the Castle, pursuing certain investigations of his own while, in the library, Mr Narroway, the lawyer, was reading the will to the assembled family. Falcon confessed that he had attached no importance to the contents of the will, taking it for granted that Lord St Blaizey would have left the bulk of his fortune to his son.

He happened to be in the great hall of the Castle, on which the library opened, when the door was flung wide, and Lord St Blaizey hobbled out. He was obviously in a tearing rage, his face twitching, and his free hand working convulsively as he dragged himself along with the aid of a stick, his damaged leg imparting a sort of stagger to his progress.

Immediately behind him was his wife, also in a state of extreme agitation, with staring eyes and a dead-white face. She was calling out 'Roderick!' in an imploring way. She tried to lay her hands on her husband; but he brushed her roughly aside, and, going to the great French windows at the end of the hall, flung them open and stood there, gulping in the fresh air as if he had been ready to choke. Helen came and stood near him, gazing at him with a look of consternation, as if she were at her wits' end to know what to do. The Chief Inspector, his presence apparently unnoticed, remained at a distance, watching and wondering what under heaven could have caused so great a pother.

For a minute or so no one else came out of the library. Then Rupert Pendexter appeared at the door, and stood, framed in the doorway, looking at his sister and her husband. On his face there were plain signs of disturbance, but not of agitation. He looked rather puzzled, Falcon said, than either angry or seriously upset. After standing there for a moment, he shrugged his shoulders, and retreated back into the library without uttering a word.

A minute later the lawyer came out, carrying a big leather satchel and a deed box. He too stood for a moment in the doorway, staring at Lord St Blaizey and his wife. Mr Narroway's countenance was not an easy one to read; but Falcon described his appearance as one of displeasure and concern. He too was obviously uncertain what to do next.

After a moment's hesitation the old lawyer advanced towards Lord St Blaizey. 'My lord,' he said, 'pray believe me that this has been fully as much of a shock to me as it must have been to you. I had no idea of what was in the will: or rather the idea which I had—and conveyed to you—of its contents has proved to be quite disastrously wrong.' He paused; but Lord St Blaizey, though he appeared by now to have regained some control of himself, said nothing at all.

'I can only say that I shall of course be ready to receive any instructions your lordship is pleased to give me, at your lordship's convenience.'

Upon that, Lord St Blaizey turned to face the lawyer. 'I can't believe it,' he said. 'My father could never have done such a thing. It . . . it . . . can't be true.'

'It is very singular, as well as very distressing,' said Mr Narroway. 'I confess I am quite at a loss to understand it.'

'It must be a forgery,' Lord St Blaizey exclaimed.

'I fear that cannot be,' the lawyer answered. 'When your lordship is more composed, I shall be ready to go into the circumstances, as far as I know them.'

'You had better explain them now—if you can explain them,' said Lord St Blaizey. 'Come to my study.'

Helen had stood all this time gazing at her husband without saying a word. But now she said, 'Shall I come too, Roderick? If you are sure you feel well enough . . .'

'No. Stay where you are,' answered her husband, in a voice that can have brought no pleasant sensation to his wife. 'Come, Narroway. I want to know how this can have happened.'

Followed by the lawyer, Lord St Blaizey stumped away, leaving Lady St Blaizey looking after them with a tragic face. They were barely gone when Rupert Pendexter again appeared in the doorway.

'Helen,' he said.

She turned towards him, her face more frightened than ever. 'No, no. Leave me alone,' she cried, and then, as he advanced towards her, turned and fled into the garden.

Rupert seemed about to follow; but the Chief Inspector called to him. 'Mr Pendexter!'

He spun round, with a startled look. 'You here?' he said. 'What do you want?'

'A word with you.'

'By all means. Let's sit down.' Rupert threw himself into a chair. 'I suppose you've gathered what has happened?'

'Far from it,' said Falcon, 'except that something seems to have upset Lord St Blaizey.'

'It has,' said Rupert, 'and I don't wonder at it. The fact is, Chief Inspector, the late Lord St Blaizey has left me most of his money. I must say it's hard on Roderick—and on my sister.'

Falcon, in telling his tale afterwards, admitted that he was taken entirely aback. He stared at Rupert Pendexter, not knowing what to say.

'It's come quite as much as a surprise to me as to everyone else,' Rupert went on. 'Till the will was read this morning, I had not the slightest idea of it. Of course, I knew he'd leave me something; but I expected something quite small

111

—a thousand or two, no more. I confess that I'm ... absolutely staggered.'

'But surely Mr Narroway must have known what was in the will,' said Falcon. 'Didn't he drop anyone a hint—to break the shock?'

'That's the queerest thing about it,' said Rupert. 'He didn't know—till this morning. You see, the will was not kept in his office. It was down here, in a locked box. Lord St Blaizey always insisted on keeping it himself. Narroway had a key—with instructions to open the box and read the will to the family after Lord St Blaizey's death.'

'But didn't he draw it up?'

'Yes, he drew up the main will; and that left everything, apart from small legacies, to Roderick. I got what I expected—a thousand pounds. Narroway, of course, read that first, and we all thought that was the end of it. But there was a codicil, practically revoking the whole thing, and making me residuary legatee instead of Roderick. I was flabbergasted.'

'But didn't Mr Narroway draw up the codicil?'

'No; and he says he hadn't the smallest notion of its existence. He thought he'd got to the end of the will, as he drew it up. And then there was another page, and he turned over, and found the codicil. He nearly fell off his chair with his astonishment. He could hardly read it out. You see, he knew the will so well he'd never looked to see if anything had been added to it.'

'When was the codicil added?' Falcon asked.

'I can't tell you the exact date. Narroway will have that. About two or three years ago, I think he said it was.'

'You're sure it's in order? I mean the codicil.'

'I'm no lawyer. Ask Narroway. He seems to think it is. Of course, if it isn't, Roderick will get the money. I half wish it wasn't in order. You see, it's awkward for me. I like Roderick; and I can see he's got a good big grievance—not against me really, because it's not my fault; but one can hardly expect him to see that just yet awhile. Besides, there's Helen. It's not at all nice, feeling you've disinherited your own sister.'

'You could always give it back,' said Falcon.

'I suppose I could—some of it. That wants thinking about. Of course, I want to do the right thing. But you see, I suppose the old man must have had some good reason for cutting out his own son, or he wouldn't have done it, would he?'

'You have no idea what his reason was?'

'Not the smallest—I mean apart from their always having quarrels. But I should say it must have been something pretty serious. The old man wasn't one to turn vindictive over trifles. The devil is to know what I'm to do next. I shall have to fish in my own lawyer, and consult him. Narroway won't do: he's been looking at me as if he'd like to strike me dead ever since he read the thing. Outraged family attorney, and all that. And I can't very well stay here, with Roderick feeling like assaulting me physically at sight. But I don't see how I can buzz back to London leaving things as they are, though I have got an important appointment in town, and I really ought to be getting back at once. It's infernally difficult for me.'

Falcon suppressed a desire to say that the acquisition of Lord St Blaizey's fortune was enough to compensate a man for quite a deal of temporary inconvenience. He only said, 'Then I suppose you'll be stopping on in the neighbourhood, if not here. You might let me know your address.'

'I will—when I've settled what to do. It's all most deucedly awkward.'

'You've an aunt in the neighbourhood, haven't you?' Falcon went on, rather maliciously. 'Perhaps you could stay with her.'

Rupert laughed. 'Aunt Sarah! Good Lord! She hates me like poison. Besides, I believe she camps out in one room and does her own washing-up. She's mad. I haven't seen her for donkeys' years.'

Falcon thought that was as much as he could get out of Rupert Pendexter for the time being. He wanted to see Mr Narroway and Lord St Blaizey, and discover whether their version of the affair tallied with Rupert's. He got to his feet and, with a reiterated request to Rupert to keep him informed of his whereabouts, walked away.

The Chief Inspector went into the corridor, where he found a manservant and asked him if he knew whether his lordship and the lawyer were still together in the study. The man said he believed they were; and his lordship had given special orders that he was not to be interrupted on any account. No, he did not know where her ladyship was to be found. Mr Landor was in his own room.

Falcon went in search of Landor, and asked him if he had heard the news. But Landor said he had heard nothing special, whereupon Falcon told him about the will, and watched for the effect.

Gregory Landor appeared to be utterly astonished. He said that such an idea as that Rupert Pendexter would get Lord St Blaizey's money had never entered his head. He had looked on the two men as close business associates, who were also on good terms personally; but no more than that. Besides, though Roderick and his father had been addicted to stormy quarrelling, he had never taken this very seriously. He had been told that all the Damians were like that; and old Lord St Blaizey had always seemed to him to be, at bottom, quite fond of his son, even though they had so little in common. He had, moreover, certainly been fond of his son's wife; and Landor found in that an additional reason for astonishment at the will.

Gregory Landor was not a person whose opinions the Chief Inspector was inclined, on general grounds, to take very seriously; but in this case his opportunities for observation had been unusually good. It was altogether a most mysterious affair, and, if the codicil had been more recent, would have been highly suspicious. As it was, of course, there was a motive for murdering Lord St Blaizey staring one in the face. At least, there was a motive, if Rupert Pendexter had known beforehand what was in the will. In that case, he had been lying barefacedly in what he had just told Falcon.

Had Rupert been lying? He had seemed straightforward enough; but the Chief Inspector reserved judgment. After the incidents of the morning, he saw that he would have to think the entire case out afresh.

(I should perhaps make plain that in this chapter, as neither Ben Tancred nor I had any first-hand information, I have taken the liberty of reconstructing the scene in accordance with what Chief Inspector Falcon told Ben over lunch, and reported to me at a later stage. In this chapter, then, the reported conversations do not purport to be more than very roughly accurate.)

CHAPTER 15

QUIS?

Chief Inspector Falcon hung about the Castle for some time longer in the hope of getting a talk with either Lord St Blaizey or Mr Narroway; but he did not like to break in on their colloquy, and they remained closeted together. Nor was there any sign of Lady St Blaizey; and Rupert Pendexter had also disappeared. Captain Galloway arrived on horseback at about noon, but left at once on finding no one except Landor free to talk to him. Finally, the Chief Inspector, having finished off his other business, decided to go back to the village for lunch, and then return to the Castle at once, in the hope that by then he would be able to get a word with Lord St Blaizey.

Thus it came about that he fell in with Ben Tancred, and agreed to take him up with him to the Castle in the afternoon. Ben, indeed, would have gone there in any case; for the new developments had decided him to seek an interview with Lord St Blaizey, and ask for permission to pursue his investigations in a less unsatisfactory way.

Ben Tancred's first reaction, on hearing the news, had been one of certainty that it pointed to Rupert Pendexter as the murderer. But on second thoughts he was not quite so confident. It was at any rate possible that Rupert's surprise at the contents of the will had been genuine, and that he had not known that Lord St Blaizey had left him heir to his fortune. It remained possible that the new Lord St Blaizey, if he had not known what was contained in the codicil, had had some part in putting his father out of the way. Helen's attitude was, when one came to consider it in that light, consistent with either hypothesis. She might insist on scouting the notion of murder because she wanted to defend either her brother or her husband from the charge.

Ben seized the chance of his conversation with Chief Inspector Falcon to see how much light the Scotland Yard man was able, or prepared, to throw on this alternative hypothesis. He had really, up to this point, no idea of what was at the back of Falcon's mind; but he felt that the Chief Inspector must have been working along some definite line, and was bound, in any case, to have investigated the alternative possibilities a great deal more thoroughly than Ben himself had had any opportunity of doing so far. Ben had not even met Lord St Blaizey, and had no idea, except from hearsay, of the sort of person he was. He asked Falcon straight out what he thought of the possibility of Lord St Blaizey having killed his own father.

The Chief Inspector shook his head. 'Apart from character,' he said, 'there's much against it. Man can't sit a horse: too much of a cripple. He can walk, and does; but he's under a big handicap for attacking anyone. No, my view is the old lord was killed riding. If so, the young lord couldn't have killed him. The blow was struck from a level with his face. Broken neck was almost certainly caused by the fall. Ergo, the murderer was riding too. That's what I think. Then there's opportunity. His lordship reached Luxulian village at twelve o'clock. Landor says he left the old man at eleven-fifteen. Lord St Blaizey couldn't have got from where the body was to Luxulian in the time. Not possibly—that is, on foot. No, doctor, he's out of it. Besides, take character. The man doesn't value money—not that,' Falcon made a gesture with his fingers. 'Fond of the old man too, unless I'm greatly mistaken. No, whoever killed him, it wasn't his son. Feel sure of that.'

Ben Tancred was inclined to accept Falcon's view. Then

who remained? 'Is it unfair,' he said, 'to ask you on what line you have been working? I mean, whom you have suspected up to now?'

Falcon took his time to answer. 'Well, there's Alfred Amos,' he said slowly.

'But you don't think he did it?' said Ben.

'No, frankly, I don't. Not as principal. Might be accessory —even instrument. But, broadly, I agree. Look higher up.'

'Yes, but where?' Ben asked.

The Chief Inspector looked at him keenly, and gave his moustaches a special twirl as he answered. 'There's her ladyship,' he said.

Ben was rather startled. He had not seriously considered Helen as the actual murderer. 'I thought you held it wasn't a woman's crime.'

'Striking the blow, yes. Though even that's possible. Short of that, I'm not so sure.'

'Is there anything to suggest she's guilty?' Ben inquired.

'There's men would have done it for her,' said Falcon. 'That Captain Galloway, for one. He was riding in the woods that morning. Or his brother. Both go trailing after my lady.'

'With her encouragement?'

'I should say so. There's been goings-on up at the Castle, so the servants say.'

'H'm. I wonder. Dangerous game, putting up your boy-friends to murder for you behind your husband's back. Of course, what you are suggesting is that Lady St Blaizey had her father-in-law put out of the way in order to get the title and the money?'

'That's the line I was working on, I admit, till this thing came along. Got to think again now. But her ladyship's been no help to me. Obstructed all she could, right from the start.'

'What about Lord St Blaizey? What has been his attitude?'

'Correct, but not helpful. Says it wasn't murder. Takes his cue from his wife, I should say. Didn't put any obstacles in my way, but he hasn't been much help.'

'You mentioned Sidney Galloway. Anything to connect him up?'

'Nothing, so far, unless he's your fair young man. The Captain was more my notion. Ugly customer, Captain Galloway.'

'Not attractive, I agree. And he could fell an ox,' said Ben. 'All the same, I don't fancy that solution.'

'Not sure I do. Seemed the least unlikely, that's all. Till this turned up. Got to consider your friend Rupert seriously now. I'm having his movements traced by the Yard in London.'

'What about my tramp?' Ben asked. 'Have you been on to him yet?'

'Tried to,' said Falcon. 'Went round to have a word with him at the old mine. Fellow saw me coming, and scuttled away up the hill. Not been seen since. My running days are over.' The Chief Inspector, with an approach to a smile, indicated his girth.

'That's just what I was afraid of,' said Ben Tancred. 'You're searching for him, I suppose.'

'Oh, yes. We'll pull him in.'

'He's our only witness, bar Sarah,' said Ben ruefully.

A waiter came in, to tell the Chief Inspector he was wanted on the telephone, from London. Falcon went out, leaving Ben Tancred and Jellicoe together. Ben asked Jellicoe, who had been a listener throughout, what he made of it.

'Well, doctor, I should say someone ought to look pretty carefully at that will, even if it is a couple of years old.'

'At the codicil, you mean,' said Ben. 'I agree. Also at Rupert Pendexter's financial position. I want you, Jellicoe, as soon as you've dropped Falcon and me at the Castle, to put through a call to your sister at the office, saying I want all the dope I can get about how Pendexter stands just now in the City. Wilson gave me a few hints; but I want more. You'd better tell her to put Gordon on to it at once. He's the best man for that sort of job. Tell him to make a quick job of it, and report to me here.' Ben went on to tell Jellicoe to have Rupert's connection with the Iridium Syndicate and with a concern called MANGO specially investigated.

'I'll see to that, doctor. You mean it would strengthen the motive, if he's in queer street.'

'Yes. If that codicil was added some years ago, and Pendexter knew it, he's had a motive for murder ever since. But on the face of it he had a motive for striking quickly; for the old man might easily have altered his will back again at any time. It's surprising he didn't kill sooner, if he meant to kill at all. That is, of course, if the codicil's genuine, as Narroway seems to think it is. The old lord seems to have been, externally, on quite reasonable terms with his son just lately. Therefore, murder two or three years after the codicil was added needs special explanation. Of course, one possibility is that Pendexter only learnt about the codicil quite recently. But another is that he's recently got into financial deep water, and that put murder into his head. Assuming, of course, that he's lying when he says he didn't know about the old man's money. That, I think, we've got to assume.'

'Yes, if he's guilty at all.'

'Well, Jellicoe, who else? Between you and me, I think that stuff of Falcon's about Lady St Blaizey and Captain Galloway being in a conspiracy is all bunk. I daresay she's no better than she should be; but I'd stake my bottom dollar she never put up that brute, Captain Galloway, to murder the old man for her. She's got more sense than that, my boy. Too much sense, perhaps. If she'd put up anyone to murder for her, it'd have been Rupert.'

'Perhaps she did, doctor,' said Jellicoe; and at the very same moment Ben Tancred struck the table with his fist.

'My hat, Jellicoe!' he exclaimed. 'I wonder if that's it. The pair of them in it, and Rupert all the time double-crossing his fair sister because he knew the money would come to him, and not to her. And she didn't know.'

'If he did know.'

'You bet he did, Jellicoe. You won't catch friend Rupert committing murder for anybody's benefit except his own. That's what put me off, at first. My hat! I do believe that must be the right notion.'

'It makes her out pretty bad, doctor.'

'Ye-es; and I don't know whether she is bad, to that extent,' Ben mused. 'I'm sure she'd do anything to shield Rupert, even if she knew he was guilty of another murder? I just don't know. I can't feel sure I know that woman, Jellicoe. I shall certainly have to make a further study of Lady St Blaizey. At present she puzzles me.'

Chief Inspector Falcon came bustling back into the room. 'That was Superintendent Wilson on the 'phone,' he said. 'Asked how you were getting on. Told him the latest—about the will. He 'phoned to say they'd traced Amos to Whitechapel, but he'd got away before they could lay hands on him. Thinks he may be hiding on a ship. Wilson says he appears to have plenty of money. Been making a bit free with it. They'll lay hands on him soon, never you fear.'

'Has anything come through about Rupert Pendexter's movements?' Ben asked.

'Nothing yet. That's the lot.'

'Then shall I run you up to the Castle now? I've got my car.'

'Glory be!' said the Chief Inspector. 'I've lost a stone since I came here, trapesing around.'

CHAPTER 16

THE WILL AND THE CODICIL

Bidding Jellicoe come back with the car as soon as he had put through his London call, and stay handy in case he was wanted, Dr Tancred followed Chief Inspector Falcon up to the front door of St Blaizey Castle. Falcon asked whether Lord St Blaizey was at liberty to see him, and they were shown into Gregory Landor's room. Ben, meeting the dead man's secretary for the first time, saw before him a rabbity little man, with a weak but rather sensitive face, mouse-coloured hair, and large owlish spectacles. Hardly, he thought, the fair young man whom the tramp had described. The Chief Inspector repeated his request for an interview with his lordship, and the secretary went away to inquire. He told them that Mr Narroway was still at the Castle, and he rather thought he and Lord St Blaizey were still together.

In a few minutes Landor came back, to say that his lordship would see the Chief Inspector at once. 'I told him you had Dr Tancred with you; and he said it was your affair whom you cared to bring along.'

'You'd better come with me, doctor,' said Falcon. 'The Super was very particular I was to give you every help.'

Thanking his stars for Henry Wilson, Ben Tancred followed Landor and the Chief Inspector down a long corridor, and was ushered into a fair-sized room, crammed with books and papers, in which two men were seated at a big table. They both got up as the visitors came in; and Ben at once noticed Lord St Blaizey's infirmity. It was plainly an effort for him to rise from his chair; and he sank down into it again immediately without shaking hands. He was a shortish fellow in the middle forties, who looked as if he had once been stout-built and strong, but had been wasted away almost to nothing by ill-health.

The lawyer, on the other hand, was a remarkably well-preserved old gentleman with beautiful silvery hair and moustache and an all-pervading glossiness like a new top-hat. He bowed, ceremoniously, before sitting down again at Lord St Blaizey's side.

'Well, Inspector,' said Lord St Blaizey, none too cordially, 'what is it now?'

Falcon introduced Dr Tancred, merely as someone who was also working upon the case. Lord St Blaizey looked at Ben, acknowledged his existence with a curt nod, and said audibly, under his breath, 'H'm, another of 'em!' and then aloud, 'Well?'

'In the new circumstances, my lord, I felt I ought to see you at once.'

'What new circumstances?' said Lord St Blaizey sharply.

'The will, my lord,' Falcon answered.

'Who told you about the will?' The tone of the question was as if Lord St Blaizey were bidding the Chief Inspector mind his own business.

'Mr Pendexter told me. I happened to meet him just after it had been read.'

Ben noticed with amusement that there was no sign of Falcon's staccato manner of speech when he was talking to a peer of the realm.

'What did he tell you?'

'That your lordship's father had added a codicil making him the principal legatee. I take it that is the case?'

'Do you?' said Lord St Blaizey. 'I don't. The thing's a forgery.'

Ben looked towards the lawyer as his client made this accusation. Mr Narroway seemed as if he had a mind to intervene. Then he thought better of it, and, with a slight shrug of the shoulders, resumed his impassive demeanour.

'That, my lord, is a serious statement,' said Falcon. 'You are in a position to back it up?'

'Of course it's a forgery,' said Lord St Blaizey. 'My father was—quite incapable of behaving in such a way.'

Ben struck in. 'What does Mr Narroway think about it?' he said.

Lord St Blaizey glared at him. 'I was expressing my opinion,' he said. 'Narroway is welcome to his own.'

'I asked what his opinion was,' said Ben.

'Tell 'em, Narroway,' said Lord St Blaizey. 'You're all wrong; but tell 'em your view.'

The lawyer said slowly, 'The signatures look to me genuine. But I am not an expert. His lordship may possibly be right.'

'Of course I'm right. What else did Pendexter tell you?'

'That the codicil had come as a complete surprise to him.'

'Liar!' exclaimed Lord St Blaizey, hammering the table with his fist. 'I was looking at him, when it was read. While Narroway was reading the will, he was watching . . . waiting.' He turned towards the lawyer. 'When you found that codicil, I saw his face. He couldn't keep it natural. He was gloating—with anticipation.'

'Then, I understand,' said Falcon, 'your lordship's view

is that Mr Pendexter forged the will.'

'Codicil, man. Be accurate. Naturally he forged it. No one else'd be likely to forge a will in his favour, would they?'

'But you are only accusing him on suspicion.'

'Heavens alive, man! Do you suppose I saw him do it? What I say is, I *know* my father never did a thing like that. He couldn't even have done it in a sudden fit of anger—not even that. As for supposing that he signed that codicil years ago, and never said a word to me about it all that time, I tell you it's ridiculous—fantastic. It's—unbelievable!

'You were on good terms with him?'

'What are good terms? We quarrelled, sometimes—he was a difficult, unreasonable man—but never seriously. Our disputes were nothing. We understood each other perfectly well.'

'But you did quarrel?'

'He wanted me to go into the banking business; and I wouldn't. That's all there was to it. I dislike business. He enjoyed it. It is a matter of taste—and conviction.'

'He never threatened to disinherit you?'

'If he did, I certainly never took it seriously. Nor did he. No, Inspector, if you are trying to work up a case on the score of my father and me not being on good terms, you're all wrong. Besides, you have not yet told me why you are subjecting me to this catechism. What have you to do with my father's will?'

'Nothing, my lord, unless it has some connection with your father's death. But that possibility cannot be overlooked.'

'It cannot,' said Lord St Blaizey. 'Until this morning, I was certain that my father had died a natural death. Now, I am not sure.'

'We are pretty certain he did not, my lord.'

'Then who do you think killed him?' said Lord St Blaizey.

'I am not yet in a position to say that, my lord.'

'Then the sooner you are in a position, the better. See here, Inspector, I want to tell you where I stand. I'm as certain Pendexter forged that codicil as I am that we're in this room. I don't mind admitting that it has been a severe shock to me. I had always regarded Pendexter as one of my friends. I've not got too many of them. But when I saw his face this morning, I knew. That's certain; and I mean to prove it. But what comes next? Pendexter always seemed to be really fond of my father. My father *made* him—lifted him up out of nothing to what he is; and he always seemed to be grateful. Now, I can believe him capable of forging that codicil; I've never thought highly of his financial morals, and his friendship for me may have been all a sham. But I don't find it easy to believe him guilty of the sheer, abominable business of killing the man who'd been his best friend in the world. It's not as if he needed the money either. He's got plenty, I always understood. But if he didn't, who did? Yet I can't believe it of him. After all, he's my wife's brother. I don't know what to think.' Lord St Blaizey ended his harangue with a deep sigh.

Ben Tancred took advantage of the pause. 'You have heard the story of Simon Pendexter's death?' he asked.

Lord St Blaizey looked hard at him. 'What do you know about that?' he said. 'Oh, are you the Dr Tancred who got my wife out of gaol?'

Ben inclined his head.

'I have always believed my wife when she told me Rupert was blameless in that affair,' Lord St Blaizey went on. 'You are suggesting that he was guilty?'

'I feel sure he was,' said Ben.

'And that it means he . . . is guilty now? I see. But he was not here at the time. He was in London, was he not?'

'We are having all that looked into,' said Falcon. 'Now that your lordship has ceased to be sure your father died a natural death, we shall rely on your helping us.'

'What I want to do first of all is to prove that this abominable codicil is a forgery.'

Narroway came in again at that point. 'The difficulty, gentlemen, is that the signatures look to me genuine. The codicil is signed by his late lordship, and witnessed by two persons both whose signatures I know well.'

'Who are they?' Ben asked.

'Two old servants of his lordship's—his valet and his

butler. They have both been with him many years and have often witnessed documents for him. They witnessed the original will.'

'Are they here, at the Castle?' Ben asked.

'No, sir. They reside at his lordship's Hertfordshire house, Longridge Park. The codicil was presumably drawn up and signed there.'

'It was not drawn up by your firm?'

'No. I have never seen it before. I was entirely unaware of its existence.'

Falcon took charge again. 'Of course, my lord, I am not concerned with the will as such, but only with its bearing on your father's death. If you doubt its genuineness, you will doubtless yourself take all necessary steps to have the signatures examined, and the witnesses questioned.'

'I certainly shall,' said Lord St Blaizey. 'Mr Narroway and I have been busy going into that already. I shall most assuredly contest the will.'

'Who, by the way, are the executors?' Ben Tancred asked.

'It is most awkward,' Narroway answered. 'The joint executors under the original will were Lord St Blaizey and myself. The codicil substitutes Mr Rupert Pendexter and Captain Abel Galloway, who is also named as a legatee.'

'Then they will have the custody of the will,' said Ben.

'As soon as they claim it, I am afraid. In the meantime, I am retaining it in my possession.'

'Can I have a look at it?' said Ben.

'If the Chief Inspector wishes,' said Lord St Blaizey.

The lawyer opened the black deed-box and drew forth the will from a long envelope. It was a long document. He passed it over to Falcon, who after looking at it for a moment, passed it on to Ben Tancred. Ben merely glanced down the first page, and then turned at once to the last. The codicil, he saw, was written on a separate sheet, in legal penmanship much like that of the rest of the document, with the signatures below.

Ben carefully compared the signatures of the codicil with those of the will itself on the previous page. Apart from what seemed quite natural minor variations, Lord St Blaizey's two signatures looked just alike. Ben Tancred, who was something of a handwriting expert, felt little doubt that either they were both genuine or, if the codicil was a forgery, it had been executed by an expert with too much skill for it to be detected by the naked eye.

He turned to the signatures of the witnesses. These had been executed for both will and codicil by the same two persons, named Henry Lamb and Robert Cuff. Robert Cuff's signature was much the same on both pages, and looked as unimpeachable as Lord St Blaizey's own. Henry Lamb's, however, showed certain differences. It was a good deal shakier in the codicil than in the main will. Ben said so.

'Ah! Poor Lamb is a very old man,' said the lawyer. 'His hand has been getting shakier for some years past. I was always surprised his lordship did not pension him off; but he preferred to keep him at Longridge with someone else to do most of the work.'

'Then you regard both his signatures as genuine?' said Ben.

'Unless they are very clever forgeries indeed.'

'Of course they are forgeries,' said Lord St Blaizey. 'We've got to prove that.'

Ben went on. 'I agree, the differences look perfectly explicable by advancing years. Of course, one can say nothing definite without microscopic examination. But the *prima facie* appearances certainly favour the genuiness of the codicil.'

'It isn't genuine,' said Lord St Blaizey stubbornly.

'If Mr Narroway's office did not engross the codicil,' Ben went on, 'has he any idea who did? It is clearly professional writing.'

'I have no idea at all,' said Narroway. 'Of course, his lordship employed other solicitors in his financial affairs; but I had always believed that we handled all his personal business.'

'The point is worth investigating,' said Ben, 'if it is decided to question the codicil.'

'I have told you I dispute it,' said Lord St Blaizey. 'I have already asked Mr Narroway to act for me in the matter. He will engage the best experts he can find.'

'I noticed,' said Ben, 'that the will was made nearly four years ago, and the codicil added rather more than a year later. Was there a previous will?'

'Yes, but it was destroyed when this one was made. It differed from this only in respect of the minor legacies.'

'Lord St Blaizey was the principal beneficiary under both wills?'

'Yes.'

'Of course I was,' said Lord St Blaizey.

Ben Tancred handed the will back to the Chief Inspector who, after turning its pages over for a moment or two, passed it back to the lawyer. 'Did Captain Galloway benefit under either will?' he asked.

'No, only under the codicil.'

'And Lady St Blaizey? Is she mentioned?'

'She gets twenty thousand pounds, under the second will. The sum was smaller under the first will. The codicil does not affect her legacy.'

'I see. And the other beneficiaries?'

'Nothing beyond minor bequests to old servants, business friends and employees, and a few distant relations. His lordship had no near relatives except his son.'

There was a silence. At length it was broken by Lord St Blaizey. 'Well, Chief Inspector, what now?'

'I will do my best, my lord,' said Falcon.

'And Dr Tancred is acting with you?'

'Well, my lord, I have been giving Dr Tancred what help I can.'

'What d'you mean? Isn't he from Scotland Yard?'

'No, Lord St Blaizey,' said Ben. 'I am a private investigator, working on my own.'

'Then what brings you into it? You fellows don't work unless someone pays you. Who's paying you to poke your nose in on this affair?'

Lord St Blaizey's manners were certainly not affable. But Ben Tancred was in no mood to take offence. 'I was asked to look into the case,' he said.

'Who asked you?'

'My relations with my client are necessarily confidential. But I may say they do not extend to the question of the will.'

'Then you refuse to say who put you on to it?'

'Yes, without my client's permission.'

'Have it your own way,' said Lord St Blaizey. 'Have you found anything yet?'

'What I have found I have communicated to Chief Inspector Falcon.'

'Then, as the principal interested party, I shall be obliged if the Chief Inspector will tell me just what you and he have found out.'

At that moment the door opened, and Lady St Blaizey came into the room. She gave a start as she saw the assembled conclave. 'I thought you and Mr Narroway were alone,' she said to her husband. Ben saw that there were haggard lines upon her face that had not been there when they met in the woods.

'Go away, woman,' said Lord St Blaizey. 'Can't you see I'm busy?' He said it in a voice in which there was no trace of love. He snarled at Helen, as if he hated the very sight of her.

Lady St Blaizey said not a word in answer, but went, with a frightened look.

'And now, gentlemen, I shall be glad to know where we stand.' Lord St Blaizey's tone was hard. There was an added ruthlessness about him as if he would not hesitate to sacrifice even his own wife.

CHAPTER 17

THE EXECUTORS TAKE ACTION

It ended, as I dare say the reader will have guessed already, in Dr Tancred finding a second employer. Sarah Pendexter had called upon him to investigate murder; and Lord St

Blaizey, with the strong approval of Mr Narroway, who was able to give a highly favourable account of Ben's standing in his profession, now authorized him to go thoroughly into the question of the will. The first thing to be done, of course, was to get a thorough examination made of the signatures; and while Ben Tancred felt a fair confidence in his own capacity to undertake this, he proposed to get as highly qualified a second opinion as he could. Then there was a great deal more to be done, even if the signatures proved to be authentic—the witnesses who had signed the codicil to be interrogated, and the firm who had drafted it to be discovered, if possible, and the circumstances of its making established to the fullest practicable extent.

In all this there was one obvious difficulty. The executors might at any moment claim possession of the will; and this could by no possibility be refused them. Neither Lord St Blaizey nor Mr Narroway had any right at all to detain the will, as soon as it was claimed. If that once happened, access to it could probably be obtained again only by starting actual legal proceedings, and getting the authority of the court for its attachment. Ben Tancred wished heartily that he had told Jellicoe to bring down with him the big portable camera which he used in many of his inquiries; but he had not expected any photographing of documents to arise in the St Blaizey case, and had with him only a small camera which he felt was inadequate for the purpose in view.

There was, Ben suggested, in the circumstances only one thing to be done. Jellicoe was probably waiting for him outside with the car. If Lord St Blaizey and Mr Narroway would agree, he and Jellicoe would at once take the will with them, and go in search of a photographer who possessed a thoroughly good camera. They would then photograph, on the largest possible scale, the vital parts of the will and codicil, and thus render their investigations largely independent of their access to the original document.

Lord St Blaizey immediately agreed to this being done; and Ben Tancred, having found Jellicoe ready with the car, soon sped off towards Fowey, where he expected to be able to get the use of a camera that would meet his need. None too soon; for they had not been gone more than a few minutes when Captain Galloway appeared at the Castle, and asked to see Mr Narroway. Somewhat to the big man's embarrassment, Lord St Blaizey and Mr Narroway saw him together; and Lord St Blaizey's attitude made it clear that there was likely to be a speedy change in the stewardship of the St Blaizey estate. The captain had come to ask for possession of the will, in order that the executors might pass it over at once to their own lawyer. Mr Pendexter, who was returning to London, would take the will up with him, and hand it over tomorrow to Messrs Pummery and Mudge, who would be acting for them. He, Captain Galloway, had come to ask for the document, because Mr Pendexter had felt a delicacy about coming, in view of Lord St Blaizey's attitude to him earlier in the day.

To this Mr Narroway answered that he too, was returning to London, and that it would surely do as well if he took the will up with him, and handed it personally to Messrs Pummery and Mudge on the morrow. He knew them, of course; they were a well-known firm, though not so exclusively employed about the affairs of the aristocracy as Messrs Narroway and Straight.

Captain Galloway, however, was insistent—as politely as it was in his nature to be. He was sorry; but he and Mr Pendexter wanted to have a look at the will together before Mr Pendexter took it with him up to town; so he would be glad if Mr Narroway would hand it over at once.

This put the lawyer into a quandary; for he did not want to inform the enemy that the document had been sent away to be photographed, or to disclose for the present his client's intention of disputing the will. But Lord St Blaizey, who was no diplomat, saved him the need for thinking out a further excuse by saying bluntly that he hadn't got the will, but that Captain Galloway should have the thing as soon as it came back, and he had half a mind to stuff it down his throat in the hope that it would choke him.

That roused Galloway's temper; and the two men stormed at each other, despite Mr Narroway's endeavours to pacify them. Obviously Galloway was very angry at the removal of the will; and, as soon as his passage of arms with Lord St Blaizey was over, he demanded from Mr Narroway to know who had got it, and where it was.

This question Narroway refused to answer, only saying that he expected it would be back sometime before evening. Galloway, who seemed to be definitely uneasy, grumbled that this would make it impossible for the two executors to consider the will together before Pendexter went back to London, and might even make it impossible for him to take it with him, or compel him, though he had important appointments in London, to remain in Cornwall for another night. Narroway said that he was sorry, but offered no solution of Captain Galloway's problem. Finally, Galloway flung out of the room, announcing his intention to wait at the Castle until the will was produced and handed over to him.

Meanwhile, Chief Inspector Falcon had not been idle. His concern, however, was still with the murder, and not with the will, except where he found that it had some bearing upon the murder. Now that he was definitely inclined to transfer his chief suspicions from Lady St Blaizey to her brother, the most urgent thing clearly was to comb the entire neighbourhood for any further sign of Rupert Pendexter's presence in St Blaizey on the fatal day. Of course, if it could be shown that he had really been in London at or near the time of the murder, that alone would suffice to prove his innocence. But that part of the investigation was in Superintendent Wilson's hands, and in the meantime it was his business to see what evidence he could pick up on the spot.

That was, necessarily, a job in the main for the local police; for the Chief Inspector had no leisure to comb the country himself. He therefore set off for Fowey, in order to put the new facts before Superintendent Usher, of the County Police, and get the requisite fresh instructions sent out. Had anyone seen Rupert Pendexter in Cornwall on or near the day of the crisis? Had Rupert Pendexter's car, of which he had obtained the number from London, been seen anywhere in the neighbourhood, or anywhere on the possible routes between Cornwall and London? At the same time, Falcon meant to infuse new energy into the hue and cry after the missing tramp, who had given Jellicoe the unhelpful name of Smith. It was now of the first importance that 'Smith' should be found; for he looked like being the most essential witness of all, if the murder case ever came into court.

Having reached Fowey, and talked the case over with Superintendent Usher, who at once proceeded to get busy over the telephone, Chief Inspector Falcon paid a call at Dr Tancred's hotel, in order to inquire whether he had come back. But there had been no word there from Dr Tancred since the morning; and Falcon was rather at a loss to know what his next step ought to be. Finally, he made up his mind that he ought to see Sarah Pendexter, as she was the one person who had so far definitely vouched for Rupert Pendexter's presence at St Blaizey on the day of the crime.

Accordingly, Falcon crossed to Polruan, and toiled up the ascent through the village in the direction of Blackbottle House. He had not so far met Sarah Pendexter at all; for Sarah's initial statement denouncing Rupert Pendexter had been made to the local police before his arrival on the scene. But he had heard enough about her to be very uncertain about the best way of handling a lady whose eccentricities were reported to stop not far short of positive insanity. Sarah would need discreet handling, Falcon knew that. The great thing would be to keep her calm, and the best hope of doing that lay in being very calm and matter-of-fact himself.

The Chief Inspector twirled his moustaches, and prepared himself for the fray. At the top of the village, he inquired the way to Blackbottle House, and was directed, not to the main approach, but to the footpath which led to it by way of the rocks. Thus it happened that he arrived, not at the front door, but, as I had done all those years ago on the occasion of my first visit, actually on the flat roof; for the reader may remember that the house is built with its back to the solid rock, so that it is possible to walk straight on to the roof from the level ground above.

Approaching thus, Falcon crossed the roof and looked

down upon the terrace which stretched across the whole front of the house. There he saw, to his great surprise, an old woman kneeling apparently in fervent prayer; for he could hear the indistinct murmur of her voice rising and falling, though he could not catch her words. He stood thus for some time, looking down on Sarah Pendexter, not quite knowing what to do, especially as he had not yet discovered any way into the house. There was, indeed, on the flat roof on which he stood a small round building with a door—old Simon Pendexter's observatory—but that was securely fastened, and did not look as if it had been opened for years, as indeed it had not. Returning from a vain attack upon it to look down upon the terrace the Chief Inspector found that the woman had disappeared. He then, by perambulating the roof, discovered the whereabouts of the front door and the means of approaching it by going back and joining the main track to the house farther from the sea. A minute or two later he was knocking at the door.

Sarah opened it herself, as she had opened it to Dr Tancred on the occasion of his visit, and asked him fiercely who he was. Somewhat intimidated by the old lady's manner, Falcon explained that he was the officer from Scotland Yard who was in charge of the St Blaizey case. Sarah Pendexter rejoined by stating, in a few well-chosen and highly uncomplimentary phrases, her opinion of the police and their methods; and only after she had got that off her chest did she invite him to come in.

Falcon was shown, not into the big room in which Sarah had interviewed Ben Tancred, but into a smaller room beside the front door, which, to all appearances, served Sarah as bedroom, sitting-room, kitchen and larder combined. It was, Falcon said afterwards, full of the mixed odours of all these apartments; and, hot as the day had been, the windows were both closed. He was not invited to sit down, and stood just inside the door while Sarah, turning her back to him, proceeded to put a kettle to boil on a primus stove, at which she pumped vigorously away. Falcon watched with what patience he could, till the old woman, still with her back to him, bending over the stove, said sharply, 'Well, what do you want? Don't stand there like a stuck pig, but tell me your business.'

Falcon said he had come to visit her because of her assertion that she had seen Rupert Pendexter leaving St Blaizey Castle woods just about the time of Lord St Blaizey's death.

'Of course I saw him,' Sarah answered. 'I told your policemen that long ago. If they were half men, they'd have caught him and hanged him by now.'

Falcon asked whether she was prepared to swear that the man she had seen was Rupert Pendexter.

At that, he said, Sarah turned round and faced him. 'Do you suppose I don't know my own nephew when I see him?' she said. 'He was riding along the road on a black horse, and then the devil came and spirited him away.'

Falcon had not been quite prepared for that. He said, 'I suppose you don't mean you saw the devil do it, madam?'

'Why not?' said Sarah. 'I often see the devil. He walks abroad among men, doing his evil work.'

'Yes, yes,' said Chief Inspector Falcon. 'But I meant really seeing him.'

'So did I,' said Sarah. 'The devil is every bit as real as I am. From the look of you, I should say he was much more real than you.'

'Doubtless, madam,' said Falcon. 'But we are not discussing theology. The question is, what exactly was your nephew doing when you saw him?'

'He rode out of the Castle woods through the gate by the lodge, and vanished round the turn of the road.'

'That is better, madam. And after that, you saw no more of him?'

'Oh, yes,' said Sarah. 'I told you. I saw the devil come and carry him away.'

'Perhaps, madam, you will explain exactly what you mean,' said the Chief Inspector.

'I mean exactly what I say,' said Sarah tartly.

'When and where did you see this remarkable thing happen, madam?'

'Does it matter when?' Sarah answered. 'I think it was

134

over here—several days afterwards—I saw it first.'

'Oh, then, you didn't really see it at all.'

'You are quite as stupid as that other policeman I talked to,' said Sarah. 'I tell you, I did see it.'

Chief Inspector Falcon gave it up. For the future, he would leave interviewing Sarah Pendexter to others.

'Thank you, madam,' he said. 'That is all I wanted to know.'

'Then be off with you,' said Sarah.

The Chief Inspector got out of the house with all speed. He was half-afraid, he told me, that if he did not, Sarah would be after him with a broom, or even riding on a broomstick, in the classical manner.

CHAPTER 18

THE WILL CHANGES HANDS

Dr Tancred, meanwhile, had hunted up the best photographer in Fowey and, after a little negotiation, secured the use of his most suitable camera. He wanted to do his photographing himself, rather than let the photographer do it, because he did not wish it to be known at present that anyone was making a photographic copy of Lord St Blaizey's will. Accordingly, having bought the photographer's acquiescence and promised to compensate him if his precious camera suffered any sort of damage, Ben Tancred and Jellicoe set to work.

Jellicoe was a highly expert photographer; and Ben himself was reasonably good. They could have done better with their own apparatus, which had been specially made for photographing documents and other exhibits needed for Dr Tancred's numerous cases; but that was in London, and the will had to be dealt with at once, before it passed out of their possession. Fortunately, the Fowey man's camera was a thoroughly good one, and they were able to make a quite sound job of it after all.

Dr Tancred was thorough. He began by taking very large-scale photographs of each signature—those on the original will and those on the codicil—including, of course, the signatures of the witnesses as well as Lord St Blaizey's. Thereafter Ben Tancred photographed the signatures again; then the entire codicil; and finally the whole will from beginning to end. This was a considerable job, as the prolix legal document ran to quite a number of pages, and each page had to be photographed in two halves—with an overlap of a line or two, in order to show the continuity.

This done at last, Ben Tancred left Jellicoe to get on at once with developing the plates, and himself set out for St Blaizey Castle in order to give the document back into Mr Narroway's hands. For the lawyer had decided, contrary to his usual intention, to remain another night at the Castle for the purpose of further consultation.

As Ben Tancred drove back, he had leisure to turn the situation over afresh in his mind. Although he had been at so much trouble to get the signatures photographed, he was strongly disposed, on the basis of his own examination, to believe that those on the codicil had been written by the same hands as those on the original will. Of course, this might only indicate that an exceptionally clever forger had been at work; but Ben was prepared to assert positively that none of the usual marks of forgery culd be detected by the naked eye. He had a good deal of experience in dealing with forged documents; and he knew well how often the forger gives himself away by hesitation. A signature carefully drawn by copying from an original is never really quite the same as the original from which it is drawn. In many forgeries the inking shows signs of the pauses made by the draughtsman in the course of his work; and even the naked eye, if it be an expert's, can usually detect these pauses, marked as they are by tiny dots and unevennesses in the ink. Ben's eye could detect none in this case. If there were any, he could rely on the camera enlargement to find them out; but he would be surprised if there were.

There remained the possibility that the forger, if there was one, had adopted the not unusual device of copying the signatures upside down—a method which, by assimilating the process more to ordinary freehand drawing, sometimes enables a clever artist to avoid the tell-tale pauses which direct copying is liable to involve. But Ben Tancred knew that this method was apt subtly to change the character of the writing; and he could see no signs of it in the case before him.

That, of course, did not dispose of the matter; for there were other ways of forging a signature than drawing directly or upside down from the original. Tracing was one way. A tracing was made from the original signature, and then transferred by faint indentation to the paper on which the forged signature was to be made. The signature was then inked in more rapidly than was possible in a drawn copy taken straight from the original. The pitfalls of this method were two. The indentation of the paper was apt to be discoverable afterwards; and the distribution of the ink, that is, the relative thickness of the lines at different points, was apt to differ markedly from that of the original. Ben had sought vainly on the codicil itself for any signs of the presence of a tracing, or any indentation of the paper. There were none; but as it was a long time since the date of the codicil, such marks might in any case have disappeared. It was, moreover, possible for the forger to remove them by artificial means.

Another method often employed by forgers was the writing of the forged signature first in pencil, the inking being done later. In this case, traces of the pencil marks, or of their having been erased, were very often left. Sometimes a pencilling escaped erasure; sometimes a tiny flick of india-rubber remained attached to the inked signature. Ben had found no signs of either of these in the present case.

Finally, the really expert forger could attempt the very difficult feat of writing the signature straight out, without a pause. This involved extraordinarily careful preliminary study of the character of the original, and resulted not in an exact copy, but in an independent work of art in the manner of the writer whose signature was being imitated. When it was really well done, it was by far the hardest type of forgery to detect; indeed, in some cases it could not be detected at all. On the other hand, it was beyond the capacity of anyone who was not a real artist at the job. Ben felt nearly certain that, if the signatures on the codicil were forgeries, this was the method that had been employed. In that event, even if he were able to point to discrepancies which indicated forgery, the prospects were none too good; for if they had been really well executed, the handwriting experts would be almost certain to disagree when the case came into the courts.

The alternative, of course, was to accept the signatures as genuine. That seemed to involve conceding that Lord St Blaizey had actually disinherited his son in Rupert Pendexter's favour—in fact, that, as far as the will was concerned, there was no case to fight. Of course, genuine wills could sometimes be fought successfully on the ground of undue influence; but nobody could really dispute, from all Ben Tancred had heard, that old Lord St Blaizey, however much his physical powers had waned, had been fully in possession of his mental faculties right up the time of his death. There was not the faintest chance, Ben was sure, of sustaining an allegation of undue influence. If the will was genuine, Rupert Pendexter would get the money, unless—

Unless he had murdered the testator. For, if he had, the law would very properly refuse to allow him, or the beneficiaries under his will after him, to profit by the consequences of his crime. No, if Lord St Blaizey had really signed that codicil, Roderick Damian's sole chance of inheriting his father's property, and not merely his title and the entailed estate, lay in proving that Rupert Pendexter was the murderer.

Ben Tancred arrived back at the Castle, and was shown at once into the room where Lord St Blaizey and Mr Narroway were still closeted together. He handed back the will, saying that he could offer no further opinion about the signatures until the photographic enlargements had been developed and microscopically examined.

Lord St Blaizey thereupon told him of Captain Galloway's visit and of his demand for the immediate surrender of the will. Ben, of course, agreed with Mr Narroway that there was no alternative to handing it over at once. He was the more glad that he had so promptly seized his opportunity, and taken the precaution of photographing the entire will, and not merely the signatures and the codicil. Whatever they decided to do, they would now have a complete document, in most respects fully as good as the original, to work from, without having to start proceedings in order to get hold of it.

Ben asked whether Captain Galloway was still in the Castle. Lord St Blaizey rang the bell and inquired. Yes, Captain Galloway was still there. The man believed he was upstairs in her ladyship's room.

'Then let me hand the will over to him myself,' said Ben. He thought the opportunity of breaking in upon Helen's *tête-à-tête* with the bearish captain was too good to be missed. Naturally, he did not explain to Lord St Blaizey that his main object was to get a look at Lady St Blaizey in Captain Galloway's company, in order to measure up their relationship. He was not yet at all sure how Lord St Blaizey's relations with his wife stood, or how they had been affected by the day's events.

Lord St Blaizey, however, made no objection to his acting as messenger; and Ben was guided by the servant up the great staircase to the door of Lady St Blaizey's sitting-room. He would have liked to break in unannounced; but he thought he had better let the servant knock and announce him. He did, however, walk straight into the room as the man pronounced his name, brushing past him without waiting for any invitation to enter.

Helen and Galloway were both standing up, facing each other. They looked as if they had been interrupted in the middle of an argument—even perhaps a quarrel. Galloway's manner was a mixture of embarrassment and defiance. He looked exceedingly uncomfortable and very red in the face. Helen, on the other hand, looked angry—very angry indeed. Her face too, was flushed; and there was about her a sense of strain that made her features seem sharper and her whole face thinner than it ordinarily appeared. Ben Tancred told himself that she had grown old in a day; she looked suddenly middle-aged and—yes—waspish.

Lady St Blaizey faced him, tapping the floor with her foot. 'Well,' she said ungraciously. 'What do you want now, Dr Tancred?'

'I am sorry if I am bothering you,' said Ben; 'I only came to hand Lord St Blaizey's will over to Captain Galloway. I understand he has been asking for it.'

'Who let you have it?' said Helen sharply.

'Your husband asked me to have a look at it. I have done with it now.'

'Narroway had absolutely no right to let it out of his possession, except to the executors,' said Galloway angrily. 'I have protested, and he shall hear more of it.'

'That, luckily, is no affair of mine,' said Ben. 'If you want the will, here it is.' He held it out to Galloway, who snatched the envelope from him, and pocketed it at once without opening it. It stuck out above the lapel of his coat.

'If Captain Galloway has got what he wants,' said Helen, 'there is no reason why we should waste any more of his time. He will be anxious to reassure his co-executor.' Her manner was bitter and angry. It made Galloway writhe, Ben could see.

'It really isn't my fault, Helen,' he said. 'You've no call to be taking it out of me. Of course, it's dashed rough luck on you. I can see that. But it's none of my doing . . .'

'Rough luck!' said Helen, with what was presumably meant to be a laugh. 'Thank you, Captain Galloway, I do not really require your sympathy.'

'Dash it all!' said the captain. 'Haven't I said I'm sorry for you?'

'That is quite enough,' said Helen, stamping. 'Will you kindly go away?'

Captain Galloway got himself out of the room like a whipped cur.

'Well, Dr Tancred,' said Helen, when he had gone. 'So you have been looking at the will. What were you looking for?'

'I think you can guess that, Lady St Blaizey. Your husband is not disposed to accept the codicil quite as its face value.'

'He thinks it is a forgery, of course. What do you think about it, Dr Tancred?'

'I am not yet in a position to form any final judgment.'

'But you think something. I want to hear what you think.'

'I think that, at first sight, it looks genuine. I can say no more than that. What view do you take of it yourself, by the way?'

'I have not seen the will.'

'Lord St Blaizey refuses to believe that his father can have disinherited him.'

'That is hardly surprising, is it?'

'You considered them to be on good terms?'

'I am not prepared to be cross-examined about my husband's private affairs, Dr Tancred.'

'Yet you are very much an interested party, Lady St Blaizey, and your husband has asked me to investigate the matter on his behalf.'

'The matter of the will?' Helen seemed as if she would have said more, but thought better of it.

'Yes, the codicil. It may, of course, prove to be connected with . . . the murder. Do you still hold to your opinion that your father-in-law's death was an accident?'

Helen shuddered. She repressed the shudder almost instantly; but it was there. 'Certainly I do,' she said. 'I fail to see how the genuineness of the will affects it.'

That, when one came to think it over, was true enough, Ben said to me afterwards. There was motive for murder, whether the codicil was forged or Rupert Pendexter a genuine beneficiary under it.

Ben switched off from that point. 'Was it a surprise to you that Captain Galloway was named as co-executor?'

'A great surprise,' said Helen. 'I had always regarded Captain Galloway rather as a servant than as an equal.'

'He is a friend of your brother's, is he not?'

'So it would appear.'

'But not of yours?'

'I have no reason to regard Captain Galloway as a friend.'

'And his brother?' Ben asked.

'I have already told you I am not here to be cross-examined.'

'Then you can give me no further help? I assume that you have Lord St Blaizey's interests at heart—to say nothing of your own.'

'You must assume what you please,' said Helen.

'And, of course, your brother's also,' said Ben maliciously.

'I see no point in continuing this conversation,' said Helen. 'I perceive that you are trying to be offensive.'

'I am a mere humble seeker after the truth, Lady St Blaizey. But I will trouble you with no more questions just now. I quite see the difficulty you are in. We shall doubtless have an opportunity of renewing the subject later.' Ben went to the door, leaving Helen standing in the middle of the room, the picture of angry perplexity—and very near the point of breakdown, Ben was sure. He felt she was ready to scratch his eyes out if he stayed—his, or anyone's on whom she could vent her bewildered rage.

CHAPTER 19

HYPOTHESES

It was clear enough to Ben Tancred where Helen, Lady St Blaizey stood. She felt sure, whether or not she had actual knowledge, that her brother had murdered her father-in-law and stolen her husband's fortune. She believed the will was a forgery, and that Rupert Pendexter had forged it, as well as murdered his benefactor and friend. But she did not know what to do. She loved her brother far better than her husband; and, furiously angry with him as she was—for had he not stolen *her* fortune in stealing her husband's?—

she was not angry enough to help in handing him over to the hangman.

Ben wondered whether she could have handed him over if she had wished. Did she merely suspect, to the point of certainty, that he had killed Lord St Blaizey, or had she in her possession evidence that could serve to convict him of the crime? If she merely suspected, her silence did not matter; for the evidence would have to be sought for elsewhere. But if she knew and had evidence behind her knowledge, could she be made to speak? Or was her knowledge even a guilty knowledge that must necessarily prevent her from speaking out the truth?

Of the forgery of the will, if it was forged, and even of its contents Ben felt certain that Helen had known nothing. It had come to her, as to her husband, as a shattering surprise. But she might know nothing of the will, and yet have some knowledge—even some guilty knowledge—of old Lord St Blaizey's death.

Ben realized suddenly, after leaving Lady St Blaizey's room, how wide a range of possibilities her attitude had opened up. Suggestions that had hardly so much as come into his calculations before were crowding now into his mind. Suppose Helen had been actually a party to Lord St Blaizey's murder, as Chief Inspector Falcon had suggested earlier on. Suppose she and Rupert had even planned the whole dastardly crime together.

Why, then, Helen had helped to plan it in the full expectation that she, and not Rupert, would derive, through her husband, the principal advantage from the murder. If that was so, Rupert had double-crossed his sister, either by forging the codicil, or, if it were genuine, because he knew beforehand, and she did not know, what its provisions were.

But, if Helen had really done such a thing, however cynically Rupert had double-crossed her since, she would be unable to betray him without incriminating herself. If that were the position, her fury was very understandable. She had made herself accessory to a murder which was her own undoing.

But there was another alternative. Lady St Blaizey might

be altogether guiltless of having conspired with Rupert to murder her father-in-law, and yet have been quite prepared to shield him against suspicion as long as the contents of the will remained unknown. That was what Ben Tancred had supposed to be the situation when he met with her in the Castle woods. But, if that had been her attitude then, by now the case was altered. For she had, Ben was sure, not known beforehand about the nature of the will. Would she still be prepared to shield Rupert in the light of this knowledge, on the assumption that she herself was innocent of any participation in the crime?

Ben came to the conclusion that such a situation might well afford a sufficient explanation of Lady St Blaizey's evident anger and perplexity. Either alternative would explain the facts, as far as he had knowledge of them. Either Helen was innocent, but furious at her husband losing the old lord's fortune, and not certain whether to reveal her suspicions of Rupert or not. Or she was guilty, jointly with him, of planning, or at least conniving at the murder—and, on that assumption, still more furious at having been monstrously gulled by her villain of a brother into participation in her own defeat, but in that case quite unable to give Rupert away without bringing retribution upon herself.

At that point, a wholly knew idea flashed suddenly into Ben Tancred's mind. He had been trying, with Jellicoe's aid, to pick up further traces of the fair young man to whom the missing tramp had seen the dark man—presumably Rupert Pendexter—hand over his horse. So far, Jellicoe had failed to find any further trace of him; and Ben, as we have seen, had spent a good deal of thought wondering who he could be—for Sidney Galloway, who could have filled the bill, seemed somehow an unsatisfying suspect. But Ben could see no one else who could have taken the part, unless it were someone who had remained so far quite outside the range of his observation.

But suppose, after all, the fair young man was not a young man in reality, but—Lady St Blaizey herself. Ben, as we saw, had found difficulty at the time in accepting the notion that Rupert Pendexter would have worked with an accomplice in so desperate an adventure as murder. But if the accomplice had been his own sister, who was notably attached to him, that difficulty became at once far less formidable. Rupert and Helen as accomplices seemed quite a possible combination.

The more Ben Tancred thought of that notion, the better he liked it. It involved, no doubt, that Helen should have been dressed enough like a young man to be mistaken for one by the tramp. That seemed to require actual disguise; but would not such disguise have been an obvious precaution? Helen, if she had been the fair young man, would have found no difficulty, alone in the woods, in transforming herself back into a young lady in a couple of minutes.

It seemed a famous idea; and Ben was thoroughly pleased with himself for thinking of it. But . . . did the times fit? That needed going over carefully again. Ben reflected. Gregory Landor said that, on leaving old Lord St Blaizey, he had ridden straight back to the Castle, and had tried to find Roderick Damian in order to tell him that his father had insisted on riding alone. He had not found Roderick, but he had found Helen—after how much delay Ben Tancred was not in a position to know. Helen, on hearing from Landor of her father-in-law's behaviour, had volunteered to ride out in search of the old man, and had apparently started off at once on her horse. According to her own story, she had then found Lord St Blaizey's riderless horse; but again Ben did not know how long she had been about it, or precisely at what hour she had informed the gamekeeper, whom she had summoned to her aid, and sent him to search the woods for signs of her father-in-law. All these times of everybody's movements on the fatal morning would have to be gone into very carefully now. On the face of them, they did not seem to allow of any opportunity for Helen to provide Rupert with a horse before the murder, or to meet him afterwards by the old mine, and receive it back from him after he had made use of it in committing his crime.

Moreover, even if the times could after all be made to fit

it, two serious difficulties remained. Why had they chosen the old mine for their meeting? Surely, if Rupert had arranged to hand over his horse to Helen after the murder, it would have been far more sensible to do this inside the Castle woods, and not to take the risk of riding, even for a short distance, along a fairly frequented public road? That was one snag; and the second seemed, at first sight, even more formidable. If Helen had ridden out on horseback to look for her father-in-law, and had then received a horse from Rupert, she would have been left with two horses on her hands. What had she done with her own horse, while she was restoring Rupert's to its stable?

Ben Tancred saw that this way of putting the problem involved assuming that the horse of which Rupert made use for the murder had come out of the Castle stables. Rupert Pendexter, according to this theory of the murder, had arrived at the point on the road above the old mine by car, and had departed by car after the crime. He had therefore needed to pick up the horse he had ridden, in order to commit the murder, as well as to get rid of it afterwards. The natural thing, if Helen had been his accomplice, would have been for her to meet him somewhere in the woods, and hand over the horse, and then to wait, still under shelter of the woods, until he brought it back to her. But this had not been done; for the horse seemed undoubtedly to have been handed back at the old mine. This seemed to make it still more difficult to work out any imaginative reconstruction of the murder which would involve Lady St Blaizey's participation. She would have had to walk from wherever she first handed over the horse to the old mine, and then, having received it back from the murderer, she would have had to ride back to the Castle.

When could Helen possibly have done all that? It must have been either before or after Gregory Landor had told her of the old lord's escapade. But it seemed inconceivable that it could have been before, unless Gregory Landor had spent a quite unconscionable time looking for Roderick Damian before he passed on the news to Helen. If, however, the whole thing had happened after Landor had given his warning, that too, was difficult enough; for it meant that old Lord St Blaizey must have ridden long enough in the woods, without being assaulted, to give Landor time to get back to the Castle and deliver his tidings, and then to give Helen long enough to ride after him, and lend Rupert the horse—and even after that time had to be allowed for Rupert to commit the murder and hand the horse back to his sister at the old mine, and then for her to change her clothes and ride back to the Castle woods, there to discover a gamekeeper, with whom she could arrange for the search for the body, and then herself to ride back to the Castle.

It was all very confusing. Moreover, if, as appeared, there had been at least one gamekeeper about in that part of the woods, it seemed an extraordinarily risky proceeding for a murderer whose cunning Ben Tancred had reason to respect. At least one gamekeeper! That started Ben on a fresh track of thought. Alfred Amos was not a gamekeeper, but a stableman, and he had declared that he had not left the stables all the morning of the murder. But had Amos seen something; and, if so, had he disappeared because what he had seen would suffice to betray the criminals if it became known? In view of Ben's conjectures about the horse, one could imagine a stableman being a most important witness. But if Amos had seen something that would give the murderer away, it seemed logically to follow that he had been bribed, and spirited away, by either Rupert or Helen, or perhaps by both. Ben remembered that Superintendent Wilson had reported from London that Amos, when the police had got on his track only to lose it again, had appeared to be in possession of plenty of money.

All this thinking was highly inconclusive, as it was bound to be, in the absence of further data. It was indispensable, Ben saw, to test his several hypotheses by establishing, as accurately as he possibly could, the times of the events that were actually known. He jotted down, as a basis for further investigation, the times he wanted. Unless Falcon could give him the precise facts he needed, he would have to get together, by the most careful questioning of every person concerned, a detailed schedule of the exact time-sequence of the known events. It was highly unfortunate, from this point of view, that the tramp was not at present available for further questioning—or Alfred Amos either. But at any rate, the best thing to begin upon was a list of the times he wanted to know.

This is what Ben wrote in his notebook that evening. I have copied it just as he wrote it there, leaving out the answers which his inquiries enabled him to fill in at a later stage.

Assumed Sequence of Events on the Morning of the Murder

Time

... Lord St B. and Landor leave Castle together.
... Landor leaves Lord St B. and returns towards Castle. (Where precisely?)
... Landor arrives back at Castle.
... Landor informs Helen, after failing to find Roderick Damian.
... Helen leaves Castle.
... Sarah Pendexter sees Rupert ride out of the Castle woods.
... Tramp ('Smith') sees Rupert hand over horse to 'fair young man'.
... Helen informs gamekeeper of finding Lord St B.'s riderless horse.
... Helen arrives back at Castle.

'There,' said Ben to himself. 'I don't know a single one of those times with any sort of accuracy. Sarah seems to have seen Rupert on the road rather later than half-past eleven; but even that is only approximate. The rest of the times are just unknown, except in the most inaccurate way. Very well, I shall have to see what I can do to fill them in. But I'm blest if I see how any possible arrangement of them can allow time for the fair Helen—not so fair just now, by the way—to have played those tricks I've been imputing to her. Am I letting my imagination run away with me? Perhaps I am. Anyway, we shall see. Or perhaps we shan't.

Really, this case gets more and more of a teaser as you get deeper into it.'

CHAPTER 20

IS IT GENUINE?

By this time Ben Tancred was feeling that he already had a good day's work behind him. After his talk with Helen, he had wandered out into the Castle garden to think; and there he had made his tabulation of the sequence of events on the morning of the murder. That done, he went back into the Castle and told Lord St Blaizey that he had delivered the will to Captain Galloway, and was now going back to Fowey to see how his assistant had got on with developing the photographs they had taken.

The attempt to answer his questions about the timing of the events would have to wait till tomorrow. So would a further talk which he wanted with Chief Inspector Falcon; for he knew that the Chief Inspector had gone off on some trail of his own, and would not be back yet awhile at The Damian Arms, even if Ben had felt disposed to go in search of him. As it was, he would just get back to Fowey in time for dinner, and could then spend the evening over the photographs, if Jellicoe had got them ready for him.

So Ben Tancred drove straight back to his hotel at Fowey, and found my telegram waiting for him, with the announcement that I proposed to come down to join him on the following day. How Ben received this I cannot say; for I have no means of knowing. But I suspect that he stuffed it into his pocket without much more than a glance, being at that moment more intent on finding Jellicoe, and discovering what progress he had made with the development of the negatives. For, if Ben has a fault, it is that when he is at work on a case, he is apt to have neither mind nor memory for anything besides.

Jellicoe had not yet come in, and Ben, having put the car in the hotel garage, went in search of him on foot. He found his assistant still toiling away at the photographer's shop, but nearly ready. Another quarter of an hour, Jellicoe said, would see him through. Ben lent a hand, and in less than that time they were on their way back to the hotel with the precious photographs. Jellicoe said that he thought they had all come out quite well.

Ben Tancred decided to postpone any examination of the photographs until he had dined. Feeling hot and dusty, he wanted a bath and a change; and both he and Jellicoe dined, for once, in dinner jackets. They were amused to observe Sidney Galloway, at another table, being entertained by a much-bedizened lady whose manners attuned ill with her years. Sidney was doing his best for her; and it looked as if he had got her well in tow. Ben Tancred did not claim acquaintance; nor did Sidney Galloway make any attempt to speak with him. He and his lady friend left before Ben and Jellicoe had finished dining—presumably for a dance, for Sidney Galloway was all resplendent in tails and white waistcoat. 'What a life!' Ben commented as they went by.

Dinner over, Ben and Jellicoe retired to a private sitting-room which Ben had ordered before the meal, and Jellicoe got out the photographs. Ben had no microscope with him; but he had an excellent pocket-lens, which he thought would be good enough for his immediate purpose. First, the photographs of the signatures were arranged on the table. There were eight of these—two showing the three signatures together, one from the original will and one from the codicil, and six showing each an individual signature greatly enlarged.

Ben began with the two signatures which purported to be Lord St Blaizey's, and studied them both carefully with the aid of his lens. There was, he was speedily sure, not the slightest sign of any of the slips that would have given plain indication of forgery. There were no pauses, where the flowing line had been interrupted and then resumed, no signs of any adherent scrap of rubber, none of any pencilled lines imperfectly removed, or of any indentation such as a photographer's copy might have revealed, even if it had been invisible to the naked eye. If Lord St Blaizey's signature appended to the codicil was a forgery, it was one of a highly superior sort, that would not be at all easy to detect, and one against which the experts would certainly not give a united or confident opinion.

Next, Ben Tancred carefully compared the two signatures. It was at once apparent that neither was an exact copy of the other. Even apart from the fact that they differed appreciably in size, there were numerous differences in the writing. The signature to the codicil was noticeably larger in proportion to the height of the letters than that of the original will. It was also somewhat less firm and bold, and the letters not quite so clearly formed; but the variation in this respect was not enough to be observable without close scrutiny. The character of the lettering was the same in both, including the distribution of the ink as between thick and thin parts of the lines; and the pen appeared to have been lifted from the paper at the same points. Under both signatures there was much the same final flourish.

Ben Tancred spent some time measuring and comparing, with the aid of callipers as well as his lens; but he was really but confirming a view at which he had already arrived. Either the signature was genuine, or it was about the cleverest forgery he had ever set eyes on. It looked to him, and seemed under every test that he was able to apply, to have been written by the same hand as the signature upon the will itself; and the authenticity of that earlier writing there was, of course, no reason to doubt. In fact, the signature on the codicil had to be treated, at any rate provisionally, as being genuine.

Ben turned to the signatures of the witnesses and, after much careful scrutiny and measurement, reached an identical result. There were, as I have mentioned earlier, noticeable differences between the two signatures of the old butler, Henry Lamb; but these were sufficiently explained by his advancing years, and there was nothing in their character to throw doubt on the genuineness of the later writing.

The signature of the dead man's valet, Robert Cuff, was exceptionally neat and precise, and practically identical in the two cases. There was absolutely nothing about any of the signatures to suggest a doubt of their having been written in both cases by the same persons.

Ben Tancred turned from them to the photographs of the full document. The writing of the codicil was, as we have seen earlier, different from that of the original will, though of the same general type. Ben felt no doubt, after studying them, that they had been written by different persons, though at certain points he detected certain similarities. There was, of course, nothing at all surprising in the two documents being in different handwritings, as they had been drawn up at different times and by different firms of lawyers —the firm responsible for the actual drawing of the codicil being still unknown.

Having extracted all the information he saw his way to getting from the study of the photographs, Ben proceeded to consider what action he should take next in the matter of the will. One thing he must certainly do was to get a second opinion, from an outstanding expert, about the authenticity of the signatures, though he was fairly well convinced that it would do no more than confirm his own. But, if the signatures were genuine, what more was there to do? Surely their genuineness carried with it full proof that the will was valid and beyond dispute. But could it be valid? Well, it *could*; but Ben was not going to accept so unpalatable a conclusion without contesting every inch of the ground.

Ben meant to leave no way untried. First, he would compare the two signatures of Lord St Blaizey with other specimens of his writing. That was easy, but most unlikely to be productive of any useful result. Secondly, he would take up the question of the witnesses. The witnessing of a will or codicil is a business involving formality; so that there would be a reasonable chance of the signatories remembering the occasion. Very well, Henry Lamb and Robert Cuff must be seen and interviewed, on the chance of their recollection of the signing of the codicil bringing some important fact to light. Presumably, in view of the aged butler's signature being on the codicil, it had been made at Longridge, old Lord St Blaizey's big house in Hertfordshire. That suggested that it would have been drawn either by a London, or by a local, firm of solicitors. Perhaps Lamb or Cuff would be able to say who had drawn it up. Or Lord St Blaizey's private secretary—that is, whoever had held that post at the time when the codicil was added. Ben made a note to inquire who had been secretary at that time, and to arrange for seeing him too, if he could be found.

All this, however, did not really promise to advance matters a great deal; for, if the signatures were authentic, whither could all these secondary investigations lead? Ben did not know; but he felt in his bones that there was something wrong about that codicil, and his only hope of bringing it to light was to grope blindly for scraps of information, in the hope of hitting on something that would put him on the right track.

For the time being, there was more to be done about the murder than about the will; for Ben badly wanted to get his questions about the exact timing of the events straightened out as far as he could. That would keep him in Cornwall; but the question of the will wanted taking up in London and at Longridge Park.

Very well; Jellicoe should try his luck at that end. Jellicoe should go up by train in the morning, pass over one copy of the photographs to Ralph Ollerton, who was the best man Ben knew of as an expert in handwriting, and then go down to Longridge Park, and get what he could out of the old butler and the valet who had witnessed the will. Curious, by the way, that Lord St Blaizey seemed not to have brought his valet with him to Cornwall. Jellicoe should find out why that was, if he could. Then, if he could discover what lawyer had been responsible for drawing up the codicil, he should see him, and find out anything that could be found. Finally, there was the question of the secretary. Ben would ask Lord St Blaizey and Landor about that in the morning, and wire to the office if he got the information. Jellicoe, of course, would keep in touch with Miss Jellicoe at the office; and she would pass it on. Jellicoe would also ask about the former secretary when he got to Longridge Park, and if possible get into touch with him. He was to ring up Ben at Fowey at ten o'clock on the following evening, whether or not he had by that time anything of substance to report.

That fixed the programme, at any rate, for the next day. Ben would be at St Blaizey, following up the timing of the murder. Jellicoe would be on his way to London, engaged principally on the question of the will. Further, Ben would have to have another talk with Chief Inspector Falcon, in order to see how far they could fix up a common plan of action. And perhaps by tomorrow Miss Jellicoe would be in a position to forward, at any rate, a preliminary report from London about Rupert Pendexter's financial affairs.

CHAPTER 21

'SHE COULD HAVE DONE IT'

On the following morning, Dr Tancred rose betimes, and saw Jellicoe off to London by the first available train. He then called at the police station, to ask whether Chief Inspector Falcon was expected there during the morning. He was told that the Chief Inspector was actually due in less than half an hour, as the Chief Constable, Colonel Gates-Cocker, had expressed a desire to hear how the case was getting on. Superintendent Usher, of the County Police, would also be present at the interview. Yes, the Chief Constable was expected at any moment; and the Superintendent was already at work in his room.

Ben Tancred thought this opportunity of presenting his letter from Superintendent Wilson to the Chief Constable too good to be missed. It would save him a journey to Bodmin; and in addition he would be able to get his talk with Falcon, if he waited. Perhaps he could motor Falcon back to St Blaizey when the Chief Constable had done with him. So he asked to see Superintendent Usher, whom he had met for a few minutes on a previous visit to the police station, and was at once shown up to his room.

Usher, a big man with a heavy face, looking as if he possessed force without much character, now rose to greet him; and Ben explained his desire to meet Colonel Gates-Cocker in order to present Superintendent Wilson's letter. A moment later, the Chief Constable himself bustled in—a small, agile man with the look of a cavalry officer all over him, silver-haired with a fine silver moustache, very well groomed and dressed in clothes cut much too dandiacally for Ben Tancred's shaggier taste. Usher presented him, and he passed over Superintendent Wilson's letter.

'I know you well by repute, of course, Dr Tancred,' said the Chief Constable, adding that he was delighted to meet him. He read the letter. 'Well, well, friend Wilson says we're to give you all the help we can. Very good. We'll do what we can. We'll take your help too, as well as give ours, eh, Usher? More Falcon's business than ours, of course; he's in charge of the case. I can't say I'm sorry. It seems to be the deuce of a case, from all I understand of it. How have you been getting on, doctor? Falcon glad of your help, I expect. Well, well. Not often we get any one murdered down here, I'm glad to say—certainly not important people like Lord St Blaizey. Very old family, the Damians. Have to mind our P's and Q's in dealing with them, eh, Usher? Well, doctor, I do hope everything is going on well. The sooner this case is off my mind, the better. How *are* you getting on?'

It had not taken Ben long to reach the conclusion that Colonel Gates-Cocker was fond of the sound of his own voice. He replied, briefly, that they had hardly got beyond suspicions yet, though there were plenty of them and to spare. He was hoping to have a talk with Chief Inspector Falcon when he had finished his report to the Chief Constable.

'You'd much better join us, and we'll talk it all over together,' said the colonel. 'No objection, eh, Usher? The more heads the better, that's my opinion, for what it's worth.

We shall have to ask Falcon whether he agrees, of course; but I'm sure he'll be delighted to have you with us. Queer chap, Falcon. I shouldn't like to carry all that fat about myself. But then I'm not likely to, either. I come of a thin family, I'm pleased to say. I don't know what my tailor would say to me if I began to develop a corporation. Still, it takes all sorts to make a world. Falcon's late.' The Chief Constable shot out the last two words in a quite different tone of voice, took out his watch, and impatiently flicked an imaginary spot of something off his elegant coat.

'I suppose you've met Lord St Blaizey, doctor,' he went on. 'He's really an excellent man, at bottom, if you understand what I mean. Of course, he's queer—cranky, I call it. Not my idea of how an aristocrat ought to behave. You see, I don't hold with Methodism myself, though there's a great deal of it in these parts. It may do no great harm among the lower classes. I express no opinion on that point. I believe in being broadminded. But I do feel a man like Lord St Blaizey ought to support the Establishment. Church and State, that's my motto. Though I don't say I'm much of a churchgoer myself. I find I need my two rounds of golf on a Sunday to keep me fit. Now, Lady St Blaizey's a deuced fine woman. No nonsense about her—ornament to the county and all that. Deuced rough luck on her, having this happen. I hope Falcon's been considerate, and not bothered her with too many questions. Fine rider, Lady St Blaizey. I suppose you've met her, doctor?'

'I've known her for a matter of twenty-five years,' said Ben. 'I knew her when she was Helen Pendexter.'

'Oh, yes. And you know her scamp of a brother too, maybe. I never could abide that feller. We've got something against him on the files here, eh, Usher? Mustn't rake that up, though, must we? Nothing to do with this business, I'm glad to say.'

'I was engaged in the Simon Pendexter case,' said Ben. 'I was young then.'

'Dear me. Were you? Now that's interesting. It was long before my time, of course,' Colonel Gates-Cocker continued. 'I know nothing about it, really. Except what's on the files.

I just happened to come across that, one day, when I was fiddling round. But that's all over and done with. I understand Pendexter wasn't in the neighbourhood when this business happened.'

'I'm not so sure of that,' said Ben.

'You don't say so. I understood from Falcon that he was up in London at the time. D'you mean he was here.'

'I can't say for certain,' said Ben. 'His aunt, Sarah Pendexter, says she saw him on the morning of the murder.'

'God bless my soul! That woman!' said the colonel. 'Why, she's mad as a hatter, my dear chap. She'd say anything. I shouldn't pay any attention to what she says, if I were you. She keeps pestering me—has for years—about some tommy-rot over some Methodist Chapel or other. The woman wants the minister evicted for heresy, or something of the sort, and thinks I can do something about it. I keep telling her it's none of my business; but it's not a bit of use. Sarah Pendexter's a pestilent female, if you ask me. Eh, Usher?'

The Superintendent started. Ben suspected he had been half-asleep, and was not surprised. 'Bit of a handful, sir,' he agreed. 'She told me this story about Rupert Pendexter, but I admit we didn't take much stock of it.'

'Quite right too,' said the colonel. 'In my experience you can't ever rely on what women say—especially women over forty. Most of 'em will tell you a pack of lies as soon as look at you. Well, here you are at last, Falcon. We've been waiting for you for hours.'

Chief Inspector Falcon apologized. He had come in by bus; and it had been late.

'We've got Dr Tancred here, you see,' said the Chief Constable. 'He said he wanted a talk with you, so I asked him to join us. I suppose you agree. Well, Falcon, where do we stand now?'

'You've heard about the will, sir?'

But it appeared that Colonel Gates-Crocker had not heard, so the position had to be explained to him. 'I must say it sounds deuced fishy,' was his comment. 'Rupert Pendexter scoops the board, eh? And Lord St Blaizey suspects forgery. So should I. Devilish nasty thing, being disinherited.'

It was Ben Tancred's turn to pass on to Chief Inspector Falcon the results of his photographing of the will and codicil. He said he could not pronounce a final opinion, but he had been unable to find anything at all that pointed to forgery.

'Wumph!' said the Chief Constable. 'Of course all that sort of stuff's your business, doctor, more than mine. You say it looks as if the thing was OK. Where does that get you?'

'No less motive for murder if it is genuine,' Falcon put in.

'Have you been able to get anything further about Pendexter's movements?' Ben asked. 'And have you located my tramp again yet?'

Falcon turned to the local superintendent. 'Anything come in yet about that tramp, Usher?'

Superintendent Usher shook his head. 'Nothing yet. But there's something from London about Pendexter.' He picked up a paper from his desk. 'The Yard says Pendexter was not at his London office on the day of the murder, but was believed there to have gone to Birmingham on business. They're looking into that now. He was certainly in London on the following day, and is believed to have returned home on the previous night. It ends "Further report will follow."'

'Aha!' said the Chief Constable. 'False alibi, eh? Upon my word, you must get that looked into, Falcon.'

'Yard will deal with it, sir,' said the Chief Inspector. 'It seems to put Pendexter distinctly more on the map as far as it goes.'

'Did he definitely tell you he was in London?' Ben asked.

'Come to that,' said Falcon, scratching his head, 'I don't believe he did. He said he'd gone back to London before Lord St Blaizey's death, and I took him to mean he'd stayed there. Didn't put it point-blank.'

'What about Amos?' Ben asked; and it had to be explained to the Chief Constable who Alfred Amos was, and how he had fled to London. He had not been caught again so far, and there was nothing further about him from the Yard.

'It seems to me, Falcon, you've been letting 'em slip

through your fingers,' said the colonel. 'It never does—that. Keep tabs on 'em. That's my motto.'

Falcon frowned. He did not at all relish this criticism of his methods. 'Dr Tancred should have told me sooner about the man Smith,' he said. 'Then I could have got on to him.'

'Or possibly, if I hadn't told you about him at all,' said Ben, 'he'd still be here. But we'll call that quits. It's vital now to clear up this Birmingham alibi of Pendexter's.'

'If he was in Birmingham on the day of the murder, he's out of it,' said Falcon.

'What've you got against the fellow, Falcon, barring his interest in the will and his being a suspicious sort of chap, anyway?' the Chief Constable inquired.

'Well, sir, Sarah Pendexter . . . ' Falcon began.

'I know all about that,' said the colonel. 'Nothing in it. What besides?'

'Nothing very definite. Dr Tancred says this tramp, Smith or whatever his name is, reports he saw a dark man hand over a horse to a fair man in the old mine just about the time of the murder. Dark man drove off in a car.'

'Anything to identify the chap as Pendexter?' asked Colonel Gates-Cocker.

'Nothing positive. Tramp says he'd recognize him again.'

'Then that's not too helpful. Who's the other chap, the fair one?'

'Don't know yet, sir. Having a man watched. Name of Sidney Galloway.'

'Never heard of him. Have you got anything against him?'

'Nothing much, sir. Friend of Rupert Pendexter, notorious sponger, and on his beam-ends. That's about the lot. Brother of Captain Galloway, who's co-executor with Pendexter under the will.'

'You don't seem to have got too far yet, do you, Falcon?' said the Chief Constable. 'I thought you Scotland Yard fellers always polished a case off in less than no time. But I guess *we* could have got as far as that ourselves, eh, Usher?'

Superintendent Usher looked up. 'I have no doubt, sir, Chief Inspector Falcon is doing his best.'

Between them, they got Falcon thoroughly riled.

'If you don't like the way I'm handling the case, sir, perhaps you would rather handle it yourselves.'

'Cha, cha, Falcon.' The colonel strutted across the room, and patted the Chief Inspector on the back. 'No offence meant. You're doing splendidly of course. Mustn't mind me. You just carry on, and catch the feller, and we'll all stand round and cheer. Get right on with it, my boy. You were saying—'

'Nothing in particular, sir.'

'Cha, cha. Well, suppose Rupert Pendexter didn't do it —I say, suppose he didn't—who do you think did?'

Falcon shrugged his shoulders.

'Open field, eh? But Rupert's your man. Then get after him. And keep me posted. I'll leave you and Dr Tancred to work the whole thing out together. Usher will let you have his room, eh, Usher? I'd like a word with you, Usher.' He bundled the Superintendent out of the room with him.

'These locals,' Falcon began, and for a full two minutes aired his grievance. Ben Tancred waited till he felt better, and then said that what he most wanted to do next was to straighten out the times of the known events on the morning of the death.

'I can give you most of 'em pretty accurately,' said the Chief Inspector. He took out his notebook. 'Let's see, what times d'you want?'

Ben read over the list that he had compiled on the previous day.*

'Can answer most of those, approximately, of course,' said Falcon. 'Call 'em over one at a time'.

Ben read, 'Lord St Blaizey and Gregory Landor leave the Castle on horseback.'

''Bout quarter-past ten, to a few minutes.'

'Landor leaves Lord St Blaizey and returns towards the Castle.'

'About quarter of an hour later.'

'Do you know exactly where they parted?'

'Somewhere near the old Castle.'

*See p. 148.

'I see. They rode out north. Then Lord St Blaizey must have turned south-east, along the ride through the wood, going more or less in the direction of St Blaizey village.'

'Well, the body was found a couple of miles off where Landor left him. You know the spot?'

'Yes. Next question. When did Landor reach the Castle?'

'About ten-forty, he says.'

'Is there any confirmation of that?'

'He put his trunk call through to London about eleven o'clock, or rather before. And Lady St Blaizey says he told her about her father-in-law riding on alone at about ten to eleven. Servants saw Landor in the Castle just about then.'

'That seems to let Landor out. He was back at the Castle probably by ten-forty, certainly by about ten-fifty. Is it proved he stayed there?'

'Yes. He was trunk-calling till a quarter-past eleven, and then at about twenty-five past he put through another call. Says he hung on for an answer till after twelve. Seen leaving the Castle again about twelve-ten.'

'Good enough,' said Ben. 'Exit Mr Landor, *qua* suspect. You've answered my fourth—when Landor told Lady St Blaizey. My fifth is, when did she leave the Castle to look for her father-in-law?'

'She says, about five to eleven. Groom who got the horse for her says he thinks it was a bit sooner. Only a minute or two, though.'

'My next is, when did Sarah Pendexter see Rupert? That's my show. We've fixed it to somewhere between half-past eleven and twenty to twelve. Then comes, when did Smith —the tramp, that is—see Rupert (if it was Rupert), with the fair fellow at the old mine? That's a blank. My man, Jellicoe, didn't get an accurate time. But it must have been only very few minutes after Sarah saw Rupert. My next is, at what time did Lady St Blaizey inform the gamekeeper of the finding of her father-in-law's riderless horse?'

'That's a bit vague,' said Falcon. 'Neither of 'em could pin it down. Before midday, the man said. She said she didn't know.'

'Who was the man, by the way?'

'Man called Hopson. He routed out some more keepers to bring in the body after he had found it.'

'He was at work in the woods near where it was found?'

'Nearer the house, I gather. Lady St Blaizey met him just by the path that goes from the Castle woods to the top of the village.'

Ben started. 'But surely,' he said, 'you're describing the very place where the body was found.'

'No, I'm not. It was found at the other side of the river—and the railway—quite near the Lostwithiel road. I thought you said you knew the place.'

That took Ben quite aback, for more than one reason. He had fully believed, that day when he met Helen in the woods, that he was surveying the actual scene of the crime. There had been the sawn-off bough that would have stretched across the path, the signs of the trampling of many feet, and . . . Helen had most assuredly led him to believe that it was the place where the body had been found. Nor was that all. Ben suddenly realized that he had felt so sure of the place partly because it was undoubtedly the exact spot Sarah had described as having presented itself to her in her 'vision' of the murder. But if it was not the real scene of the tragedy after all, then Sarah's 'vision' could be eliminated once and for all, and—Helen had been deliberately misleading him.

Ben got out his Ordnance Map, and made the Chief Inspector point out the places he had mentioned. Yes, the spot where Helen had met the gamekeeper was just by the place he had hitherto taken for the scene of the murder, whereas the actual place where the body had been found was some way off, and he had not visited it at all. It was up the right-hand fork that he had not taken when he entered the woods from the Lostwithiel road.

'But,' he said to Falcon, 'the ground was all trampled, and there was a bough sawn off at just about the right height.'

'Always sawing off boughs, in woods,' said the Chief Inspector. 'As for trampling, I dare say some boys had been having a game there. Always trespassing round that end of the woods, I'm told. Nice and handy for the village lads.'

Ben Tancred was annoyed with himself—not that it probably made much difference. The actual scene of the crime did not appear to matter. Still, he would assuredly visit the real place, now that he knew where it was.

'My last question,' he said, 'is, when did Lady St Blaizey get back to the Castle?'

'Round about a quarter past twelve.'

'That saves a lot of trouble,' said Ben. 'The question is, what to make of it. Assume Rupert left the woods at eleven-thirty or soon after. He wouldn't have lingered after the murder, if he'd done it. The place being within a minute or so of the road, that would put the murder just before— say about eleven-twenty or eleven twenty-five, with a few minutes' margin either way.'

Falcon agreed.

'But it couldn't have taken Lord St Blaizey the best part of fifty minutes to ride from where he left Landor to where he was found.'

'May have ridden around anywhere,' said Falcon.

'Yes, or had quite a long talk with his murderer before he was killed. Or, of course, we may be wrong about the time of the murder. Now for the next point. I'm wanting to get as clear as I can about Lady St Blaizey's movements. Unfortunately, I don't see how we can time any of them between her leaving the Castle a bit before eleven, and getting back about twelve-fifteen.'

'What are you getting at?' said Falcon.

Ben told him. He was wondering whether Lady St Blaizey could possibly be the 'fair young man' whom Smith had seen. He explained his difficulty in believing that Rupert Pendexter, if he had meant to kill Lord St Blaizey, would have risked having an accomplice—unless indeed that accomplice had been his sister. If it had been she, the idea that suggested itself was that Lady St Blaizey had lent her brother her own horse while he went to meet the old lord, rode along with him, and committed the murder, and must afterwards have met him in the old mine to receive back the horse, while Rupert Pendexter made his escape in the car that he had left parked in readiness nearby. The question was, could she have done it in the time?

'Let's try to reconstruct it,' said Ben. 'Say ten fifty-five, or thereabouts, Lady St Blaizey leaves the Castle, dressed as usual for riding. She rides straight to some point near the Lostwithiel road, and meets Rupert. How long would that take?'

'Quarter of an hour, I should say.'

'Then put it at about eleven-ten, when they meet. Rupert gets the horse, and joins Lord St Blaizey, presumably by appointment. You haven't found anything bearing on that, by the way?'

'Not a thing. Not for want of looking.'

'Then we've got to suppose that Lady St Blaizey dressed herself up to look like a man.'

'Why on earth? Sounds fantastic to me.'

'Because she doesn't want to be seen, as herself, anywhere near the old mine.'

Falcon shrugged his shoulders. 'Bit far-fetched, if you ask me.'

'I'm not saying it's true. I'm only trying it out, as a hypothesis that does at least cover the known facts. Let it go at that, for the moment. Lady St Blaizey then has plenty of time to walk to the old mine, and be ready to get the horse back from Pendexter at about half-past eleven.'

'Why didn't she get it back in the wood without risking crossing the road?'

'That, I agree, is a very serious difficulty. Still, we feel sure that someone met Pendexter in the old mine. Then we have to suppose that Lady St Blaizey rode back into the wood, changed her clothes again, "discovered" the riderless horse, or rather pretended to, and then galloped off and told Hopson. She had plenty of time to do that before noon, and still get back to the Castle by twelve-fifteen.'

'Plenty of time, I admit,' said Falcon. 'But a damn fool game to play all the same. It don't make sense—not to me.'

'It does sound a bit fantastic, by the cold light of reason,' said Ben. 'More fantastic than I supposed, till I tried it out on you. But . . . it is possible. The times make it possible. By the way, what was the medical evidence about the time of death?'

'Usual thing,' Falcon answered. 'Pretty vague. Doctor saw the body about a quarter to one. Dead from one to two hours.'

'There's nothing to be got out of that, then. What are you on to now? Apart from hunting for Smith and Amos, that is?'

'Keeping an eye on the two Galloways,' said Falcon. 'I still fancy Sidney as the fair young man—if your tramp's tale isn't just bunk. Still combing the Castle staff in the hope of getting something more out of them. As I told you, I've hunted the whole place for any sign of a letter making an appointment.'

'In fact,' said Ben, 'we're both a bit stuck. At any rate, till your people can lay hands on Amos.'

A constable came in to say that Falcon was wanted on the telephone. The Chief Inspector had the call switched through to the room where they were. 'The Yard speaking,' he said to Ben.

Then Ben listened to one end of a conversation which was so laconic at the end he could hear that he could only make out that some one had been found. 'I'll come up,' he heard the Chief Inspector say.

'They've got Amos,' said Falcon at last. 'Detaining him in London. They've nothing, of course, actually to arrest him on. I'm going up to town at once.'

'I've half a mind to come up with you,' said Ben. 'But I think I won't. If you get anything, will you 'phone through here at once?'

'Right. I'll 'phone Usher, and tell him to pass it on to you if you look in.'

'Good hunting, then,' said Ben. 'Let's hope things are beginning to move at last.'

CHAPTER 22

RUPERT PENDEXTER'S LETTER

Ben Tancred's programme had been disarranged. In view of what Falcon had told him, there was no need for him to spend the rest of his morning in trying to get evidence about the timing of the events on the morning of the murder. Nor was there anything further to be done about the will till Jellicoe had made his report. The Chief Inspector, moreover, had been very positive that no evidence was to be found at the Castle of anyone having made an appointment in the woods with old Lord St Blaizey; and Ben thought it unlikely that he would find anything of that sort where Falcon had failed.

What should his next step be? He had been tempted to go up to London with the Chief Inspector precisely because he was rather at a loss; but Falcon could interview Amos just as well without him, and would in any case probably bring him back; and if anything came of the interview it might be just as well for Ben to be on the spot at St Blaizey in order to follow it up at once. It looked like being a day of waiting, till either Jellicoe or the Chief Inspector produced some more news.

Well, there was at any rate one thing he could do. He could pay a visit to the actual scene of the murder as pointed out to him by Falcon. It was a queer business, that—Helen having bamboozled him about it, and Sarah's 'vision' having seemed so plausible when after all she had visualized the murder in the wrong place.

Ben got out his car, and drove off to St Blaizey. Leaving the car outside The Damian Arms, he walked up the road towards Lostwithiel till he came again to the gate leading into the woods, with the deserted lodge beside it. Suddenly it occurred to him that if his rather fantastic hypothesis was correct, and Helen had changed her clothes in the woods after leaving the Castle, the empty lodge would have been a very convenient place in which to make the change.

He pushed the gate open, and went up to the front of the cottage. The front door was locked, and looked as if it had not been opened for years, for creepers had grown right across it. He made his way round to the back, and was surprised to find obvious traces of recent occupation. Behind the lodge was a little garden, quite trimly kept. An open verandah ran along the back of the building, and under it were a table and a couple of chairs.

Ben entered the verandah, noting french windows leading into a room beyond. He went up to them, and looked in. The room was furnished, with a big table in the middle, strewn with papers, and all round it were bookshelves. He pushed at the french windows; but they were fastened.

Ben left the verandah, and went to the back door of the cottage. He turned the handle, and the door opened. He went in, entering straight upon a kitchen that looked as if it had been long deserted; for dust lay thickly everywhere. He opened another door, and found himself in the room which he had seen through the french windows.

A minute or two was enough to tell Ben what the room was. It was full of books about anthropology, ethnology and similar subjects; and the papers on the table seemed to be bits of unfinished ethnological work. They were typed, and he saw on a chair a portable typewriter. Evidently, the place was used by the new Lord St Blaizey as a study. Presumably he liked getting away from the Castle, in order to secure absolute solitude for his work. Ben remembered that Roderick Damian had written quite a lot—and quite well—about anthropological subjects. His favourite pursuit had been field investigation of tribal customs, till he met with his disabling accident.

An interesting find, yet hardly helpful. Or was it helpful after all? Helen Damian would have known that her husband would not be at the cottage that morning; for he had gone off early in the opposite direction to see a friend at Luxulian, before attending his Methodist meeting at Lostwithiel later in the day. The lodge would thus have been an excellent place for Helen if she had wanted to make an assignation, or for changing her clothes if she had needed to do so. But, even if his far-flying guess were right, it was most unlikely she would have left any traces of her presence.

Nevertheless, Ben hunted the empty cottage from floor to ceiling in the hope of lighting on something to help him. And in the end he found something, though it was by no means what he had expected to find. Thrust between the pages of a book lying on the big table in Lord St Blaizey's study he found a letter. It was addressed to Roderick Damian, and closed, in the absence of an envelope, by being folded in three, and then tucked in. Ben repressed a scruple, and unfolded it.

Dear Roderick,
I came here in the hope of seeing you, and reaching some agreement. Really, you know, this cannot go on any longer. As you are not here, I shall have to see you up at the Castle, but in case you get this first, let me tell you that, in my view, your conduct is indefensible. I assure you positively you are quite wrong in your suspicions about Helen, as you have been told again and again by everyone whose judgment you ought to value. If I fail to see you today, I will run down again in a few days' time. I want to get back to London this evening.

Yours,
Rupert.

Ben Tancred stared long at that letter, wondering what on earth to make of it. There was no heading, and no date. The obvious thing, of course, was to take it to Lord St Blaizey, and ask him when it had been received and what it meant. But would Lord St Blaizey, though he had employed Ben's services over the will, be really pleased to discover that the detective had been rooting about among his private papers? Ben, with some experience now of his lordship's little ways, felt quite certain that he would go right off the deep end.

Ben made a copy of the letter and put it back where he had found it. He was about to leave the cottage, when he heard footsteps approaching. He looked out of the window, and saw no less a person than Rupert Pendexter coming along the path. Ben thought quickly. There was no possibility of concealment in the room where he was, or of getting out of the cottage without being noticed. He slipped quickly into the kitchen, and retired through it into the dusty front parlour, just as Rupert Pendexter turned the handle of the backdoor.

Ben wondered what to do. Where he was, he could hear, and see, nothing. He waited a minute or two, and then very quietly opened the door leading into the kitchen a little way. The kitchen was empty. Either Rupert had already gone away, or, more probably, he was in the study. With the utmost precaution against noise, Ben Tancred opened the backdoor and slipped out, avoiding the path that would have brought him into full view of Lord St Blaizey's study. He had barely time to get behind some thick bushes, which grew close up to the corner of the cottage, when Rupert Pendexter appeared at the backdoor, and stepped out. At the same moment, Ben Tancred's sharp ears caught the sound of other footsteps—the unmistakable sound of a lame man walking unevenly with the aid of a stick. A second later, Rupert also apparently heard them, for he stood still with the air of listening. Lord St Blaizey, hobbling painfully along with his thick stick in his left hand, came into view round the corner of the cottage, and saw Rupert awaiting him. Ben watched the two men intently, as they stood for a moment facing each other, with some paces between them, without speaking a word. Rupert's back was half-turned to him, and Ben could not see his expression; but he marked the heavy scowl on Lord St Blaizey's face.

At length Rupert Pendexter broke the silence. 'I came here, Roderick, because I felt I must see you alone.'

Lord St Blaizey's scowl deepened. 'You can write to my lawyer,' he said. 'I've finished with you.'

'But really, Roderick, this is too absurd. You must see it

wasn't my fault your father treated you as he did. I'm ... jolly sorry it happened ... like that. Honour bright, you know, I hadn't the very faintest idea he meant to leave his money to me. I never said a single word to him about it, or he to me. You can't blame me for it, Roderick. It's rotten luck on you ...'

From Lord St Blaizey's throat proceeded a menacing growl, 'You forger!' he said, 'I'm wondering whether you aren't a murderer as well.'

Rupert's voice was plaintive. 'For God's sake, Roderick, don't say such things. You must know they aren't true. Your father was the best friend I ever had.'

'And this is how you rewarded him, you smooth-faced hypocrite.'

'I make every allowance for you,' said Rupert. 'You aren't yourself. Or I couldn't put up with your saying such things. But the plain fact is, Roderick, you and I have got to come to terms.'

'I make no terms with scoundrels,' exclaimed Lord St Blaizey.

'Do try to be reasonable,' said Rupert. 'Your father has left me his money. There's no altering that. But I am prepared to settle a good round sum on Helen, so that she can keep the place up properly, and you won't need to be worried about money for the rest of your life.'

'Do you suppose,' said Lord St Blaizey, with deep, slow malevolence, 'I would touch a penny at your hands if I were dying in a ditch of starvation? As for Helen, she has made her bed, and she must lie on it.'

'But, look here, Roderick. I suppose you must think what you choose to think about me, though I swear to you you're absolutely wrong. But I can't have you imagining these absurd things about Helen. There's no truth in them, not a single word.'

'I know how to deal with my own wife,' said Lord St Blaizey.

'That's just what you don't know. I tell you it is absolute nonsense about there being anything between Helen and Abel Galloway—or anyone else. You don't expect her never to speak to a man, do you? I tell you there's nothing in it.'

'I propose to divorce her,' said Lord St Blaizey, with ominous quietness this time. 'She has disgraced me.'

'Rubbish!' said Rupert. 'Absolute rubbish! You ought to know better than to believe a word a man like Amos says.'

'I can use my own eyes, thank you.'

'Let me tell you, Roderick, that if this does come into the divorce court, you'll not merely lose your case. You'll be laughed out of court, and every decent person will cut you.'

Lord St Blaizey said nothing. He turned and spat upon the ground.

'In any case,' Rupert went on, 'I'm not going to let your ridiculous fancies stop me putting a proposition to you. It's a generous offer, and it won't remain open if you are fool enough to start proceedings against Helen. Come, Roderick, if you'll drop all this nonsense, I'll settle a hundred thousand pounds on Helen right away; and I won't object if she wishes to transfer some of it to you. You just think it over. If you turn it down you'll be a pauper. You'll drag your family name in the dirt; and every decent person'll say it serves you right. Come, Roderick, you used to be fond of Helen.'

Lord St Blaizey's face was convulsed. He made sounds of inarticulate fury. He raised his stick, as if to strike Rupert, but, unable to keep his balance without it, fell to the ground. Rupert sprang forward to help him to his feet; but he cried to him to keep off. Painfully he regained his feet, and without another word hobbled to the back door of the cottage, and slammed it shut behind him.

Rupert Pendexter stood for a moment staring after him, with a look of deep perplexity on his face. Then, muttering something to himself, he strode away round the corner of the cottage, and disappeared from Ben Tancred's view.

Ben had again to think quickly. Should he confront Lord St Blaizey and ask for an explanation of this extraordinary interview, and of the letter that appeared to have led up to it? Or should he . . . Ben made up his mind. He made his way round through the bushes to the front of the lodge, avoiding the path past the window, and emerged in time to see in the distance Rupert Pendexter walking away in the direction of the Castle. Ben went after him. At the sound of his footsteps, Rupert turned and faced him, looking him curiously up and down.

'Dr Tancred, I believe?' he said. 'If so, we meet again—after many years. My sister told me you were taking an interest in us again.'

Ben admitted his identity. He stared curiously in his turn at Rupert, who looked astonishingly calm after his stormy interview. 'I'd been hoping for a word with you, Mr Pendexter,' he said.

'Fire away, then,' said Rupert, 'I'm listening.'

'You know what brought me down here?'

'I gather my old fool of an aunt set you on to me because she had got it into her head that I murdered Lord St Blaizey.'

'That is so,' said Ben. 'I gather you deny the accusation.'

'Need I say anything, Dr Tancred? Isn't it for you to find out whether I did or not?'

'That is what I am endeavouring to do. You were at any rate seen near this spot on the morning of the crime.'

'Remarkable; for I happened to be some hundreds of miles away.'

'Where, if I may ask?'

'It is hardly my business to tell you; but if you care to inquire at the offices of the Metal Securities Trust in Birmingham . . .'

'That is being done. We will take it that you deny the murder. Whom do you suspect of it?'

'Shall we say my aunt, Dr Tancred? It seems only fair to return her suspicions in kind.'

'I will bear your accusation in mind,' said Ben gravely. 'But that was not really what I wanted to talk to you about. Since I have been down here I have got the impression that relations between Lord and Lady St Blaizey are . . . a little strained. Can you tell me anything about that?'

'Only that you're wrong,' said Rupert. 'Roderick is a bit of a boor, as to manners; but he and Helen are devoted to each other.'

'As you were explaining to Lord St Blaizey just now.'

Rupert Pendexter flushed red. 'Oh, you were listening to us, were you? I might have guessed. Well, if you know all about it, why ask me?'

'You expressed the view that Lord St Blaizey's suspicions were unfounded.'

'So they are. The whole thing's a ridiculous mare's nest. There's nothing between my sister and Captain Galloway—nothing at all. It's simply that my brother-in-law is insanely jealous.'

'I understand Captain Galloway is a friend of yours. Your co-executor, is he not?'

'Oh, Galloway's all right up to a point. As you know so much, you'd better know the lot. My sister has been bored stiff down here, and she let Galloway trail round a bit after her. He presumed on it, and she sent him away with a flea in his ear. That fool, my brother-in-law, got to know about it, and jumped to quite wrong conclusions.'

'Who told him?'

'What does it matter? It's nothing to do with anything you're investigating. Lord St Blaizey put you on to trying to prove the will was a fake, didn't he? How are you getting on about that?'

'It *looks* all right,' said Ben.

'Because it is all right. You can't get round that. My brother-in-law'll only be wasting money he hasn't got if he tries to dispute it. You must have seen for yourself the signatures were in order.'

'Why do you suppose Lord St Blaizey disinherited his son?'

'You didn't know him, did you? I did, very well. He and Roderick did nothing but quarrel.'

'But you had no idea of what he had done about his will?'

'It was the surprise of my life—not his cutting out his son, but his leaving the money to me.'

'It will doubtless come in handy?'

'Doesn't money, always? But probably you heard me offer to give some of it back.'

'On conditions, yes. Would you mind showing me the

place where the body was found?' Ben made this sudden exhange of subject with a purpose.

'Where it was found? I don't think I know exactly. Somewhere quite near here, wasn't it?'

'You haven't seen the place?'

'No. Why should I?'

'Curiosity. I'm just going there. Care to come?'

'No. I've got better things to do. So our roads part here.' They had just come to the fork in the path, where one way led towards the Castle—the route Ben Tancred had taken on his previous exploration—and the other towards what Ben now knew to be the place where the body had been found. Ben took the fork to the right, while Rupert went on his way in the direction of the Castle.

So Rupert Pendexter, despite his disclaimer, knew perfectly well where Lord St Blaizey's body had lain. Otherwise, how could he have known that their paths diverged?

Ben Tancred had plenty to think about as he went along, looking for the scene of old Lord St Blaizey's murder.

CHAPTER 23

AN EMBARRASSING INTERVIEW

This, Ben said to himself, must be the real scene of the murder. That tree, right on the verge of the path, showed the mark of a sawn-off branch much at the same height as that other one Ben had found. Here too the ground had been trampled, and Ben's experienced eye could follow the traces of an exhaustive search in the surrounding undergrowth. The Chief Inspector, Ben remembered, had found there what he believed to be the weapon which had been used to strike the blow.

Ben surveyed the scene. Well, he had seen it now; and much good seeing it had done him! He stayed about the place for some time, hunting vainly for anything the police might have overlooked. He found nothing. Moreover, this second setting was wholly unlike that which Sarah had described. Undoubtedly, her 'vision' had been of that other sport which he had at first supposed to be where the murder had been done.

Ben Tancred slowly retraced his steps to the fork in the path at which he had parted from Rupert Pendexter. Thence he went, not towards the Castle, but back in the direction of the lodge. He walked round the side, and saw Lord St Blaizey sitting dejectedly on the verandah, poking the ground in front of him savagely with his stick. He did not observe Ben's approach until he was almost beside him. Then Lord St Blaizey looked up and saw his visitor.

'Dr Tancred! What brings you here?'

'I thought I might find you here. I want to speak to you about a somewhat delicate matter, I am afraid. You asked me to take up the question of the will's genuineness.' Ben described the steps he had taken. 'Of course, I can form no final opinion yet; but the codicil looks genuine.'

'It cannot be genuine,' said Lord St Blaizey.

'I am not saying that it is. But I am very doubtful of the possibility of successfully challenging the signatures in court. I am now awaiting a second, very expert, opinion. But that is my present view.'

'Then there's no point in discussing it further till your expert reports.'

'Not that particular matter, I agree. But there are others. There is a bare possibility that the signatures may be genuine, and yet the codicil may be open to challenge.'

'How?'

Ben shrugged his shoulders. 'I am having the witnesses interviewed, and trying to find the lawyer who drafted it.'

'Until you do, I still see nothing to discuss.'

'Lord St Blaizey, may I speak quite frankly to you? I have taken certain liberties of which I fear you may not approve.'

'I'll tell you that when I know what they are.'

'I overheard your conversation with Rupert Pendexter.'

'Then you know what I think of him,' said Lord St Blaizey grimly.

'He made you an offer.'

'And I refused it. I may add that I am not disposed to discuss my private affairs with anyone.'

'Not if they have a bearing on your father's murder?'

'They have no such bearing—if you mean my relations with my wife.'

'Let us hope not. I was referring rather to your relations with her brother. Lord St Blaizey, I found this retreat of yours this morning entirely by accident. I ventured to explore it. On the table I found a letter. I took the liberty of reading it.'

'I should most certainly resent your meddling with my letters, Dr Tancred. But I fail to understand what you mean. I keep no letters here.'

'There was a letter addressed to you by Rupert Pendexter here this morning. It was sticking out of a copy of Tylor's *Primitive Anthropology*, on your table.'

'I know of no such letter.'

'Nevertheless, it was there. I put it back as I found it: so I presume it is there still. May I look?' Ben stepped in through the french windows, which were now open. He picked up the book; but the letter was gone. 'Upon my word,' he said, 'it's vanished.'

'I have received no such letter,' said Lord St Blaizey. 'You must have made a mistake, Dr Tancred.'

'I assure you I didn't. Pendexter must have taken it away. He was in your room this morning before you arrived.'

'I shall lock it up in future. My papers are private.'

'I regret if I have offended you, Lord St Blaizey. A detective cannot afford always to observe the conventions. This letter seemed to me important: so I took a copy of it.' Ben handed Lord St Blaizey his copy of Rupert's letter.

Lord St Blaizey took the paper with an air of distaste, and read it through. 'I never saw the thing till now,' he said.

'Yet it was there in the book. When were you in your room here last, before today?'

'Not since my father ... was murdered. The evening before, in fact.'

'Could the letter have been here then?'

'Impossible. I was reading Tylor that night.'

'Then we know it was put here after that.'

'Was there no date on it?' Lord St Blaizey asked.

'No. We must see if we can date it at all on internal evidence. It seems to refer plainly to ... certain matters affecting Lady St Blaizey.'

'I prefer not to discuss that.'

'Solely in relation to the date,' said Ben. 'I am afraid I must ask you when this trouble over Captain Galloway came to a head. I mean, could Pendexter have written to you in those precise terms before the murder?'

Lord St Blaizey hesitated before answering. 'This is extremely distasteful to me,' he said. 'The answer is, Yes, he could. But he did not. He had left the Castle for London before ... I discovered my wife's relations with Captain Galloway.'

'But you did discover them before your father's death?'

'The day before. Is all this really necessary, Dr Tancred?'

'I am sorry; but it is necessary. Then either this letter was written after your father's death, or Pendexter was about here at the time of the death, when he was supposed to be in Birmingham, or London.'

'I see your point. But the letter could have been written at any time subsequently.'

'Quite. But Pendexter was undoubtedly away from St Blaizey till he came down for the reading of the will yesterday morning. Do you know when he arrived?'

'Yes, he travelled by the night train, and got to the Castle after breakfast. He certainly didn't come down here before the will was read. Besides, he could have talked to me then, if he wanted to. No need to write a letter.'

'Then it comes to this. The letter was written either between now and yesterday after the will had been read, or Pendexter was in the neighbourhood unknown between the night before your father's murder and his open return yesterday morning. It hardly seems likely he wrote it yesterday, or why should he come down this morning to remove it? No, what looks most likely is that it was written actually on the day of the murder; and, if so, it's a most valuable clue. If the date can be established, it proves his presence.'

But, though Ben Tancred tried hard to get more positive internal evidence out of the letter, as to the time at which it had been written, he could get nothing more decisive than that. It was no easy matter to get Lord St Blaizey to put up with this inquisition, which he plainly continued to resent. That made it all the harder even to hint at the other matter which he felt, nevertheless, it was impossible to leave unsaid. Ben decided to take the bull by the horns. Tact, he felt, would not help in dealing with Lord St Blaizey.

'You remember what Falcon and I told you about the fair young man whom the tramp saw in the old mine?' Ben said.

'Yes, what of it? Have you found out who he was?'

'Lord St Blaizey, has it occurred to you as possible that the "fair young man" might have been . . . your wife?'

Lord St Blaizey rose from his seat, and sank back into it again, gasping. For a moment, he was taken too much aback to say a word.

'Good God, no!' he said at last. 'Whatever are you suggesting?'

'Nothing definite, my lord. I merely wanted to know whether such an idea had crossed your mind.'

'Such an idea is unthinkable.'

'Yet the starting of divorce proceedings just now might lead people to connect your wife's name with the murder. Forgive me for speaking plainly. But there the fact is.'

'It is monstrous,' said Lord St Blaizey.

'People will say it,' said Ben Tancred.

'But you are not suspecting such a terrible thing?'

'That is not the point. If you start proceedings for divorce, I am telling you what will be said.'

'But there is no connection.'

'Captain Galloway is co-executor under the will. The connection will be inferred.'

'But this is abominable,' said Lord St Blaizey. 'Do you think I have not suffered enough? Heaven knows I have pleaded with her. God forgive me, I have tried to put my conscience to sleep.'

'It would surprise me greatly if you were right about her relations with Captain Galloway.'

'She has been seen with him—in the woods.'

'On whose evidence?'

'One of the men on the estate came and told me. He saw them. I was . . . deeply shocked.'

'I should think twice before trusting Alfred Amos's word.'

'You mean . . . I would give my right hand not to believe it.'

'They have found Amos—in London. Chief Inspector Falcon has gone up to town to interrogate him.'

'About my private affairs? He has no right.'

'No. About the reason for his flight. He had money. You did not give it him?'

'I gave him nothing.'

'Someone bribed him to run away.'

'I know nothing about it. He came to me of his own accord. He said he regarded it as his duty.'

'And expected to be well rewarded for it, I make no doubt,' said Ben. 'From all I hear of Amos, I should place no reliance on what he said.'

'Would to God I did not.'

'Then do nothing for the present. Take no step about Captain Galloway until this graver matter is cleared up.'

'Good God, Dr Tancred! Are you saying that you suspect my wife of murder?'

'Say rather of knowing more about it than she has yet been persuaded to tell,' said Ben.

Lord St Blaizey buried his head in his hands. 'But I entirely refuse to believe her capable of such a thing. God help me!'

'Let us hope you are as right in that as I think you are wrong where you do suspect her.'

'Dr Tancred, you have said things to me that I could never have believed I should allow any man to say. Let me say something to you. If I thought my wife had any part in conniving at this abomination—which I am sure she had not—I should kill myself. I could not bear it. But she did not . . . You have no evidence. You can have none. Nothing at all. It is . . . impossible.' His voice trailed away. He sat, staring into space, with all the anger gone out of him.

Ben Tancred was not enjoying himself at all. He had not meant the interview to reach so awkward a situation. 'Of course,' he said, 'there is no suggestion that Lady St Blaizey actually killed your father.'

Lord St Blaizey's voice rose to a shout, cracked, and sank almost to a whisper. 'I should hope not,' he cried. 'Not that. For God's sake, leave me alone.'

Ben took him at his word. He crept away, as he told me afterwards, feeling like a dog with its tail between its legs. He had no heart for further investigation just then. He went back to St Blaizey, collected his car, and drove out into the country for a quiet think.

CHAPTER 24

MR SMITH EXPLAINS

There was no more progress made that morning as far as Dr Tancred was concerned. Frankly, he told me afterwards, he was fagged out, nervously exhausted, and he went to sleep in a field and, when he woke and looked at his watch, found that it was after half-past five. He had gone without lunch; but he was not hungry. He sat on where he was, thinking the whole thing over, and trying to make up his mind what he really thought. Somehow, that very embarrassing talk with Lord St Blaizey had made him a good deal less inclined to suspect Helen of complicity in the murder. His identification of her with the fair young man now seemed to him to rest on an extraordinarily flimsy set of suppositions. But, apart from that, there was nothing at all to cause him to suspect Helen. Or was there? At any rate, nothing more than a vague instinct; and Ben was a person who held that his instincts were quite as often wrong as right.

He became conscious of something moving near him. Where he sat, the shadow of a haystack screened him from view. But someone was walking near, making a rustle of loose straws as he advanced. A figure came into view round the corner of the haystack—the unmistakable figure of an habitual tramp, with his tattered, ill-assorted garments gleaned from anywhere, and his pervading odour of stale tobacco and unwashed human combined.

Ben was wide awake in an instant. He drew a bow at a venture. 'Mr Smith,' he said, 'if I am not mistaken.'

The tramp, hearing his voice, hovered doubtfully a moment, as if about to run away. Then he thought better of it. 'What if my name is Smith?' he said. 'It's a free world, ain't it?'

'An optimistic view, Mr Smith,' said Ben. 'Very far from it, I should say. But I agree it is a world in which people are sometimes very difficult to find when they are wanted.'

'No one wants me, that I know of,' said the tramp. 'I'm one of the great unwanted, I am. I used to be a clerk, till I got the sack. Then I was one of the unemployed, till they cut me off the dole and started asking too many questions. So now I'm a gentleman of leisure. Who may you be?'

'I think my assistant, by name Jellicoe, had a word with you the other day somewhere close by the old copper mine.'

'Oh, him,' said the tramp. 'Well, I told him what he wanted, didn't I?'

'And he rewarded you with five shillings. Now I can do better than that.' Ben held out a ten-shilling note. 'This to begin with, and possibly more to come, provided you don't get lost again.'

'Anything to oblige,' said Mr Smith. 'D'you mind if I sit down?' He suited the action to the word, and, drawing out a very foul pipe, asked Ben Tancred if he happened to have any tobacco on him.

Ben handed over his pouch of Gold Block; and the tramp filled up his pipe, and, having borrowed a match, lighted up. 'Good stuff, this,' he said. 'Give a chap like me a fine day, and a pipe of baccy, and a five pound note in his pocket, and what more can he ask? That's what we tramps are supposed to be thinking; but I can tell you, in the light of my own experience, he can ask for a good bit more than that.'

'He can be asked one or two questions,' said Ben, 'and answer them—before he gets even a ten-shilling note. For example, you told my friend that you saw a dark man ride up to the old mine-workings on a horse, and hand it over to a fair young man who afterwards rode off on it.'

'Well, what if I did? Wasn't it all gospel truth?'

'That's what I want to know,' said Ben. 'What time of day was it when you saw those people?'

'I'm not much of a one for time,' said the tramp, 'my watch having gone what you might call the way of all flesh. About the time a chap begins to think the pubs'd be opening, if only he had the price of a drink.'

'Is that as near as you can put it?' said Ben. 'Very well, describe the dark man.'

'He was a well-dressed bloke. About forty, I should say. You know, the sort that looks as if he'd never done without a square meal in his life and thought the world was made for him. As a matter of fact, I saw the same man again this morning.'

'Where?' said Ben.

'In those woods, up by the big house,' said the tramp, cocking a finger towards the Castle woods in the distance. 'He was with a female.'

'Describe the lady.'

'Oh, she was fair and hoity-toity, and much the same age as him. Bit of a turned-up nose, and a high voice like as if she owned the universe.'

That sounded very much like Lady St Blaizey.

'And what about the fair young man?' Ben asked. 'I want you to describe him too.'

The tramp chuckled. 'If you'll hand over that ten-shilling note,' he said, 'or mebbe make it a pound, I'll see what I can do.'

Ben flicked the note towards him. 'Fire away,' he said.

'Want the gospel truth, mister?'

'What else?'

'Then I'll let you into a secret. That fair young man was a what-you-may-call-it.'

'A what?'

'A will-o'-the wisp. Creature o' the imagination,' said the tramp. 'I made him up.'

'You made him up! Do you mean to say he wasn't really there at all?'

'That's about the size of it. Your young fellow seemed all keen after some sort of a story: so I threw in the fair young man, free, gratis, and for nothing.'

Ben's exasperation got the better of him. 'You abominable rascal!' he said.

'Here, mister, none of that. A bit of romance often adds a spice to life. Your young fellow was no end pleased when I told him about that fair young man.'

'Did you invent the dark man on the horse too?' asked Ben, bitterly.

'Of course I didn't. He was real—all except the horse. Your man put in that bit. Asked me if I'd seen a dark chap on a horse. Well, I had seen a dark chap, only he was running. But I threw in the horse to oblige.'

'Will you kindly tell me what you really did see?'

'Relying on your well-known generosity,' said Mr Smith, 'I will. This is gospel truth, and no frills to it. I was sitting in one of them sheds by the old mine when I saw this dark fellow, same as I described him, come along, looking in the deuce of a stew. He was running hell-for-leather, as if the devil was after him. He went right past where I was without spotting me, and shinned up the bank on to the road; and then I heard him starting up his car and driving away.'

Ben Tancred produced a photograph of Rupert Pendexter. 'Is this anything like the man you saw?' he asked.

'That's the identical bloke. I'd swear to him in a million.'

'That really is the truth, is it?'

'Honour bright. You're not the man I'd be trying to put off with things that wasn't true, after you treating me—

183

shall we say generous—only then you'd have to make it a quid.'

Ben Tancred ignored this sally. 'There was no one with him at all? No one met him? And he hadn't a horse?'

'Right every time,' said the tramp. 'But he looked as if the devil was after him.'

'And you really saw this man again this morning?'

'Ain't I telling you? Gospel truth, that is, too.'

'Why on earth did you tell my man that other story?'

'Just came out of my head, like,' said Mr Smith. 'Besides, I always like to oblige. I'm one for variety, I am.'

'Well, you've done a great deal of harm,' said Ben. 'Did you know the police had been searching for you for days?'

'Hadn't an idea of it. I did see a bloke that looked as if he was looking for someone down at the old mine. He was a fat bloke, and I didn't fancy his face. So I hopped it.'

'Well, mind you don't hop it again,' said Ben. 'You stay where I can find you the next few days, and there'll be a couple of pounds for you. More, if I have to keep you longer than that.'

'You can count me in, my lord. At a quid a day—even allowing a reduction on taking a quantity—I don't mind how long I stop.'

'Where'll I find you, then?'

'I'm residing in the Old Castle at present. Palatial, but draughty.'

'Will you stay there? That'll suit me.'

The tramp bowed. 'Thine till death do us part,' he said. 'You can count on Billy Smith.'

'Your real name?' Ben asked.

'Why not? Somebody has to be named Smith, don't they?'

Which is, after all, undoubtedly true.

CHAPTER 25

WHO BRIBED ALFRED AMOS?

That really was a facer. So the fair young man was a sheer figment of Mr Smith's too-fertile imagination. All Ben Tancred's fanciful reconstruction of the crime was down-fallen like a house of cards. The entire case against Helen, flimsy as it now appeared always to have been, was blown clean away like morning mist. Ben felt that Chief Inspector Falcon would have the laugh of him when they next met. But, more than that, he felt he had put himself in a most unfortunately false position with Lord St Blaizey.

Still, if the tramp's revised story could be believed, it confirmed Rupert Pendexter's presence on the scene of the crime. For now Billy Smith had positively identified Rupert as the man he had seen. The letter, the tramp's story, Sarah's story—all pointed to Rupert having been present near the scene of the crime. But ... Good Lord, he'd nearly overlooked that—Sarah said she had seen Rupert on horseback; but now the tramp asserted that he had been on foot. That made the confusion worse than ever. 'Riding as swift as the wind.' That was what Sarah had said. Of course, it had to be admitted that Sarah was an unreliable witness; but really ... Ben did not know what to make of it all.

He drove back to Fowey in a condition of bewildered confusion of mind, in which his usually acute brain obstinately refused to work at all. There he found me, Paul Graham, eagerly awaiting him. I had come straight to the hotel from the train, and inquired for Ben, or if any message had been left for me. There was none; and I found that Ben had not even booked me a room. I was hurt; but I tried charitably to suppose that, through some accident, he could not have got my wire.

At last Ben drove up to the hotel, and flung out of his car. As I dashed to meet him I could see that he was upset. 'Hallo, Ben,' I cried, 'here I am.'

Devotion to truth compels me to chronicle Ben's reply. 'Good Lord, Paul,' he said, 'I'd forgotten every word about you.'

'Then you did get my wire?'

'I believe I did.' He began fumbling in his pockets. 'Why, here is the damned thing.'

'And you never booked me a room. Luckily they were able to squeeze me in.'

'Well, now you are here,' said Ben, 'what about dinner? I missed my lunch.'

'Is that what's the matter?' said I.

'That, and the fact that I'm a fool and a goop and a juggins and anything else you like to call me.'

'My dear Ben,' I cried in consternation. 'Whatever has gone wrong? You're generally so pleased with yourself.'

He gave a snort, and made for the door. 'I'll feel better after a bath,' he said. 'Hang on for me.'

I ordered a brown sherry, and waited impatiently till he came back. 'Now you must tell me all about it,' I said. 'I'm dying to hear.'

'Then you'll jolly well have to wait. I'm not going to say a word about the blasted thing till I've dined, if then.'

I followed him, rather chastened in spirit, into the dining-room. I had seldom seen Ben Tancred in so black a mood. We dined none too cheerfully, Ben squelching every effort I made at conversation. Not even a bottle of the hotel's best wine, a Chambertin of 1923, seemed to brighten him up. After dinner he glowered at me over coffee on the terrace, and still refused morosely to tell me anything at all about the case.

At last word came that he was wanted on the telephone —from London. At that, he sprang up with alacrity, and I waited impatiently for his return. He was a good long time away; but when he did come back, his manner had entirely changed. His moroseness had gone: he looked keyed up for action.

'That's a lot better,' he said. 'That was Chief Inspector Falcon, 'phoning from Scotland Yard.'

'You must tell me,' I cried. 'Remember, I haven't heard a single word since you wrote.'

He began to tell me then; but he was barely launched on his story when the boy in buttons summoned him back again to the telephone. Another call from London had just come through.

Ben was even longer away that time. He came back saying, 'That was Jellicoe—about the will. Nothing much yet from that end.'

Then at last Ben sat down to tell me the whole story, pretty much as I have related it in the foregoing chapters, though I have filled in some of the details from information which I got out of him later on, when the case was all over, bar the shouting. He came last of all to what Falcon and Jellicoe had just been telling him over the 'phone.

'This man, Amos,' said Ben, 'has looked almost from the first like being the really crucial witness. Of course, one had to reckon with the possibility that he'd run away simply because of the girl he'd got into trouble; but I never thought that was it really. And it wasn't. I doubt if he's come clean even now, but he's spilt enough to be getting on with.

'First of all he was bribed to run away. We had guessed that; but now he's admitted it.'

'Who bribed him?'

'Helen. Your lady-love that was.'

That was a blow. I said, 'Don't Ben. That's not a thing to be raking up after all these years.'

He laughed. 'All right, Paul. Anyway, she gave him a fat wad of money to be off and not let the police find him.'

'But why?'

'He says, because he saw her being made love to by Galloway, and giving as good as she got, and threatened to go and sneak about her to her husband.'

'But you told me he did tell Lord St Blaizey. Beside, the police couldn't do anything to him about that.'

'Quite; but I don't suppose the fair Helen knew he'd spilt the beans. And I'm convinced it's nothing like the whole story. So's Falcon. I suspect that what she really bribed him for was something altogether different. But at present Amos is sticking to that story, which has the advantage, as you say, that the police can't get him over it. Though he did let drop one other thing.'

'Which was?'

'He did say at one point that he could have told a much nastier tale about my lady if he'd had a mind. Then he seemed sorry he'd said it, and dried up.'

'And the Scotland Yard man couldn't find out what he meant?'

'No, but he's bringing him back here at once. It seems he got dead drunk in a pub down in Limehouse, and had all his money stolen. So he's on his beam ends again, and quite glad to get his fare paid back home.'

'And that cheered you up, Ben?'

'It did. I'm beginning to see light now, I think. Though some bits are in a pretty muddle still. I'm worried about that tramp, Paul.'

'What had Jellicoe to say?'

'Not a great deal about the will. He'd been to Longridge, and found both the servants who signed it. But they said they'd witnessed far too many papers for the old lord to be able to tell them apart. They remembered witnessing the original will, because Lord St Blaizey explained to them what it was; but they couldn't call to mind anything about the codicil. They may never have known what they were witnessing—probably didn't. And Jellicoe couldn't find out anything about the lawyer who drafted it. I let him down a bit there, by the way. I promised to find out who was old Lord St Blaizey's private secretary at the time, and then clean forgot. He found out, though, from the old butler. It was a man named Verdon. Jellicoe's discovered where he lives now, and is going after him tomorrow.'

'A bit disappointing, all that,' I commented.

'One last item,' said Ben. 'They say in the City Pendexter's in a financial jam. Made a muck of his speculations just lately, and is in a pretty bad hole. It's not widely known; but the man I put on to look into it says he's no doubt it's true. The Iridium Syndicate's going west, they say, unless somebody can put up a lot more money pretty soon.'

'More motive,' said I.

'Yes,' said Ben. 'Rupert did the thing, I feel sure of that. But I'm blest if I see yet how to prove it. Besides, was he on horseback, or wasn't he, when he left the woods to make his escape? That's what's bothering me most.'

'It's very confusing,' said I.

'It is. The question is, can one trust that infernal tramp's evidence even now? My hat, I'd like to skin that fellow alive. But Amos will be here tomorrow morning; and I'm looking forward to having a go at him. I've a feeling that his story, if we can get the whole of it, ought to help us a lot.'

On that we retired to bed; and, whatever happened to Ben Tancred, I know I slept the sleep of the just.

CHAPTER 26

RUPERT PENDEXTER'S ALIBI

It was time, Ben felt, for a new stocktaking. That was what he told me when he came into my room very early the next morning, fresh from a swim, to find me still in bed. Ben sat beside me, on the edge of the bed, and began talking, as he said, in the hope of getting things a bit sorted out.

'You know, Paul, this case has too many ramifications. There's the murder, and there's the will; and then there are Lord St Blaizey's matrimonial troubles thrown in just to make it all harder. The whole thing's full of blind alleys, too. There's Sarah, with her preposterous "visions"—which, all the same, one can't bring oneself quite to ignore. There's that tramp, Smith, spinning yarns just to amuse himself, so that you can't be sure when he's telling the truth and when he's simply romancing. There are people like Sidney Galloway who sometimes look as if they were going to fit in somewhere or other, and sometimes as if they were the merest red-herrings across the trail. There's Reuben Amos, with his mysterious informant, who is so positive Lord St Blaizey was never murdered at all. I must have another go at him, Paul. I've been rather neglecting Reuben Amos, I'm afraid. Really, Paul, it's a brute of a case; and I still don't quite know what to make of it.'

'You aren't doubting Lord St Blaizey was murdered?' I asked.

'No, not that, or, really, that Rupert Pendexter murdered him. That's not the difficulty. The problem is to get a clean case one can possibly hope to convict him on.'

'Well, why not try to sum up what you have got against him? That might clear the air.'

'Motive . . . he gets the money. Possible further motive . . . he stands a chance of saving his sister from the divorce court.'

'I don't quite see that,' said I. 'How do you mean?'

'By getting the whip hand of Lord St Blaizey and bribing him not to divorce her.'

'Then you do think she was carrying on with Galloway?'

Ben shrugged his great shoulders. 'Carrying on, of course,' he said. 'Whether to the point that would make a divorce possible, I simply don't know. I should rather doubt it. I shouldn't have thought the Captain was her meat. But anyhow, it leaves a pretty tangle.'

'In what way exactly?'

'We'll come back to that later, if you don't mind. Let's stick to Rupert for the moment. We've dealt with motive. Money . . . and he needs it badly. Possibly something about Helen too.'

'Opportunity next?' I suggested.

'Well, we're a bit weak there. Sarah says she saw him, on a horse. The tramp, Smith, says he saw him, or someone very like him, not on a horse, but on foot, running. The tramp's earlier version put him on a horse, and threw in the fair young man.'

'Now exploded as a myth,' said I.

'Yes, if we accept Smith's second version. But do we? If

we do, what do we make of Sarah? Smith's first story fits in with hers. His second doesn't.

'I see that,' said I; 'but . . .'

'Then there's Rupert's Birmingham alibi. We still don't know what the Yard has done about that. But it's crucial. If friend Rupert really was in Brum, bang goes the whole case against him.'

'Then he can't have been.'

'Let's hope not; but he must have done something he thinks pretty cute to make people believe he was. Then there's the codicil. One feels in one's bones it must be a fake; and yet, I can't see a thing wrong with those infernal signatures.

'I tell you what, Paul,' Ben went on. 'I've sucked the case dry at this end, and got nowhere. The rest's not here; it's in Birmingham, or London. I shall have to go up. But the nuisance is, that means missing Amos. Falcon's bringing him back here, this afternoon. He may be the vital link in the chain after all. But I can't be in two places at once; and I don't like leaving this end quite unguarded. All the same, I'm going to Birmingham today. I can't wait any longer for the police to clear up that point.'

I was deeply disappointed, and the words slipped out of my mouth. 'But I've only just arrived,' I said.

Ben grinned. 'Sorry, my lad,' he said; 'but this isn't a pleasure jaunt. Which is it to be? Are you stopping here, or coming with me to Brum, and then probably London?'

'Could I be any use if I stopped here?' I said.

'Frankly, I doubt if you could,' said Ben. 'There's nothing to do here unless something fresh happens, apart from seeing Amos, and I don't think you could tackle that. And if anything does happen . . .' Ben left his silence unfinished.

'Then I'll come with you, if I may,' said I. 'How are you going?'

'Aeroplane, if I can get one. If not, train, I suppose. The devil of it is that it's Saturday, and the Lord knows if one'll be able to find anyone in Brum at the week-end. This office of Pendexter's is sure to be closed.'

I suggested that Ben might wire to Jellicoe to go to

191

Birmingham from London in order to save time, and go himself to London, where he could tell Jellicoe to meet him and report. But Ben had obviously a hunch that he wanted to study that Birmingham alibi for himself.

He left me then, and I dressed and went down to breakfast. Ben was busy trunk-calling, and I ate my meal alone. At last he came into the now deserted coffee-room.

'I've fixed up a plane from Plymouth,' he said. 'We'll drive over there, and leave the car. We should get to Brum in time for a late lunch, with any luck. And then we must take our chance of finding anyone we want.'

'But you said that the Metal What-ever-it-is office would be all closed up,' said I. Internally, I was in a panic; for I had never travelled by aeroplane in my life. Far sooner would I have stayed on at Fowey, or gone back to London by the homely train, to meet Ben there when he had done in Birmingham what he had to do. But I could not say so; where Ben went I felt I must follow, if he would accept me as his companion.

'I've been on the 'phone to Rupert Pendexter just now,' Ben answered me. 'I told him frankly I was going to Birmingham to look into his alibi, and he said he wished me good hunting. I got out of him the name of the man he says he was with in Birmingham on the afternoon Lord St Blaizey was killed, and the place where he had lunch, and so on. So we have got something to go on. We shall have to rout the man out at his home, I expect. Well, Paul, I'll be ready in ten minutes. Will you?'

I was, at any rate, ready in a quarter of an hour, leaving everything behind me except a small suitcase; for Ben, he said he would certainly be coming back to Fowey. He motored me to Torcross, and we crossed by the ferry and drove on to the Plymouth aerodrome. Feeling sick already, I got into the private aeroplane which Ben had managed to command over the telephone from Fowey.

I do not propose to describe that journey. The day was beautifully fine and calm, and Ben said that, but for me, he would have thoroughly enjoyed it. But I was as sick as a dog; and when at last I crept out of the aeroplane at

Birmingham, I felt as if I didn't care who had killed Lord St Blaizey, or indeed about anything at all except finding a quiet place to die.

Ben, however, after putting through a telephone call from the aerodrome, dragged me off to a restaurant, where I watched him make a hearty lunch. A couple of brandies did something to restore my manhood; and by the time that Ben, back at the telephone, had located the manager of the Metal Securities Trust at his private address, and fixed up an appointment with him, I felt almost human.

We had lunched in the hotel, adjoining the Midland Station, which Rupert Pendexter had named to Ben as the place where he had lunched on the day of the murder. Accordingly, after lunch, Ben spent some time inquiring of the staff, with the aid of his photograph, whether they remembered Rupert. But the hotel was a big place, and pretty busy at lunch-time except at the week-end; so that we failed to get any information at all. Rupert Pendexter might have been there, but nobody was able to remember him. Ben said we might have to try again later on, if we could not get what we wanted in other ways. But he was not hopeful.

We got a taxi; and drove out to Edgbaston to see John Lamont, the manager of the Metal Securities Trust. He proved to be an American, lean, small, and business-like, and not too friendly at having been kept away from his Saturday round of golf. He inquired rather brusquely what he could do for us.

Ben was very frank—I thought, too frank. He said straight out that he was investigating old Lord St Blaizey's murder, and that it had become important to trace Rupert Pendexter's movements on the day of the crime. He had come to ask for Lamont's help, as Rupert said he had been with him that day, and had referred us to him for confirmation.

The manager opened his eyes pretty wide at that. 'Are you suggesting Mr Pendexter had anything to do with killing Lord St Blaizey?' he asked. 'If so, the idea seems to me—well, fantastic. They were the closest friends.'

'I'm not suggesting anything,' said Ben. 'I merely want to know whether he was here, as he says.'

'I've told the police that already,' the American answered.

'Then you won't mind telling me over again.'

'I do mind, because you are wasting my time as well as your own. Still, as you are here—yes, Mr Pendexter had an appointment with me on that afternoon at the office.'

'And he kept it?'

'I'll say he did.'

'At what hour?'

'He named no time when we fixed it up. By my recollection, he came to the office in the mid-afternoon. Say, well before four o'clock. He was with me an hour or so, and then he went back to London.'

'How?'

'By train, I believe.'

'He came to see you on business?'

'Certainly. He made the appointment by telephone.'

'When was the appointment made?'

'The same morning. About noon, I think. At all events, before lunch.'

'Was the business important?'

'He thought it so, I presume, or he would not have come.'

'But you did not? You were surprised at his coming?'

'Well, it did cross my mind we could have settled it just as well over the 'phone.'

'Do you know where he called you up from?'

'London, I think. To the best of my recollection he said he was speaking from London. I do remember it was from a call office, or at least, I think so, from the way the call came through.'

That was the sum total of Lamont's information. Clearly, unless he was lying, and there was no reason at all to suppose he was, Rupert Pendexter had been in Birmingham on the day of the murder.

At least, he had been there in the afternoon by four o'clock at the latest. Was that in any way reconcilable with his having been at St Blaizey the same morning, leaving it, if Smith's information could be relied on, soon after half-past eleven by car? Neither a car nor a train could possibly have enabled him to make the journey in the time. It is true that Ben and I had breakfasted in Fowey, and been in Birmingham for lunch. But we had come by aeroplane. Had Rupert made the journey by the same means? If he was really guilty, there seemed to be no other possible way.

From Edgbaston Ben dragged me back to the hotel, where he spent another half-hour trying to get information to confirm or disprove Rupert's assertion that he had lunched there before seeing Lamont—which, by the way, was clearly inconsistent with his having trunk-called from London round about noon. Again Ben got nothing for his pains. No one remembered Rupert. Thence we went back to the aerodrome; for surely, if Rupert Pendexter had arrived at Birmingham by air, it should be easy to trace his coming, whether he had travelled by a regular air-liner or by a private plane. But the aerodrome had no news for us. No private plane had landed there on the day of the murder, apart from those belonging to local fliers; and there was no air-liner whose time of arrival fitted in. The only liner from Plymouth to Birmingham had left long before Rupert could possibly have reached the Plymouth aerodrome if he had committed the murder.

Before we left for London by train, Ben called up a man —a private detective—who had occasionally done a bit of work for him in Birmingham, and instructed him to make a further attempt to pick up Rupert Pendexter's traces either at the hotel or at the aerodrome. But he had not much hope that anything would come of this. On the way up to London, he wagged his head at me and said that he was damned if he knew how Rupert had managed it, and was even beginning to be doubtful whether he had not all the time been barking up the wrong tree.

As for me, I was tired out, and I fell asleep. Ben woke me with a nudge at Euston, and carried me off to his flat, where he expected to find Jellicoe awaiting him.

CHAPTER 27

BEN TANCRED'S THEORY

Jellicoe was waiting for us at Ben's flat. But the news he had to give us was none too reassuring. Ralph Ollerton, the handwriting expert, had pronounced the signatures to the codicil to be unquestionably genuine. He said that in his opinion it was quite useless to attempt to contest the point, and he felt certain that, for once, any other expert would agree.

Jellicoe had also seen Maurice Verdon, who had been Lord St Blaizey's secretary at the time when the codicil was dated. But Verdon said he had heard nothing of any alteration being made in his employer's will. That, however, he did not regard as surprising; for Lord St Blaizey had not been a man who took his employees readily into his confidence. As for the lawyers who might have been employed to draw up such an instrument, he would have expected Mr Narroway to have done it. Otherwise, he had no idea. He did mention several firms of solicitors whom Lord St Blaizey had employed on work connected with his companies; and Jellicoe had already got in touch with these, only to be told that none of them had drawn up any will or codicil on his behalf.

As to the witnesses to the codicil, Jellicoe, as he had told Ben over the 'phone, had seen them both, and got nothing out of them, except that they did remember witnessing the will, but had no recollection of the codicil, though they might easily have witnessed it without knowing what it was, among the many papers they had been called upon to sign. Robert Cuff, the valet, had said that only a day or two before his lordship left for Cornwall he had been called upon to witness at least a dozen documents. Mr Pendexter had brought them down from London, as he often did in these latter days, when his lordship did not go nearly so frequently to his office, preferring to do most of his business at Longridge Park. He and Mr Lamb had been kept signing things quite a while, but neither then nor on other occasions had he any notion of the nature of the documents he signed. They were business papers of some sort, but that was all he knew about them.

Finally, Miss Jellicoe had got in some further reports about Rupert Pendexter's finances. These strongly confirmed the impression that his affairs were in a mess. He seemed to have been speculating heavily on his own account in iridium and other commodities, without the backing of Mangans' Bank; and there was a rumour that there had been a quarrel when old Lord St Blaizey had got wind of his doings. MANGO, too, was said to be in difficulties, on account of the large backing it had given to the Iridium Syndicate. At all events, people in the know had been saying that Pendexter's luck seemed to have deserted him at last, and that he would not find it easy to extricate himself without the help of Lord St Blaizey's money.

'Which,' said Ben, 'he has very opportunely made his own.'

'But Ollerton's opinion means that the codicil is genuine, doctor,' Jellicoe answered.

'That,' I put in, 'gives him all the more reason for murder.'

'But what if his alibi is genuine too?' Ben asked gloomily.

Ben told me, when it was all over, that there was no moment in the whole case when he felt so near giving up in despair as when we had that talk in his office after our trip to Birmingham. I heard the discouragement in his voice, and saw it in his manner, at the time; and after Ben's remark about the alibi, there was a long silence. Ben broke it at last.

'All the same,' he said, bringing his fist down on the table with a resounding bang, 'I don't believe in either of them.'

'Of what?'

'In the alibi, or the codicil. And, if they are fakes, it must be possible to prove it. As for the alibi, there are only two possibilities, unless it is really watertight. One is that Lamont is a liar, which I don't believe. He seems honest. The other is that Pendexter did get to Birmingham by aeroplane after the murder.

'As for the codicil, if it is a fake, we've got to get to the bottom of it, however cleverly it may have been done. What Jellicoe has told us has put an idea on that point into my head. It lets me see how the will could be a wrong 'un, and yet the signatures be as unexceptionable as Ollerton makes them out.'

'I don't see that,' said I.

'Don't you see,' said Ben, 'that the codicil may have been among the papers Lamb and Cuff signed only a few days before Lord St Blaizey was killed?'

'But it's dated years ago.'

'Suppose it's dated wrong.'

'But Lord St Blaizey signed it.'

'I have no doubt he did.'

'Then it's genuine.'

'Not if he didn't know what he was signing. See here, Paul. We know the old gentleman was as blind as a bat. If Pendexter brought him down a big sheaf of business papers to sign, do you suppose he read them all? The man was his regular business deputy—always bringing him things to sign. What was to hinder him from slipping in one extra one, and getting the old gentleman to sign it, without an idea of what it was? Then he could get both Lamb and Cuff to witness it, and, hey presto, add a wrong date to make it look less fishy, and the thing was done. There was an indisputable codicil, with genuine signatures, and no means at all of proving it was a fake.'

'By joke, doctor,' said Jellicoe. 'I do believe you're right.' His face had lighted up as Ben was speaking, but now it fell. 'But can it be proved? There must be a way of showing it up, surely.'

'That,' said Ben, 'is indeed the problem. Friend Rupert, I fancy, has given us yet another proof of his ability. Well, Jellicoe, suppose for the moment I am right. How *are* we to set about proving it?'

Jellicoe shook his head. 'I don't see how we can, doctor, unless Lamb or Cuff can remember that particular paper when he sees it.'

'I doubt that,' said Ben. 'But there is one thing. You remember the signatures.'

'Got the photos here, doctor.'

'Fetch them.'

Jellicoe got the photographs of the will, and spread them out on the table.

'Now,' said Ben, 'there's just one thing about those signatures that strikes the eye. On the codicil, Lord St Blaizey's signature is a little shakier than on the original will, and Henry Lamb's a good deal shakier. Make anything of that?'

'We explained it by the difference of date, doctor,' Jellicoe answered. 'They were both getting pretty old.'

'Just so. Then there is just the possibility of being able to establish the date of either signature by comparison with others made by the same person at known dates. For example, to take the larger difference, if we could show that Henry Lamb's signature in the codicil is much more like his writing now than his writing of three years ago, at the alleged date of its making, that would give us at least the beginnings of a case.'

I ventured to put in a word of doubt. It didn't seem the sort of point a jury would make much of.

'Oh, quite,' said Ben. 'I'm not building on it at all. But if these two men, Lamb and Cuff, were confronted with the actual document, I do think it possible they might be able to say, from the look of their signatures, even if no one else could positively say, whether they were made quite recently or a couple of years ago. They might not be able to tell from our photographs; and yet, they might know if they had the actual document in front of them.'

'That involves getting hold of it,' I said, 'and I imagine the executors will not give it up if they can help it.'

'True,' said Ben. 'Of course, we can make them produce it, if we take the case into court. But we want the thing now; and I see no means of getting even a sight of it. Yet,' he went on meditatively, 'I must get hold of it somehow, if I'm to have a dog's chance of catching friend Pendexter out. You know, Paul, I feel pretty sure this hunch of mine must be right. It's the only way the codicil could have been faked so as to be passed with an absolutely clean bill by a man like Ollerton.'

'Where is the will now?' I asked.

'Either still in Cornwall, in Galloway's hands or Pendexter's if he's still there, or with Pendexter's lawyers, I suppose, if he's come up by now and handed it over. Galloway said when he claimed it from us that Pendexter was bringing it up to town, and putting it into the lawyers' hands. They're Pummery and Mudge, quite sound people, I believe. But they won't let us have it, even if it is in their hands.'

'Mr Pendexter is in London, doctor,' said Jellicoe. 'I saw in the paper this morning he was taking the chair today at some business-men's luncheon.'

'Then he mut have travelled up yesterday. Wonder if I can get hold of him. Nothing like taking the bull by the horns.' Ben flicked over the pages of the telephone directory. 'Belgravia 020202,' he said. 'See if you can locate him, Jellicoe.'

Jellicoe went into the adjoining room, and came back in a few minutes to say that Rupert Pendexter was on the telephone himself.

Ben took off the receiver.

'That you, Mr Pendexter? Dr Tancred speaking. Would it be convenient if I came round to see you for a few minutes?' A pause while Ben listened. 'No, I won't keep you long. It may interest you to know I've been to Birmingham . . . Oh, yes, Lamont says you called on him that afternoon . . . Just one or two small points you might help me to clear up . . . What's that? . . . No, I had no idea she was in London . . . Very well, I'll come round at once.

'He's agreed to see me,' said Ben. 'Do you want to come, Paul? It must be quite a while since you and friend Rupert met.'

Of course I jumped at the chance. I felt it was a real privilege to be allowed to watch these two formidable antagonists face to face.

CHAPTER 28

A VISIT TO RUPERT PENDEXTER

Rupert Pendexter did not recognize me—or said he didn't; but I should have known him anywhere, though it was a far cry from the mere boy of twenty-five years ago to the confident business man of today. His flat was the height of luxury, but not, by my judgment, in the best of taste. The decorations were garish, and the pictures much too, shall we say, modern for me. Rupert was in a velvet smoking-jacket which, I must admit, became him very well. Ben's rough tweeds and my rather ruffled lounge suit looked quite out of place in Rupert's splendid apartment.

'Well, Dr Tancred, take a drink and a seat, and then tell me what it's all about. I don't think I know your friend, do I? . . . Oh, Mr Graham, is it? I remember. Mr Graham and you still hunt in couples, then? What'll you drink? Whisky? Right. Mix your own. Quite decent cigars those. Oh, you prefer a pipe. By all means. You won't mind if I smoke a cigar.'

Rupert Pendexter was very voluble; but he seemed to me by no means wholly at his ease. Ben Tancred and I were settled at length in two big armchairs, while Rupert remained standing with his back to the fireplace.

'Well?' he said. 'What's the trouble this time?'

Ben came to the point at once. 'Have you any objection to letting me have another look at Lord St Blaizey's will?'

'Still barking up that tree, Dr Tancred? I've not the smallest objection, naturally. But I thought you'd probably photographed it already.'

'You have it here?' Ben asked.

'As it happens, I have. I should have handed it over to my lawyers; but I couldn't get up to town until this morning, and then I had no time to hand it over. I shall be taking it round to them on Monday morning. Of course they will be getting our letters of administration at once.'

'Then, if I may look at it now,' said Ben, 'that'll be a great help.'

'I don't see how,' said Rupert; 'but you're welcome to what you can make of it.' He grinned as he spoke, almost as if he were challenging Ben Tancred to get to the bottom of his cleverness, and fully confident of Ben's failure. Then he got up and went out of the room, taking a bunch of keys out of his pocket as he went. A minute later he came back, with a long envelope in his hand. He handed it across unopened to Ben, who opened it and took out the will.

'You don't happen to know what firm of lawyers drafted out the codicil, do you?' Ben asked.

'As I didn't know the thing existed,' Rupert answered, 'that's hardly likely, is it? No, I'm afraid I've no idea.'

Ben slowly turned over the pages of the document. Then, having studied each page intently for a minute, he suddenly held the document up to the light, and again scrutinized each page in turn.

'Looking for what?' Rupert asked. There was a jaunty insolence about his manner that infuriated me.

'For anything I can find,' said Ben. 'It doesn't do to miss any chances, does it?' He finished his examination, and then slowly folded up the will, and put it back into its envelope. 'I'm going to ask another favour. Are you prepared to give your lawyers instructions to let me inspect the will again, with anyone I choose to bring along with me?'

'Handwriting experts, I suppose,' said Rupert. 'You're wasting your time; but have it your own way. I'll give you a note to my lawyers, telling them to let your people look at it, if that's what you want. I've nothing to conceal.'

'Thank you,' said Ben. 'That's very helpful of you.'

'Any other little thing you'd like, while you're about it?'

'A little more information. Mr Lamont says you called on him in his office at about four o'clock.'

'Earlier, I think. I should have said it was about half-past three. I went round as soon as I'd finished lunch.'

'You lunched at the hotel adjoining the Midland Station, I believe.'

'I told you that before. Surely they remember me? I gave the waiter a big enough tip.'

'Yet you seem to have been forgotten. How did you arrive in Birmingham—by train or by car?'

'By train—from Euston. I got in just about in time for a late lunch.'

'You arranged the appointment by telephone, did you not?'

'Yes, what about it?'

'I should like to know where you were when you 'phoned.'

'I was at Euston.'

'Lamont said you 'phoned at about noon.'

'Oh, no. Earlier than that. The train left at twelve o'clock.'

Clever of him, I thought. That just fitted in. He could have telephoned then. But I was sure he was lying. Ben continued his questions.

'You visited no one else before seeing Mr Lamont?'

'No. I just had a leisurely lunch, and then strolled round to Lamont's office. I was with Lamont at about half-past three.'

'And afterwards you returned to London at once?'

'Yes, by the same route. Would you like me to send for my man to inform you that I got back here the same evening?'

'It is unnecessary. You deny, then, that you were in Cornwall at all that day?'

'Absolutely.'

'Then perhaps your man could help by telling us whether you were at home on the previous night.'

'As it happens, he couldn't, because I wasn't at home.'

'Then where did you spend the previous night, Mr Pendexter?'

'That, Mr Tancred, I will leave you to find out, not because it is of the smallest importance, but because I am really getting a bit tired of your questions.'

'You were away in your car the previous day?'

'Was I? I quite often am.'

'Can I have your authority to ask your chauffeur about the movements of your car during the days before and after Lord St Blaizey's death?'

'Really, Dr Tancred, you have the most colossal cheek. But as you're certain to ask him whatever I say, and as I should hate him to get into the habit of taking bribes, you have my permission to ask him any damned thing you like.'

Ben remained quite unperturbed by Rupert Pendexter's manner. He went on to get particulars about the chauffeur's name and address. Rupert, it appeared, had a private garage in a mews nearby, and the chauffeur, by name Colley, lived in rooms over the garage.

'Then I think that's the lot,' Ben said at last. 'Except that you said something about Miss Pendexter's being in London. Does that mean you have seen her?'

'It does. The old harridan had the effrontery to call on me at my office, and charge me with being a murderer in front of my secretary. I told her, unless she made herself scarce, I should send for the police to remove her.'

'What did she come for, do you know?' Ben asked.

Rupert laughed—a nasty laugh, I thought it. 'Acting on the usual instructions,' he said, 'or so she told me. She was *guided* to come. I think "guided" is the word, isn't it? If you can persuade the woman to let me alone, I shall be greatly obliged to you. I should hate to have to get the old lady certified; but it might come to that, if she makes herself a plague.'

Ben said that, if Sarah Pendexter came to see him, he would certainly counsel her against badgering Rupert. I could see that he was perplexed about the reasons for Sarah's visit to London, and wondered how much more had happened in the course of her visit to Rupert than he had thought fit to tell us. But Rupert volunteered no further information; and a few minutes later we were back in the street.

'Too late to go hunting up that chauffeur now,' Ben said. 'He's probably in bed, long ago. And tomorrow's Sunday. Really, Sunday is a curse, from the detective's point of view. I wonder how many murderers have got off scot free because the detective had to kick his heels over a Sunday, with everybody out of town, all the places he wanted to make inquiries in shut up, and everyone except the criminal taking a day off. If ever I commit a murder, Paul, I'll do it the last thing on Saturday night, and make sure of a full twenty-four hours' start.'

On that note of pessimism we went home to Ben's flat to bed; for I had said nothing to my wife about my coming back to London, and so I was to stay with Ben, at any rate, for the one night. Tomorrow, Ben would make up his mind whether to stop on in London and try to clear up the question of the will, or to go back to Cornwall. A good deal would doubtless depend on what more Chief Inspector Falcon had managed to get out of Alfred Amos, who was now presumably back with him at Fowey, and might by this time have been persuaded to come clean, or at least cleaner —if, indeed, he had really anything more to tell.

At the flat, we found that Falcon had 'phoned up while we were out. Jellicoe had taken the call, but the Chief Inspector had refused to say more than that he wanted to speak to Dr Tancred himself. As Dr Tancred was out, he would 'phone up in the morning, before ten o'clock.

I had half expected that, since Sarah Pendexter was in London, there would have been some word from her to Ben before we got back. But there was no message, or sign of her; and we had no idea where she was staying, or indeed whether she had not already gone back home after her passage with Rupert.

'Bed,' said Ben.

I agreed; for I was tired out. 'What were you looking for,' I asked, 'when you held the pages of the will up to the light?'

'I should have thought you could have guessed that,' Ben answered. 'I fancy friend Rupert did. It'll probably come to nothing; but you might use such wits as you have in thinking out what it was.'

On that problem, then, I fell asleep. Ben, I supposed, must have been looking to see if the paper bore any signs of tracing or erasure that might bear out the idea of forgery. But hadn't he looked for that sort of thing before? I was nearly certain he had told me so. Then had he, for some reason, wanted Rupert Pendexter to see him looking? That was as near as I could get to it, and it wasn't very near after all.

CHAPTER 29

EXIT SIDNEY GALLOWAY

Ben lifted the receiver and listened . . . 'Good God!' he said. 'I'll come down at once.' Thereafter the man at the other end did nearly all the talking; and from Ben's occasional questions and responses I could form no idea of what it was all about. But I could see that Ben was mightily excited, and taken quite by surprise.

At last the conversation ended. 'What's happened?' I asked.

'Sidney Galloway's been murdered. They've found his body in the old Castle.'

'Who killed him?'

'Falcon says there's not a thing to show. Our friend the tramp discovered the body, by the way, and came in thoroughly scared to find Falcon or me and pass on the news. That was yesterday evening. But Galloway had been dead a good time when he was found. Dr Andover says he must have been killed some time on Friday.'

'How was it done?'

'Another broken neck. Looks as if he was shoved over the battlements of the old Castle. He's badly smashed up by the fall, Falcon says.'

'Then mightn't have been an accident?'

'Falcon says no. He was hit over the head with a bit of rusty iron. They've got the weapon, and there's blood on it, and traces of rust in the wound.'

'But why should any one want to kill Sidney Galloway?'

Ben made his favourite gesture. He shrugged his shoulders. 'My dear chap, if we knew that, we should know everything. That's what we have to find out. As a mere conjecture, because Galloway knew too much about something connected with the other murder.'

'The fair young man with the horse,' I exclaimed.

'But was there such a person? Smith says he invented him.' I confess that for the moment I had quite forgotten the tramp's withdrawal of his earlier statement. But I persisted. 'Perhaps there was. Perhaps Smith's first story was the true one after all.'

'The Lord alone knows,' said Ben. 'If so, he took me in properly, and set me a pretty puzzle. If the fair young man and the horse did exist, that reinstates Sarah's story about seeing Rupert.'

'That must be right,' I said. 'It all fits in, then.'

'I wish it did,' said Ben. 'Anyway, it means going back to Cornwall at once. We'll go down to Plymouth by train, and pick up the car there.'

'And what about things at this end?'

'We shall have to leave them to Jellicoe now. You go and pack, Paul, while I see Jellicoe and tell him what to do.'

An hour or so later, Ben and I were in the train for Plymouth. Ben refused to discuss the case, and plunged into a trashy novel he had brought with him. I controlled as well as I could my impatience to be back on the scene of action. I felt certain things were moving swiftly towards a climax now.

We picked up the car in Plymouth, and drove not to Fowey, but straight to St Blaizey, for Ben wanted to see Chief Inspector Falcon at the earliest possible moment. We found him actually at The Damian Arms, with Abel Galloway, who seemed to be in a fine fury, for his voice was plainly audible in the passage.

'I've had about enough of your infernal incompetence,' he was roaring. 'Go and find the murderer, instead of badgering me about things that aren't any business of yours.'

Ben knocked at the door, and entered, with me following at his heels.

'What d'you want?' said Falcon. 'Oh, it's you, doctor. Come right in. Know Captain Galloway, don't you?'

Abel Galloway glared at Ben Tancred. 'Let's hope you've got some sense,' he growled. 'This fool of an inspector seems to think I murdered my own brother.'

'No accusation been made—none at all,' said Falcon. 'Much better if Captain Galloway would keep his head.'

'Much better if you'd find out who bashed in my brother's instead of asking me fool questions.'

'Who do *you* think killed your brother, Captain Galloway?' asked Ben.

'The same devil that killed Lord St Blaizey.'

'Any reason for thinking that?'

'Yes, I have a reason, as I was trying to tell your half-witted inspector when you came butting in. Sidney knew something. He told me so.'

'Do you know what he knew?'

'No, I don't. But I know this. Sidney owed me a tidy sum of money, and on Thursday he came and paid me the whole lot back. He said he knew where to get plenty more too—from where that lot came from. I tried to find out how he got it—I supposed it was from one of those aged harridans he always had trailing after him. But now I think differently. He got it from the murderer—for not giving him away.'

'And who is the murderer, Captain Galloway?' Ben repeated his question.

'I don't know. If I did, I'd go and bash his head in for him. But it's your job, to find out that, isn't it?'

'You have no suspicions, then?'

Galloway snorted. 'Of course I have suspicions,' he said. 'Who wouldn't have suspicions?'

'You are Mr Pendexter's co-executor under Lord St Blaizey's will,' said Ben.

'What's that got to do with it?'

'Did you know he had made you an executor?'

'I hadn't the faintest idea till Pendexter came and told me.'

'When was that?

'After they read the will, of course. He didn't know either till then.'

Ben abruptly changed the subject.

'You do not suspect Pendexter of having killed your brother?' he asked.

'Pendexter! Good heavens, no! Why on earth should he want to kill Sidney?' Galloway's surprise was evidently genuine.

'Then I suppose you must suspect Lord St Blaizey,' said Ben slowly. 'Because there's no one else for you to suspect. Is that what's in your mind?'

'Of course it's in my mind. I guessed he had killed his father all along.'

'You told me that you believed Lord St Blaizey had died a natural death.'

'Well, so I did, at first—till I got thinking. Then I felt sure his son had done it.'

'Why?' said Ben.

'For his money, of course,' Galloway answered. 'And then he found he'd been done out of it after all. It serves him right, too, with his dirty, spying ways, and his snivelling Methodist talk about his infernal conscience. Never trust a Dissenter, that's my motto. Of course he killed him.'

'Is that Mr Pendexter's opinion too?' Ben inquired. 'I mean, does he think Lord St Blaizey murdered his father?'

'Of course he does. The thing's obvious. Besides, Rupert's a good sort. It riles him to see the abominable way the man treats his wife. Rupert can't stick the fellow.'

'Still, that's a long way off accusing him of murder. There's been some trouble between you and Lord St Blaizey recently, hasn't there?'

'If you mean that the man accuses me of having immoral relations with his wife, there has,' said Galloway savagely. 'Of course, that's all complete nonsense from beginning to end. Sidney was a great deal more friendly with Helen than I ever was.'

'But you call her Helen?' said Ben.

'Why the hell shouldn't I? If I'm to be accused of carrying on with every woman I call by her first name . . .'

'No one's accusing you. But it's important to get this thing straight. Do you know Lord St Blaizey has been

209

threatening to start divorce proceedings, with you as co-respondent?'

'Then he'll be laughed out of court. Look here, Dr Tancred, I know it's not a bit of good talking to this fool inspector; but I give you my solemn word there's nothing in it. You don't seem to be quite so much of an ass as he is.'

Falcon exploded. 'Keep a civil tongue in your head, Captain Galloway, or . . .'

'Or what? I'm not frightened of you, you ball of suet. You let me alone, and get on with your job.'

'If you say another word, Captain Galloway, I'll put you under arrest.'

'And a pretty fool you'll look if you do. Pah! I'm sick of the sight of you. If you had the brains of a rabbit, you'd have had the murderer under lock and key days ago, and Sidney'd be alive now. Arrest me! You nit-wit!' Captain Galloway strode out of the room, banging the door behind him as he went.

'Our friend seems to be out of humour,' said Ben.

'I'll humour him,' said the Chief Inspector. 'Talking that rubbish about Lord St Blaizey, and as like as not he committed both murders himself.'

'Oh, no. I don't think that,' said Ben mildly. 'I think the gallant captain's bad temper is quite genuine—and strongly supports his innocence. But let's put him out of our heads for the moment. I want to know where we stand.'

Falcon told us, more fully than had been possible over the 'phone. On the previous evening, Smith, the tramp, had come in to the village, and reported that he had found a dead body lying on the ground just outside the wall of the old Castle. He did not know who the dead man was, but had seen him before in the neighbourhood. Falcon, after sending a messenger to Dr Andover, had gone up at once to the place with Smith and the local constable; and Falcon had at once recognized Sidney Galloway. The body had been lying, as Smith had said, among some heaps of old building stone at the foot of the main wall of the Castle. It had been badly battered, and had evidently fallen from some height. Entering the ruin, Falcon had noticed a winding stair in a turret near by, leading up to the top of the main wall, where there was a ruinous chamber with its outer wall broken away. Here there had been signs of some masonry recently dislodged; and the Chief Inspector had found a rusty iron bar, on which there were unmistakable traces of blood.

Dr Andover had arrived shortly after that, and examined the body where it lay. His conclusion was that death, which had been immediate, had been due to the fall, but that shortly before death the victim had been struck savagely over the head with some rusty implement, which had left its traces in the wound. Shown the iron bar found by Falcon, he had agreed that the wound could have been made with just such a weapon.

Falcon had gone carefully over the ground, but had discovered nothing else that seemed to have any bearing on the murder. The iron bar was not likely to have taken any fingerprints; and in any case, they would have disappeared before he found it. Death, said Dr Andover, had occurred at least twenty-four hours previously, and probably longer.

'I saw Pendexter in London yesterday,' said Ben Tancred. 'Do you know when he left here?'

Falcon did. Rupert Pendexter had been driven to Par Junction on Friday in one of the Castle cars, and had caught the evening train to London. The train left at ten twenty-five.

'So that, if Pendexter killed him, it was done before ten on Friday evening, at the latest. Do you know when Sidney Galloway was last seen alive?'

'He was seen driving through St Blaizey soon after two o'clock on Friday; in the direction of his brother's house. Of course, that's the way to the old Castle too. Captain Galloway denies that Sidney visited him at all that day.'

'If we believe that, presumably he drove to the old Castle. What about his car?'

'Found, abandoned in a field, just nearby,' said Falcon. 'Nothing in it.'

'Any papers on the body?'

'A lot of letters from female admirers. Nothing to throw any light on this business.'

'What about his rooms? You've tried them?'

'And drawn blank. More letters—and lashings of photos of his female friends. Nothing else. Except that he paid a couple of hundred into his bank on Thursday.'

'In addition to repaying a substantial loan to his brother. Come, there's not much doubt what that means.'

'Blackmail.'

'What else? The question is, what did he know that made him too dangerous to leave alive?'

'I should say he knew the murderer.'

'Quite. So should I. The question is, has his knowledge died with him? Do you know who his chief friends were?'

'Middle-aged women needing excitement. And Lady St Blaizey. No one else I know of.'

'Then try the middle-aged women. Or have you?'

'Had a shot at one of 'em, without any luck. Got the addresses of two more I've not got hold of yet. Her ladyship refuses to talk at all. Just says she knows nothing about it, but looks like a ghost.'

'And Lord St Blaizey? How does he take it?'

'Nohow. Looks pretty badly under the weather too. He's in the deuce of a bad temper.'

'H'm. Not surprising,' said Ben. 'But we mustn't let this business make us forget everything else. What about Amos? Has he spilt any more beans yet? Where is he, by the way?'

'At home. I'd nothing really to hold him on. He refuses to talk.'

'And Smith? Get any more out of him?'

Falcon scratched his head. 'Frankly,' he said, 'I don't know what to make of Smith. He says he won't say another word about anything till he's seen you. Seems to have something on his mind; but he won't even confirm that story of his you passed on to me.'

'I don't wonder,' said Ben, and told the Chief Inspector how the tramp had given him quite a different version of his story when he had questioned him from that which he had given to Jellicoe earlier on. 'Do you know where Smith is now?' Ben asked.

'Said he'd be back at the old mine if you wanted him,'

Falcon answered. 'Didn't fancy the old Castle since he found the corpse.'

Ben suggested that they should go up and have a word with the tramp at once, if he could be found, and Falcon agreed. So the three of us set off for the old mine; and when we got to the track leading to it Ben went ahead by himself, for fear of frightening Smith away if we appeared in force. Soon he came back, and beckoned to us to come on. 'He's here,' he said; 'and for what it's worth, he promises to tell us the truth this time.'

The tramp had a fire in an old basket. He was sitting on the ground beside it. I thought he looked badly scared, though he still kept up his jaunty manner. 'What, three of you?' he exclaimed, as we approached his retreat. 'Well, the more the merrier. Sit down and make yourselves quite at home. This is Liberty Hall, this is.'

Ben sat down on an old log. Falcon and I remained standing.

'See here, gentlemen,' said the tramp. 'I reckon you've got a bone to pick with me, but what I'm a-going to tell you now is gospel truth. I don't hold with murder—at all events, when the murderer leaves his corpses lying about in my sleeping quarters. Now listen to me. You know that chap you found with his head all bashed in.'

'Sidney Galloway?' said Falcon.

'I don't know his name. But what I do know is, he was the identical chap I seen here that morning you was asking me about.' He turned to Ben Tancred as he spoke.

'Which man? The man who went off in the motor car?'

'No. T'other bloke. The fair one that went off with the horse.'

'But you told me there weren't two men,' said Ben. 'You said that stuff about the horse was all a fairy tale.'

'Why, so I did,' said the tramp, 'and it grieves my heart to be thinking of leading you astray. But the fact is, my tongue's always running away with me. Besides, in this case, I had my reasons. I always try to play fair; and when a chap gives me a quid to say I didn't see him, why, then I didn't see him. Leastways, not till he was dead, and it couldn't matter to him whether I saw him or not. I reckon you'll be annoyed with me, but please to bear in mind I asked you to make that ten bob of yours a quid, because when the betting's what you may call even, I'm one that tells the truth.'

'Do you mean to tell me your first story was true? You did see Pendexter ride up on a horse and hand it over to Sidney Galloway, and then Pendexter drive off in his car, just as you told Jellicoe? Is that what you mean?'

'I name no names,' said the tramp; 'not knowing any. But the dark fellow whose photo you showed me came riding up on the horse just as I said, and the fair one led the horse away, and then the dark chap went off in his motor car, same as I told you at the time.'

'And Sidney Galloway bribed you to say you hadn't seen him?'

'The fair fellow gave me a quid, if that's what you mean. The dark 'un didn't give me nothing, so I didn't feel any call not to let on to you about seeing him. And I'll tell you another thing now. I seen that fair chap talking to a lady in the woods—very fine lady she was, too—only he asked me not to mention that either. Because they were fair carrying on.'

'What lady?' Ben asked.

'Same lady I saw the dark young man a-conversing with, same as I told you before.'

'Helen!' I exclaimed.

'Does he mean Lady St Blaizey?' asked Falcon.

'He does,' said Ben.

'In my opinion, she ain't no lady,' said Mr Smith. 'I don't hold with doings.'

Well, it did look as if Smith were really telling the truth this time. That meant definitely that Rupert's alibi was a fake, or rather that he must have travelled to Birmingham by aeroplane—for there was no other way in which the journey could possibly have been made in the time. But, if he had, it must be possible to prove it; for he must have started from somewhere and landed somewhere not too far from Birmingham, presumably at an aerodrome. That was clearly Scotland Yard's affair; they had means of tracing such things which no private investigator could command. As we walked back to the village, Falcon agreed to take on that part of the task, at once, while Ben proposed to go in chase of some more of Sidney Galloway's female admirers, in the faint hope of getting some further light on the secret for which it seemed clear he had been killed.

Ben and I got back to Fowey late and hungry. Over a cold supper and a bottle of Burgundy we agreed that Rupert Pendexter was quite the most elusive criminal in our experience. Over a tumbler of hot rum afterwards, Ben confessed that he was almost in despair of catching him. I went mournfully to bed. It would be really too dreadful if Rupert were to get clean away with two more murders. For I had not the smallest doubt that he had killed Sidney Galloway as well as Lord St Blaizey. I felt as certain of that as that he had murdered old Simon Pendexter twenty-five years before.

CHAPTER 30

BEN OFFERS A RECONSTRUCTION

Ben Tancred said to me, 'You know, Paul, I don't think I've ever managed to see this case quite straight. There are reasons for that: it's so amazingly full of cock-eyed people. What with Sarah Pendexter seeing "visions", and Mr Smith spinning fairy tales just for the pleasure of hearing his own voice, and Lord St Blaizey all in a dither because he thinks his wife is having an affair with Abel Galloway, whereas it's more likely to have been with his brother after all, it has been quite extraordinarily difficult not to get all muddled up oneself. The result is that, instead of our getting clearer as we find out more facts, the tangle keeps on getting worse and worse.

'As far as I can see, Paul, there's only one thing to be done. I've got to think the whole thing through again right from the start. I've got to reconstruct what I do believe really happened, in such a way that all the scattered facts we know about can be made to fit in. And then I've got to see what remains unexplained, what other facts *must* be true if my reconstruction holds; and I've got to go and look for the evidence for just those missing facts—or, of course, for proof that they aren't facts after all. In which case we shall have to start all over again.

'Now, Paul, what are the facts, as we actually know them at present?'

With that preamble Dr Tancred plunged into a complete review of the case. I shall try to compress it here, because a good deal of what he said would involve repetition of earlier chapters. But I shall try to put down just the essential points; and before this book is published I shall ask Ben to go over them and make sure that I have got them right.

Ben began by enumerating the things that had somehow to be fitted into his projected reconstruction. He started off, of course, with the known circumstances of Lord St Blaizey's death, which I need not enumerate again. Then he went on to the more intractable points. I shall put them down *seriatim* for the reader's attention:-

The First Murder

1. Sarah Pendexter says she saw Rupert Pendexter *on horseback* ride out of the Castle woods on to the Lostwithiel road at about eleven-thirty, on the morning of Lord St Blaizey's murder.

2. The tramp, Henry Smith, says he saw Rupert (for I think we can accept the identification) in conversation with Sidney Galloway near the old mine at about the same time. He says Galloway went off towards the road leading the horse, whereas Rupert scrambled up the bank and went off in a car. At one stage he denied seeing Galloway, who had bribed him not to give him away; but he now asserts that

he did see both Sidney Galloway and Rupert on horseback; and we believe he is now telling the truth.

3. Sarah Pendexter says she had a 'vision', whatever that means, of Rupert actually murdering Lord St Blaizey; but as she put her 'vision' in a spot where the event did not happen, I think we can safely discount that part of her story.

4. Alfred Amos says that Helen St Blaizey bribed him to run away. He says this was because he saw her being made love to by Galloway.

(At this point I asked Ben, 'Which Galloway?' And he said, 'Upon my word, Paul, I don't believe we know. We assumed it was the Captain, but of course it may have been Sidney after all. That would fit in with what Smith said about seeing them together. It may turn out to be quite an important point.' I glowed with pleasure at the thought that my question might contribute, however humbly, to the solution of the mystery.)

5. Reuben Amos says he knows from a lady that Lord St Blaizey wasn't murdered at all.

6. Helen also assures us that there was no murder.

7. Lamont, of the Metal Securities Trust, says Rupert Pendexter was with him in Birmingham at four o'clock on the day of the murder. Rupert says three-thirty; but the point is not very material.

Those seven points all relate directly to old Lord St Blaizey's death. Now about the will.

The Will

8. Ralph Ollerton, who is a first-class expert, says—and I agree—that the signatures to both the will and the codicil are genuine.

9. Lamb, the butler, and Cuff, the valet, were in the habit of witnessing numerous documents for Lord St Blaizey. Rupert Pendexter often brought him documents for signature to Longridge Park.

10. Rupert actually brought a batch of documents to be signed and witnessed a few days before Lord St Blaizey left Longridge for Cornwall—that is, within a week or two of his death.

11. The codicil was undoubtedly written in a professional law clerk's handwriting; but we have been unable to trace the firm which drew it up.

12. Rupert Pendexter says he knew nothing of the contents of the will or codicil till he heard them read at St Blaizey Castle. Captain Galloway, the other executor, also denies that he knew.

13. Mr Narroway, the family lawyer, also denies all prior knowledge of the codicil.

14. Young Lord St Blaizey entirely refuses to believe that his father could have disinherited him, and especially that he could have done so more than three years ago (as the codicil is dated), and have concealed the fact from him ever since.

15. The will and codicil were not kept at the lawyers', but in a locked box which old Lord St Blaizey had with him at the Castle at the time of his death. Narroway knew about this box, and had a key to it, with instructions about finding and reading the will.

16. Rupert Pendexter and Captain Abel Galloway were joint executors under the codicil, but neither was an executor under the original will.

'So much for the will,' said Ben Tancred. 'Now we come to the murder of Sidney Galloway; and the plain fact is that we don't know a single thing about it, except where and by what means he was killed. All we have is this:

THE SECOND MURDER

17. Sidney Galloway became suddenly flush of money after Lord St Blaizey's death. He repaid a large loan to his brother, or so Captain Galloway says; and he also paid two hundred pounds into his bank.

18. Sidney Galloway's car was found parked in a field near the scene of his murder.

19. Smith found the body on Saturday night.

20. Sidney Galloway was killed at least twenty-four hours before he was found.

'Then there are one or two facts that don't fit in under any of the three heads:

In General

21. Young Lord St Blaizey has been threatening to divorce Helen because of her relations, real or supposed, with Captain Galloway.

22. Alfred Amos had got a young woman at the Castle into trouble.

23. Young Lord St Blaizey had a standing quarrel with his father because he refused to go into business and succeed to his position at the head of Mangans' Bank.

25. Rupert Pendexter wrote a letter to young Lord St Blaizey, which Lord St Blaizey denied having seen. It referred to Helen's relations with her husband. The conditions under which the letter was written have still to be explained.

'Now there,' said Ben, 'are the facts as far as we know them. It seems to me we've got to piece them together into some sort of a connected story before we can hope to make any further progress. Let's try to make a reconstruction, knowing well that we may get it wrong, but, at any rate, trying to fit in all the known facts, unless we think we have good reason for distrusting any particular person's story. You'll agree that, in the case of Smith, I'm right in following his first and third stories rather than his second. That means accepting his statement that he was bribed by Sidney Galloway not to give him away.

'We begin with old Lord St Blaizey riding out with his secretary, Landor, in the Castle woods, and then sending Landor back to the Castle to put through a trunk call to

London, and riding on alone.

'As it was unusual for the old gentleman to ride alone, we assume that he had a reason for wishing to be alone on that particular occasion.

'We assume that he had an appointment to meet the man who murdered him, and that he wanted to meet him alone.

'Falcon has tried to confirm that by hunting for any letter making an appointment, but he has not succeeded. Probably either the letter has been destroyed, or the appointment was made by word of mouth.

'We assume that the murderer met Lord St Blaizey; and from the nature of the blow that unhorsed him, we seem justified in assuming that the murderer was also on horseback. If we regard Rupert Pendexter as the murderer, that fits in with the fact that Sarah saw him riding out of the Castle woods, and that Smith saw him hand over his horse to Sidney Galloway by the old mine.

'But at this point a series of highly interesting questions comes up. According to Smith, Rupert Pendexter made his escape in a car, after passing the horse over to Sidney Galloway. Then, did he arrive in a car, and subsequently provide himself with a horse? If so, how did he get the horse, and whose horse was it? Did Galloway provide him with it? Sidney Galloway, Falcon tells me, definitely had no horse of his own, though his brother had. Was it Abel Galloway's horse? What did Sidney do with it after taking it over from Rupert?

'Now, there you have a perfect cloud of questions to which we can return no positive answers. The most plausible reconstruction is that Sidney Galloway supplied the horse, since he took it away afterwards, and that it came either from the Castle stables or from Abel Galloway's place. That makes Sidney Galloway an accessory both *before* and *after* the fact, unless he supplied the horse without knowing that Rupert meant murder. In that case, he is still probably an accessory *after* the fact.

'But, as I've said before, I can't believe that Rupert would have made Sidney Galloway his accomplice in planning a murder. Therefore I have to reject the notion, plausible as it is, that Sidney Galloway supplied the horse. Then who did? I can conceive of only one possible person with whom Rupert might have conspired in such a matter.'

'You mean . . . Helen?' The notion still shocked me, I confess.

'I do mean Helen,' Ben went on. 'But if Lady St Blaizey supplied the horse, one would have expected her also to take it away. That is why, at one stage, I was inclined to identify her with the "fair young man". Smith's positive identification of Sidney Galloway washes that notion out, as indeed does Sidney Galloway's murder. How, then, did Sidney Galloway come to be an accomplice?

'Two possible explanations suggest themselves. The first is that Lady St Blaizey was Rupert's original accomplice, but that for some reason we do not know she found herself prevented from carrying out her part of the plan by receiving the horse back, and that she turned in desperation to the man whom we have now some reason to suspect of having been her lover. In that case, Lady St Blaizey and not Rupert Pendexter brought in Sidney Galloway as an accomplice—a far likelier supposition, I think you will agree.

'But there is a second possibility—that Sidney Galloway, accidentally present on the scene of the crime, saw Rupert commit the murder and threatened to betray him. Rupert thereupon offered to buy him off, and availed himself of his help for getting the horse returned. That is pure conjecture, of course; but it is the notion I like the better, though we must, of course, keep both possibilities in mind.

'That brings me to the car in which Rupert Pendexter made off. Whose car was it? We have been assuming that it was Rupert's own, and I am expecting from Jellicoe the results of his visit to Rupert's chauffeur about the movements of the car. But it has occurred to me since that the car may have been not Rupert Pendexter's but Sidney Galloway's.

'Now we come to Alfred Amos. I shall be seeing him today, with Falcon; and a great deal may yet depend on what he can be persuaded to tell. I do not believe that his running away was because of anything he knew about a love affair between Helen and either of the Galloways, though, of course, that may have entered in. I believe he knows something of importance about the murder; and, as Lady St Blaizey bribed him to run away, I think we can conclude that it is something that would incriminate either her or her brother, or, of course, both of them. But what is it? This time I see three possibilities. Either Amos saw the murder, or he saw Rupert escaping, *or he knows something about the horse*—in which case, as he is a stableman at the Castle, it probably came out of the Castle stables.

'Points five and six we can only ignore for the moment. But obviously point seven is crucial. If Rupert Pendexter committed the murder and got to Birmingham by four o'clock or earlier, he travelled by aeroplane, and that must be capable of being found out, by Scotland Yard, if not by me.

'Now, that reconstruction, wrong as it may be at many points, at any rate, gives us certain lines we can follow up. I must try to get the truth out of Amos, with the advantage of knowing more or less what I am looking for. Then I must tackle Sidney Galloway's ladies. And, I think, above all, I must try to trace the movements of that horse both before and after Rupert handed him over to Sidney in the old mine. *The more I think of it, the more the horse seems to be the very centre of the whole thing.*

'As for the will, Jellicoe has that in hand in London, and until he's able to report further progress there is nothing more to be done.

'Finally, about the second murder. If Sidney Galloway was killed on Friday afternoon, which is consistent with the medical evidence, Rupert Pendexter could have killed him. We know he did not leave for London till fairly late on Friday afternoon. But I don't believe we shall get much more light on Sidney Galloway's murder, till we are a lot nearer to the truth about Lord St Blaizey's. We can assume that the one is consequential on the other. Clear up the main case, and the lesser one will fall into its place in the puzzle.'

So far Ben's reconstruction seemed to me sheerly masterly, though of course it had to leave a great many loose ends still to be tied. Except that I could not bring myself to believe that Helen was in any way guilty of even conniving at so terrible a crime as murder, I felt sure that Ben had got most of the story right. I was in a far happier mood when he had poured it all out to me, sitting again on the edge of my bed very early that Monday morning, than I had been when I went to sleep thoroughly discouraged on the Sunday night. So was Ben more cheerful; for I think that from the moment he had made that reconstruction, he no longer doubted his ability to bring the Pendexter case to a successful issue. There was indeed a great deal still to be done; but from now on Ben could see his way right to the end of the road.

CHAPTER 31

THE BOOK OF AMOS

Chief Inspector Falcon and Ben Tancred went together that morning to interview Alfred Amos again. They found him digging in the back garden of his cottage; for no arrangement had been made for him to resume his work in the Castle stables. Amos did not look at all pleased to see his visitors; indeed, after a growl of greeting, he turned his back on them and went on sullenly with his work.

Falcon tried browbeating him; but he utterly refused to talk. He would reaffirm in a surly way what he had already told the Chief Inspector; but he would add nothing to it. Yet he gave Ben the very definite impression of a man uncertain as well as uneasy, and of one who could be got to talk if only he were being tackled in the right way, and by someone he did not regard so instinctively as his natural enemy as a policeman.

At length Falcon gave up the attempt; and Ben, who had

stood silent while it was being made, did not try his hand in the Chief Inspector's presence, but manœuvred him out of Amos's garden and accompanied him back towards the village. The Chief Inspector was manifestly depressed; for from his point of view the case, complicated now by the second murder, seemed to be standing still. He told Ben he proposed to go in at once to Fowey to see whether any fresh news had come in; and Ben arranged to meet him again at Fowey Police Station by lunch-time and compare notes. Ben was expecting a telephone call from London before then, having arranged that either Jellicoe or Miss Jellicoe should ring him up at his hotel at half-past twelve. Before then, he had a couple of hours before him, and he meant to put them to good use in trying to test his new reconstruction of the crime.

Ben would greatly have preferred to see Amos first of all without the Chief Inspector; but it had been impossible to reject Falcon's proposal that they should go together. Ben could only hope that his first appearance in the policeman's company had not destroyed his chance of getting Amos to speak. As soon as Falcon had gone, we went straight back to Amos's cottage to try our luck again.

Alfred Amos was still in his little garden; but he was no longer at work. He was sitting wretchedly on an old packing-case, with his head between his hands, staring at nothing and obviously trying in vain to puzzle out a problem that was too hard for him. He looked up as he heard our feet on the path; but he did not rise. He sat glaring at us, looking the very picture of misery.

'Well, Mr Amos,' Ben began, 'now the policeman has gone perhaps we shall get on a bit faster.'

'Ain't you another on 'em?'

'By no means. A policeman is unfortunately prevented by law from offering an innocent witness a suitable reward. I am not. You must not expect me to reward you on the scale of what you got from Lady St Blaizey. But I understand you have lost that: so perhaps a couple of pounds would not come amiss to you.' Ben, as he spoke, drew a couple of notes for a moment out of his pocket, and then promptly put them back.

'I told that policeman all about her ladyship's carryings-on with that Galloway.'

'Quite. But that's not what I want to know about. I am not interested in Captain Galloway's doings.'

'It wasn't the Captain. It was Sidney I was telling about. Him as used to be sec'tary up to the Castle.'

That cleared up one doubtful matter for Ben without any need for putting a direct question. But he said, 'That point does not concern me. I want you to tell me exactly what you know about the morning of Lord St Blaizey's murder.'

'Who says I know anything about it?'

Ben said nothing. He took the two pound notes again out of his pocket—and again put them back.

'It's worth a tenner, what I know,' said Amos.

'Two pounds, or nothing,' said Ben decisively. 'Nobody'll offer you a penny, except me; and the police'll have you up in court, and make you tell it for nothing.'

'Can't you make it a fiver?' said Amos.

'No.' Ben had plenty of experience in dealing with people of Alfred Amos's type.

There was a long silence. Then, as Ben said no more, Amos said at last 'OK. Hand over that two quid.'

'When you've told me, not before.' Another pause. Then Amos said, 'It's about a horse.'

'I know that,' said Ben. That startled Amos. Ben went on. 'Whose horse was it?'

'Her ladyship's mare. She didn't want no one to know she'd been a-riding of her that morning.'

'You mean earlier, before she went out to look for Lord St Blaizey?'

'Yes, it was just after the old lord started out for his ride.'

'Tell me exactly what happened.'

'It was like this. Her ladyship comes down to the stables, where there was no one but me at the time, and orders out Bessie. That's her ladyship's own mare, same as Flossie, which is her other, she keeping the two for her own use. Her ladyship tells me she's riding over to Luxulian way to see someone; and when I'd got Bessie ready, off she rides.'

'What time was that?'

'Mebbe a quarter to eleven, or thereabouts. Well about twenty minutes later I happens to be round the other side of the Castle, and I sees her ladyship walking along one of the paths in the wood, without any horse. So I makes bold to go up to her ladyship, and I asks her if there was any mischief come to Bessie, being a favourite of mine, so to speak. And she looks at me as if she would a liked to wipe me off the face of the earth, and as good as tells me to be minding mine own business. So I goes back to the stables, wondering a bit what'd happened, but not making much of it, same as you wouldn't if you'd been in my place. I gets on with my work, and, upon my word, about twelve o'clock up rides that Mr Galloway, who's been and got himself murdered, and a good riddance if you ask me, and blest if he wasn't riding on Bessie same as if she belonged to him. He don't see me, and he jumps down and shoves the mare into her stable, and starts taking off the harness. So I goes up to him, and I asks him what he reckoned to be doing. And he goes all white about the gills, and he says her ladyship says he was to bring the horse back for her, because she was busy.

'I didn't make much of that at the time, though it set me wondering a good bit. But when I heard how his lordship had been killed out riding, and how it wasn't an accident same as they thought it was, I began to put two and two together. So, in the end, I goes to her ladyship, and puts a bold face on it, and tells her what I seen, and asks her what she was wanting me to do. And her ladyship, if I make so bold, gets in a terrible stew, and gives me a pot of money to go right away and not let the police be asking me any questions. So off I goes, same as her ladyship told me, and I done my best; but what's a man to do when he's set on and robbed by a lot of murdering thieves up to London and all brow-badgered by a pack of policemen, till he don't know how to call his soul his own?'

That, with a lot more rigmarole that doesn't matter, was Alfred Amos's story; and I think you will agree that it was pretty interesting, and carried Ben a good long way towards turning his reconstruction into a solid demonstration of fact. We could now take certain of Ben's conjectures as definitely established, though the precise meaning of the facts which he had elicited still remained obscure. We could be sure that the horse Rupert had been riding had been Helen's horse, and that she had supplied him with it, and we knew now that Smith had told us the truth about the fair young man, and that Sidney Galloway had received the horse from Rupert and returned it to the Castle stables.

That looked bad for Helen; but I still fought obstinately against the idea that she could have been a party to her father-in-law's murder. I suggested to Ben that she could have had no idea when she lent Rupert the horse that he was meaning murder, however chivalrously ready she might have been to shield him after the murder had been done. Ben wagged his head at me, and admitted that I might be right—though he couldn't approve of my moral attitude. We were getting on now, he said; but we were still a long way off being certain of what had really happened.

What was to be our next step? One possibility was to confront Helen St Blaizey with our new knowledge, and see what she had to say. But Ben wanted, if he could, to be surer of his ground before he tackled Lady St Blaizey. He made up his mind to make another attempt upon the old cobbler, Reuben Amos, who had so firmly asserted his absolute assurance that Lord St Blaizey had not been murdered at all. It was at any rate possible that a second murder, following so sharply on the first, might have affected Reuben's attitude.

We went, then, back to the village, and found Reuben Amos at work as usual in his little shop. The old man looked, Ben said, older than before—older and more careworn. Certainly he struck me, who now saw him for the first time, as old and frail.

Ben plunged to the heart of the matter at once, by asking him whether he still maintained his conviction that Lord St Blaizey had died a natural death.

'Eh, but I don't know what to be thinking,' was the answer.

'Sidney Galloway did not die naturally, at all events,' said Ben.

The old man heaved a deep sigh. ''Tis grievous to think of him, cut off in the midst of his iniquities,' he lamented. 'Aye, 'tis a weary world, and full of raging lions seeking whom they may devour.'

'And your informant,' said Ben, 'who told you so positively Lord St Blaizey's death was an accident . . . what does she say now?'

'Alas, poor lady, I fear she's in a sad way.'

'It was Lady St Blaizey, wasn't it, who told you she knew her father-in-law had died by misadventure?'

Amos made no answer: so Ben went on. 'You said she told you she saw the accident happen and was so frightened that she ran away instead of fetching help. What I can't understand is how she came to tell you a thing like that. Of course, it wasn't true; but why did she pretend to make you her confidant over it?'

'It is not for me to be breaking a lady's confidence.'

Ben tried a conjecture. 'I suppose Alfred Amos told you about Lady St Blaizey's horse and about Sidney Galloway bringing it back to the stable.'

Amos was surprised out of his calm. 'Man, you know about that?' he said.

'Oh, yes; and I assume you must have spoken about it to Lady St Blaizey, and, in order to keep you quiet, she made up this fairy story about seeing the accident and being so frightened that she ran away.'

'You're sure what she said was not true?'

'I'm dead sure. She didn't kill Lord St Blaizey; but she knows very well who did.'

'Then I'll not be one to keep back the truth as I know it. You are right, master, Alfred Amos did go for to tell me what he had seen, and I did speak of the matter to her ladyship, and she tell me what I was saying to you before. But if it was not an accident at all, and her ladyship was deceiving an old man . . .'

★

There, again, you have the gist of Reuben Amos's part of the story—all helping to build up the now formidable case against Helen, as even I had to admit. For even I, now, had to agree that Helen had lied and bribed, and been deeply implicated. But I would not have her made out a murderess. Besides, was it conceivable that she had really aided Rupert to kill Lord St Blaizey, when Rupert's one motive for the murder was to appropriate to himself the fortune that his sister had every right to expect would come to her own husband? It simply could not be so, I told Ben.

'But she didn't know that,' Ben answered. 'If Helen helped Rupert to kill the old man, you can be sure she had no idea what was in the codicil.' This was not complimentary to Helen; but I could not help admitting that it might explain a great deal.

CHAPTER 32

THE NET BEGINS TO CLOSE

After that, Ben and I drove in to Fowey, and got back to The Three Cutters just before noon. We had not been in more than a few minutes, which Ben used in calling up the police station to invite Falcon to come round to lunch at the hotel, when word came that Jellicoe was on the telephone from London. Again, I had to control my impatience as well as I could till Ben came back from taking the message. I tried to read his face as he came towards me in the lounge; but it expressed neither satisfaction nor disappointment. Still, his first words were reassuring. He said, 'We're still getting on.'

'About the will?' I asked eagerly.

'No. There's nothing more to report about that yet. Jellicoe's ringing up again later tonight. It's about Pendexter's chauffeur.'

'Oh!' said I, rather disappointed; for I was far more curious about what Ben was doing over the will—a subject on which he remained obstinately uncommunicative until his ideas had been put to the test.

'Jellicoe has seen the chauffeur,' Ben went on. 'Pendexter's car was definitely not down in these parts on the day of the murder. It was in London, and it met his train from Birmingham that evening.'

My face fell. That didn't look at all promising, I felt.

'But the day before the chauffeur drove Pendexter out to Longridge Park—you know, Lord St Blaizey's Hertfordshire place. Pendexter has a cottage there, in the grounds, and he said he meant to stay the night. Usually, the chauffeur says, Pendexter keeps him on such occasions to drive him back the next day. He can always garage the car and get a bed at the big house. But on this occasion Pendexter sent him home to await further orders in London. Only, as it happened, he didn't go.'

'Why not?'

'The car broke down; and before he got it fixed up it was too late to go back. So he decided to stay the night, and ask his employer for further orders in the morning. But when he went round to the cottage the next morning, Pendexter had gone away.'

'All the same, I don't see how it helps. Unless you've found out where he went.'

'I'm keeping the best till the last,' said Ben. 'As the chauffeur was poking about round the cottage, a man came up, and asked him what his business was. The chauffeur said he was looking for Mr Pendexter; and the man said he'd gone off early in his private aeroplane.'

'Good heavens, Ben.'

'The man turned out to be the mechanic who looks after it for him. He hasn't had it long, it seems, and the man, who had taught him, seemed a bit doubtful about his flying it alone. Pendexter, it seems, had been keeping the fact that he owned the thing dark; and no one up at Longridge Park knew anything about it. He didn't keep it on the estate, but at an aerodrome a mile or so away. Of course, now we know that, it's simple to get the number, and find out whether Pendexter flew it in his own name, and whether it can be traced as landing anywhere near Fowey or Birmingham on the day that interests us. Jellicoe has put Scotland Yard on to that. He got on the 'phone to Wilson at once; and he says Wilson's as keen as mustard.'

Of course, any lingering doubt that may have been in our minds about Rupert Pendexter's guilt was finally dispelled by the news that he possessed a private aeroplane of his own. But I wondered why Rupert, if his chauffeur possessed this highly incriminating knowledge, had been so ready to give Ben permission to question the man. Ben at once supplied the answer. 'Of course he had no idea the chauffeur knew anything about his having a plane. As it happens, the chauffeur didn't mention to him that he had been delayed at Longridge overnight, or say anything about having met the mechanic. He wouldn't, you know: servants practically never let on to their masters how much they really know about them.'

At that exciting point Falcon came bursting in, obviously full of news. 'We've traced that car at last,' he said. 'I mean, the one Smith heard being started up on the road above the old mine. Only it wasn't Pendexter's car, as you supposed: it was one Sidney Galloway had borrowed from one of his lady friends. It was found by the police, abandoned on the edge of Red Moor beyond Lostwithiel. They informed the owner, and Sidney Galloway came out and collected it. That was the day after Lord St Blaizey was killed.'

'Then,' said Ben, 'now we know where Pendexter parked his aeroplane that morning. He left it on Red Moor, in some deserted place, probably walked to St Blaizey and committed the murder, and then got back to his plane in Galloway's borrowed car.'

'What's all this about Pendexter's aeroplane?' said Falcon.

Ben told him, and added that Superintendent Wilson had the matter of tracing the aeroplane's movements already in hand up in London. Naturally Falcon was as excited as we were; and he agreed that it removed the last possible doubt of Rupert Pendexter's guilt.

'But I've got some more news for you,' said the Chief Inspector. 'I've been on to that secretary fellow, Landor, again; and with the aid of some third-degree stuff, or near it, I've made him come across. Seems the fool's been cherishing a hopeless passion for her ladyship, or he'd have spoken before. He now says he heard her fixing up with the old man to meet someone for a talk in the woods on the day he died. Landor didn't hear who it was; but something else he heard gave him an idea, when he heard of the old man's death, that there was something wrong, and that his ladylove was mixed up in it. He says he didn't suspect her of anything more than knowing who the murderer was. In fact, he tried to tackle her about it; and I reckon the lady bewitched him, and got him to hold his tongue. Then the second murder shook him up proper, and he came across in the end, with a bit of coaxing—especially as he seems a bit off Lady St B. since he heard Lord St B. threatening to divorce her over Captain Galloway.'

It was curious to notice how, under stress of his excitement, Falcon quite threw off his usual staccato way of speaking, and consented to talk, for once, like an ordinary mortal.

It was all clicking together now. There was another of Ben's conjectures confirmed. There had been an appointment for Lord St Blaizey to meet his murderer in the woods, and—what went ahead even of Ben's conjectures—Helen had been the person who made the fatal appointment.

The three of us, at a table well out of earshot in an alcove, talked the case over at great length again over lunch; and now Ben laid his entire theoretical reconstruction before the Chief Inspector. So much of it had been confirmed already that the rest of Ben's imaginings had acquired powerful reinforcement. But, as Ben himself admitted, there were one or two things that still quite obstinately refused to fit in. By far the most intractable was that letter of Rupert Pendexter's which Ben had found on Lord St Blaizey's study table in the old lodge. Ben put the difficulty something like this.

'When I found that letter, and Lord St Blaizey positively said it had not been there the day before the murder, it seemed to be at any rate highly likely that Rupert must have put it there actually on the morning of the murder. But, when one came to think it out, that was quite incredible. Pendexter had been at immense pains not to let anyone know he had been in the neighbourhood of St Blaizey on that day. Would he, then, have tried to see young Lord St Blaizey and, on failing to find him, have left a note that gave plain proof of his presence? That made sheer nonsense; and therefore I knew it couldn't be true.

'Then what was the truth? It could only be that the note was written after the murder—in fact, after Rupert Pendexter's open return to St Blaizey for the reading of the will. That would put it not sooner than the Thursday morning. You remember it bore no date. Now, I found it on Friday morning. I think the truth must be that Rupert wrote it, probably on the Thursday, and then on the Friday thought better of it and came and took it back—not, however, before I, in a most ungentlemanly fashion, had read and copied it. That being so, it ceases to have any value as evidence in relation to the crime, though finding it, and making a mistake about its date, did actually help me at that stage, because it seemed to confirm our idea of Pendexter's having been on the scene of the crime.'

Falcon and I both agreed that Ben had offered the only possible explanation.

'And now,' said Falcon, 'where are we? Far enough for me to be seeing about a warrant for Rupert Pendexter's arrest?'

'I should say so,' Ben answered, 'especially now we know the man has an aeroplane of his own, and can make a good quick getaway if he has any idea we are thinking of laying him by the heels. Of course, the case isn't nearly complete yet. But I fancy the rest is only a matter of time and hard work.'

Falcon agreed to that. He would at any rate get on the phone to Superintendent Wilson in London, and see what Wilson thought of the expediency of an immediate arrest in the light of the latest developments. Wilson, he said, would very likely get the warrant made out, but might summon him to London before making a final decision about its execution.

'And Helen,' I said. 'You won't arrest her, will you?'

'Talk to her first, anyway,' said Ben Tancred. 'Not you, Falcon, if you don't mind. You'd have to warn her; and that'd mean you'd get nothing. Leave her to me for the moment. It ought to be an amusing interview. Do you want to come with me, Paul?'

I drew the line at that. It was one thing—and bad enough —to see the net closing around Helen; but it was another and a far worse to attend voluntarily while Ben Tancred exercised his wits upon a woman to whom I had once proposed marriage. Then, too, Helen Pendexter had been in peril of her life; but on that far-off occasion Ben and I had been on her side. Now, Ben was to be her persecutor-in-chief; but there was no need for me to stand by and hand him the thumbscrews.

The last thing Ben did with the Chief Inspector was to arrange for him to call up Scotland Yard at once in order to have a close watch set on Rupert Pendexter. Above all, the place where he kept his aeroplane was to be found and watched, and he was to be detained for inquiries if he made any attempt to get away by that means. For, unless this were done, there might be danger in Ben's coming talk with Helen. If she realized that the game was up, her first thought would surely be to get into touch with Rupert, and bid him fly the country without an instant's delay.

CHAPTER 33

TWO TRYING INTERVIEWS

'I reckon the case is about finished at this end. The rest's in London,' Ben Tancred said to me when Chief Inspector Falcon had gone away. 'I'm going to see the fair Helen, as

I told Falcon; but there's no need now for me to be bothering with Sidney Galloway's female friends. We can leave the police to handle them. I'm going up to London by the first train I can get after seeing Lady St Blaizey. I don't want to miss being in at the death.'

'But what about the car?' I objected. 'Surely you aren't leaving it here?'

'That's where you come in, my faithful friend,' said Ben. 'I want you to drive me over to the Castle; and then, if you don't want to come in, you can wait outside. Then I want you to drive me to the nearest station where I can pick up the London express. Probably Par—we'll look it up in a minute. Then, if you will, I'd like you to bring the car up to town for me. It'll be all right if you arrive tomorrow.'

I confess I was a little hurt by Ben's proposal. I wanted to be in at the death just as much as he did; but here he was proposing to leave me behind, so that I might arrive in London only when it was all over. But Ben has always been able to make me do anything he wants to; and though I am sure my face betrayed my disappointment, I agreed without making any objection.

Ben softened the blow. 'I expect you'll be in plenty of time for the last lap, Paul. And you'll be really helping if you'll do this for me.'

So that was that. I drove Ben over to the Castle, and waited while he was informed that Lady St Blaizey was at home, and would consent to see him. Then, at his request, I drove to the village and trunk-called his office in order to inform Jellicoe of his change of plans. Jellicoe, however, was out, busy with some business about the will; and Miss Jellicoe took the message. I told her that Ben expected to be back home at latest at about half-past six the next morning, after a night in the train; but if he could he would catch the afternoon express from Par and be in London late that very evening.

When I had done that, I drove slowly back to the Castle; but there was no sign of Ben as yet. It was half an hour before he emerged, looking uncommonly pleased with himself, and told me to drive straight to Par—for we had already taken all our things from the hotel at Fowey. He would be in time after all to catch the earlier train.

Of course I was all agog to hear what had happened in the course of his momentous interview with Helen. But there was no opportunity for more than the briefest outline before we reached Par, only just in time for the London express. In what follows, then, I am giving you not the hurried *résumé* I had to be content with at that stage, but the much fuller account of the conversation that I extracted from Ben later on, when we met again in London.

Ben said that Lady St Blaizey looked even more ill and haggard than when he had seen her before. He said he felt almost sorry for her, but none the less determined to get as much of the truth out of her as he possibly could. Questions, he was sure, would be of no use. The only course was to tell her straight out how much he knew, and leave it to her whether to refuse to talk to him, or to attempt to offer anything in her own defence.

So he began by telling Helen, in so many words, that he knew positively, and could prove by evidence, that she had arranged for Rupert Pendexter to meet old Lord St Blaizey in the Castle woods on the morning of his death. At that she attempted a denial, looking, Ben said, as if she could have killed him gladly for his knowledge. He ignored her denial, and went on to tell her that he knew how she had taken her horse out of the stable and lent it to her brother, and how Alfred Amos had met her returning to the Castle on foot. He told her what he had discovered about Sidney Galloway's meeting with Rupert by the old mine, and about Galloway bringing the horse back to the stables afterwards. He told her how Rupert Pendexter had borrowed Sidney Galloway's car, and driven it to where he had left his aeroplane hidden on the Moor.

All through this recital, he said, Helen St Blaizey sat and stared at him with growing horror on her face. Having told her so much, he came to the real point of his talk.

'You see, Lady St Blaizey, that most of the facts are by now fully known. Your brother's arrest in London is only a matter of hours. He is already closely watched, and has no chance of getting away. Now, as the facts stand, you have to realize that you, as well as he, are very deeply implicated . . . No, let me finish what I have to say. To put the matter quite bluntly, there are two possibilities. When you helped your brother to meet Lord St Blaizey alone that morning, either you did not know that he was planning murder—*or you did know*. On the face of the evidence, it will be widely believed that you did know.'

'Of course I did not know,' Helen burst out. 'I mean, how could I know? It is wicked of you to say that Rupert killed my father-in-law. He did not. I tell you he did not. It was all an accident. I know nothing about it.' She faced Ben Tancred, with white face and staring eyes, like an animal at bay.

'It was not an accident, and you know it was not. At the least, you are an accomplice after the fact, in a case of murder. Nothing can save you from standing in the dock on that charge. The only question, Lady St Blaizey, is whether you will not have to face a still more terrible charge.'

Helen's face had gone grey. She was shuddering. 'I knew nothing,' she said, 'except that Rupert wanted to meet him alone. I arranged that, I admit. There was nothing wrong in arranging for them to meet.'

'But afterwards,' Ben went on ruthlessly, 'when you knew how Lord St Blaizey had met his death you concealed your knowledge. You abetted the murderer—knowing him to be a murderer.'

'I did not know,' said Helen. 'I do not know now. You are telling lies—lies—nothing but lies.' There was a silence, which Ben did not break. 'Besides,' said Helen, 'it is absurd. As if I should have helped Rupert to steal my money.'

'I think you did not know then that your brother had forged a codicil to the will.'

'Of course I did not,' said Helen. The look on her face changed suddenly to one of calculation. 'Do you mean you can prove the will was forged?'

'I am not here to answer that question,' said Ben. 'In any event, the law does not allow a murderer to profit by his crime.'

'Then you have not proved it. He has been too clever for you. He is too clever for everyone.'

'Not too clever to be hanged, Lady St Blaizey.'

'But they can't hang him. Surely there is no proof. There can be no proof. Oh, whatever else is true, Dr Tancred, I swear to you I am innocent.'

'Innocent of what, Lady St Blaizey?'

'I had no idea . . .' she stopped in mid-sentence.

'That your brother meant murder? I am rather inclined to believe you. But your only chance of making a jury believe you is to tell quite frankly everything you know.'

'And help to hang my brother? You say he will be hanged!' Helen was wringing her hands.

'He presumed on your loyalty so far as to rob you of your fortune. Will you stand by him after that?'

'You have no right to torture me,' said Helen, with a gesture of repulsion.

'Your brother did not stop short of a second murder when he saw his safety threatened. Your brother killed Sidney Galloway. Do not forget that, Lady St Blaizey. And you helped him. You kept silence even after he had killed . . . your lover.'

Helen blazed. 'How dare you say such a thing? You are trying to trap me. Oh!' She buried her face in her hands, and began to sob hysterically.

Ben told me that he felt no pity for her then. As for me, I was all pity, long before Ben had reached this point in his gruesome recital of his brutality. He stood waiting, till her sobbing died down. Then he said, 'I am speaking to you for your own good, Lady St Blaizey. You will realize, when you are calmer, that I am giving you good advice. Your one chance of escape is to tell all you know, and throw yourself on the jury's mercy. That is, if your guilt goes no further than you have admitted already.'

'I . . . I have not admitted anything,' Helen managed to say.

'Oh, yes. You have admitted a great deal. And you will have to admit a great deal in court, when the trial is held.

In the meantime, my last word of advice to you is to tell your husband the whole truth. He had better learn it from you than from others.'

Helen St Blaizey had lost control of herself for a moment; but now her self-possession was gradually coming back. She again looked Ben Tancred in the face. She said, in a voice steady and tightly controlled. 'And, if I admit what you call everything, what will be done to me? Will they put me . . . in prison?'

'Assuming that you had no hand in planning murder,' said Ben, 'but were only an accomplice after the fact, lying in order to save your brother, a judge will probably be lenient with you. I can say no more than that. Well, Lady St Blaizey, I have said my say. Think it over, and you will see for yourself that I am right.'

With these parting words Ben left her. When he told me about it all afterwards, I was furious with him. 'You didn't play fair, Ben,' I told him. 'The best advice to her was to deny everything, and simply burst into tears when anyone asked her a question. If she does that, almost any jury can be relied on to let her off.'

Ben chuckled. 'My dear Paul,' he said, 'don't I know that? She'll have realized it for herself by now. Catch her owning up, or giving herself away, when the trial comes! But my one hope of getting anything out of her was to take her by surprise, put the wind up her thoroughly, and then play the heavy father. See what I made her admit by doing it.'

'You were abominable,' I said.

'She deserved every bit of it,' said Ben, with another chuckle. 'I only wish I could have given her a still more uncomfortable half-hour. That woman ought to be gaoled at the least; and if I know my British juries she'll get off scot-free. Good heavens, Paul, you must see she richly deserved all she got—and more. '

I refused to admit it; but in cold blood afterwards I could at any rate see Ben Tancred's point of view.

However, that wasn't the end of his doings at the Castle that afternoon, or he would not have kept me waiting so long. In the hall downstairs, the butler told him that his lordship had heard he was with her ladyship, and had expressed a desire to see him before he left. Ben had no desire to meet Lord St Blaizey just then; but he couldn't very well refuse. He was shown into the library, and found himself face to face, not with Lord St Blaizey, but with Sarah Pendexter.

'Dr Tancred!' said Sarah. 'What are you doing here?'

'I might reply in the same terms, madam. I was told Lord St Blaizey was here.'

'I too have come to see Lord St Blaizey.' There was a pause. 'I have been in London, Dr Tancred,' said Sarah.

'So I heard,' Ben answered. 'Your nephew told me you have been there.'

'I went to Scotland Yard,' Sarah continued. 'I told them the detective they sent here was a fool. But they refused to listen to me. I have been expecting you to let me know how you are getting on.'

'I was about to do so. I expect Rupert Pendexter will be arrested tomorrow, if not today.'

'The Lord be praised!' said Sarah, lifting up her hands. 'He will be hanged? Tell me he is certain to be hanged. Thanks to you, Dr Tancred. I was guided to call upon you, and the Lord heard my prayer.'

'I believe there is enough evidence to convict him, madam,' Ben answered coldly. 'Until today, we were only groping; but now everything is clearing itself up.'

'I can see him,' said Sarah gloatingly. 'I see the gallows, and the hangman with his face of death. They are bringing him from the prison. He is walking between two warders with that wicked smile on his face to the last. I can die content, now that I have been vouchsafed that vision.'

Ben said he had never conceived so horrible a sight as Sarah Pendexter's rapt face, as, with her hands clutching like claws at space, she uttered this extraordinary rhapsody. Then she descended to earth. 'You must tell me what I owe you, Dr Tancred, for getting him hanged.'

It was Ben's turn to make a gesture of repulsion. Nothing would have persuaded him to touch a penny of the appalling old witch's money. 'Nothing, madam,' he said sharply. 'It is enough that justice is done, without our exulting over it.'

'But you must let me pay you,' said Sarah, 'or it will not be *my* triumph.'

'You only confirm my determination, Miss Pendexter,' said Ben. 'You don't owe me a penny.' He walked out of the room without another word, and escaped from the Castle without seeing Lord St Blaizey. For he felt that his other employer, too, might start talking to him about blood-money if they met. Ben Tancred, for once, almost hated his profession as he joined me in the car.

CHAPTER 34

THE SAGA ENDS

From that point my story rushes on swiftly to its end. As I had no part in any of the remaining incidents, I can report them briefly; for, with one great exception, everything is really over now, bar the shouting. That one great exception, of course, concerns the will.

By the time Ben Tancred got back to London, Jellicoe, acting on his instructions, had brought the two witnesses, Henry Lamb and Robert Cuff, up to London, and, in the offices of Rupert Pendexter lawyer's, had shown them the originals of the will and codicil. The question Jellicoe had to put to them both was this. Could they throw any light on the date at which they had actually put their signatures to the codicil?

To that form of the question both men returned a negative answer. They paid little attention to the numerous papers they were called upon to witness: there was no means by which they could tell one from another.

Thereupon Jellicoe put the question in a different form. Could they, by looking closely at the actual signatures, form any idea of the time when they had been written? Handwriting did change with time, so that people were often startled when they saw their own writing of some years before. Could either Lamb or Cuff distinguish between their signatures of more than two years ago, and their signatures of today?

To that question Jellicoe got one negative and one doubtful answer. Robert Cuff, the valet, could not tell the difference at all. Henry Lamb, on the other hand, said that his own signature looked to him as if it had been made recently, but he could not feel quite sure. Certainly, he could not swear to such a thing. Cuff also opined that Lamb's signature of three years ago had been distinctly less shaky than the writing on the codicil; but that, of course, was a mere opinion, which would not be likely to carry any weight in a court of law.

So far, Ben's questions had produced no more than a doubt. But his next venture was much more fortunate. Ralph Ollerton, the handwriting expert, had been equipped with samples of Rupert Pendexter's writing, as well as with the photographed copies of the will. He had been asked by Ben Tancred to say whether the actual text of the codicil could be identified as Pendexter's writing.

For—this being one of the points Ben had kept up his sleeve and bade me think of for myself, because I knew it fully as well as he—Rupert Pendexter, in the old days of Simon Pendexter's murder, had been a lawyer's clerk, and had presumably learnt to write the legal script.

Ralph Ollerton's report had come in before Ben Tancred returned to London. Yes, there were distinct points of subtle resemblance between Pendexter's hand and that in which the codicil was written. He could not say quite positively that they had been written by the same person; but he would be prepared to testify in court to the resemblance, and to suggest that the identification was highly probable. He did not, however, believe that his testimony would carry conviction with a jury. The two scripts were, superficially, quite unlike; and some rival expert could probably be found to declare that they had not been written by the same hand.

That strengthened the presumption in favour of forgery; but it left us still far short of legal proof. But Ben Tancred's last long shot gave us even that, though it must be admitted that, clever as he was to think of it, only sheer luck enabled him to get his proof. Jellicoe's third instruction as to find the makers of the paper on which the codicil was written and to discover from them, if possible, at what date the paper had been made. Ben, when he held the pages of the will and codicil up to the light in Rupert Pendexter's flat, had been memorizing the watermarks, with the aid of which Jellicoe was at once able to find out who had made the paper of the later document.

With a representative of the firm, he then visited Rupert's lawyers, and, again relying on his authority from Rupert, got the will produced for inspection. The paper-maker was at once able to declare that his firm had only been making the precise sort of paper on which the codicil was inscribed for less than one year. The paper was practically the same as that on which the will had been drawn up; but there was a small difference in the water-mark, and that was conclusive as to the date when the paper had been made.

That, of course, finally settled the question of forgery; for the codicil could not possibly have been drawn up at the date engrossed upon it, and as the date was actually included in the text there was no possibility of it having been added subsequently.

I am conscious that, at this stage of my narrative, this masterly stroke of Ben Tancred's is bound to come as something of an anti-climax; for the codicil really ceased to matter when the proof of murder made Rupert unable to benefit under it. I am not lawyer enough to know what would have happened if the codicil had not been shown to be a forgery. Would old Lord St Blaizey's fortune have reverted after all to his son? Or would it have gone to Rupert Pendexter's heirs—that is, presumably, to Lady St Blaizey? Or would the lawyers have got the best part of it, and been still arguing about it today? At all events, Ben's ingenuity and patience settled the matter once and for all. Lord St Blaizey duly inherited his father's property under the original will, about whose authenticity there was, of course, no dispute.

For the rest, there is little to tell. Before Ben Tancred arrived in London, Superintendent Wilson, acting on Falcon's message, had issued a warrant for Rupert Pendexter's arrest, and a warrant was also issued for Lady St Blaizey through the Cornish police. Helen, the moment Ben had left her, had telephoned to Rupert in London, and begged him to fly for his life; and Rupert was actually arrested as he stepped out of his car beside the shed near Longridge where he had his aeroplane in readiness for his escape. Helen was arrested at St Blaizey Castle by Superintendent Usher, Chief Inspector Falcon having left at once for London after his telephone talk with Scotland Yard.

By the time I got back with Ben Tancred's car, Rupert Pendexter was safe under lock and key, and the case was all over, except for the trial. Scotland Yard had located the aerodrome where Rupert had landed on the occasion of his dash to Birmingham to set up his *alibi* after the murder; and, as the news of his arrest went round the City, the crazy edifice of Rupert Pendexter's financial ventures came crashing down in ruins, spreading devastation among the innocent as well as the guilty.

As for the trial, it ended as it was bound to end, with Rupert Pendexter, debonair and defiant to the last, receiving the judge's sentence with an ironical bow. Nor was Ben mistaken about Lady St Blaizey's fate. She pleaded not guilty, and went into the witness-box, where she broke down so piteously at every inconvenient question, that the jury acquitted her with as little hesitation as they felt in condemning her brother to death. Lord St Blaizey was less impressionable. He and his wife never lived together after the trial. I am told that he made her a small allowance, and that she inhabited a boarding-house somewhere in Belgium under an assumed name until her premature death, last year, which set me free to write this record.

As for Sarah Pendexter, I saw her sitting through the trial, positively gloating as every fresh count in the indictment against Rupert came to be pressed home. She did not mind Helen's acquittal in the least; for all her vindictiveness spent itself upon her nephew. When sentence had been pronounced, she marched out of court triumphantly, fell down in the street outside, and died of heart failure. If heaven and hell exist, I wonder which way Sarah went. She had her qualities; but in her latter days at any rate she was plainly mad. Let us hope no such vindictiveness pursues her as she meted out to her despicable nephew. *Requiescat in pace* —if for such as Sarah Pendexter there is ever peace.

So, after two volumes, I came at last to my journey's end. Ben Tancred is sure to tell me I have made a hash of the whole story, and after what some of the reviewers said about my first volume I have no hope that they will think very highly of its successor. All I can say is that I have done my best, and that, whatever the reviewers may say, I shall never weary of singing my friend Ben Tancred's praises. As for Rupert Pendexter, no one I think will doubt that he richly deserved his fate. He was a wicked man; and for a whole quarter of a century he enjoyed, apparently without one twinge of conscience, the fruits of an abominable crime. But at the last his sins did find him out. For Helen, who sinned, I am sure, only because she loved him too well, I have only pity. She paid, I think, despite her acquittal, a higher price than him. But I must give over moralizing, and write at last to the Pendexter Saga the simple words

THE END